FISSION

FISSION

A NOVEL OF ATOMIC HEARTBREAK

LESLIE R. SCHOVER

SHE WRITES PRESS

Published in 2026 by
She Writes Press, an imprint of The Stable Book Group

32 Court Street, Suite 2109
Brooklyn, NY 11201
https://shewritespress.com
Library of Congress Control Number: 2025918196
ISBN: 979-8-89636-056-8
eISBN: 979-8-89636-057-5

Interior Designer: Kiran Spees

Printed in the United States
This is a work of fiction. Names, characters, places, and incidents are either products of the author's imagination or are used fictitiously. Any resemblance to actual persons, living or dead, is purely coincidental.

For my parents, Janet and Don, with love and respect for their fifty years of marriage.

1: August 1942

Staccato baby sobs made a discordant counterpoint to the spritely opening of Haydn's Concerto in D Major. Doris's hands continued the melody automatically as she scanned her audience. What kind of philistine brought an infant to a concert? Then she awoke and realized she was not sitting at the piano, swaying in her pink organza gown with the fabric rose at the neckline. Instead, she wore a stained nightie and lay in her sweaty bed, next to a bassinet holding her one-month-old daughter. She groaned. Playing with the Chicago Symphony had been her prize three years ago for winning a local piano competition. That perfect rapport with the orchestra and conductor had been the high point of her life.

A crescendo of wails reminded her that the last few months were the nadir. The air was already stale and humid, the slight breeze from the open window wafting in a rancid whiff of a neighbor's frying eggs. Doris threw off her blanket and padded over to lift her baby onto a makeshift changing table. She fumbled with the tiny diaper, sized for preemies like Barbara, who had been born five weeks early. The tip of a safety pin scratched the baby's thigh. Barbara scrunched up her face and gave an even more penetrating cry. "Sorry." Doris stroked the red trail with a gentle finger and swiped it with a soapy cloth before lifting Barbara's feet to clean her bottom and slide a new diaper under it. She pinned the diaper snugly closed without further incident and picked Barbara up. "Your mother is a bumbling amateur."

Now for the bottle. She was getting better at that ritual. As she mixed the formula, Doris cursed her mother's gynecologist, Dr. Melman. "May you rot in hell, you quack!—Not you sweetie," she reassured her oblivious daughter. Doris's parents had been furious when she and Rob came home the previous October and announced they had married at Chicago City Hall. "What about finishing college?" her father, Samuel, demanded.

"Of course I will, Papa. Rob has an essential job, so even if we declare war, he won't be drafted. We've rented a one-bedroom near the university." Samuel had nevertheless forbidden Rob to spend time at the house until Sophie, Doris's mother, could arrange a wedding at the synagogue. In the interim, Sophie set up a visit to Dr. Melman.

"If you're not pregnant, Doris, why the rush to get married?"

"Mama, I love Rob and we want our own apartment. I've told you over and over again that I am not pregnant."

"Fine," Sophie sniffed. "Then let's have Dr. Melman examine you. If you're going to be a married woman, you should see a gynecologist."

After the indignity of Doris's first pelvic exam, the bald and elderly doctor handed the speculum to his nurse, who dunked it in a tub of disinfectant. "Get dressed, young lady, and Nurse Rose will bring you into my office." Doris sat in front of Dr. Melman's massive desk, cringing at the wet gel in her panties and trying not to fidget. He frowned and wrote a note on lined paper in Doris's chart, a brown cardboard folder with a metal fastener. "I'm sorry to tell you, Mrs. Friedman, but not only are you not pregnant—"

"I never said I was. It was my mother who insisted on this appointment."

"Well, lucky she did. I'm afraid you have a tipped uterus. One of the worst I've ever seen. I think you are extremely unlikely to conceive."

"You mean I can't have babies? Ever?"

"You are infertile, Mrs. Friedman."

Doris had no imminent plans for motherhood. She was hoping to become a concert pianist, or at least to apply to law school once she finished her bachelor's degree. Still, she wept for hours when she got back to her parents' house. She met Rob for dinner and told him the bad news.

"Maybe we shouldn't go ahead with the second wedding," she said.

Rob leaned across the table and wiped away a tear. "We're already married. Let's not worry about children now. If the doctor's right, we can always adopt a baby."

Rob and Doris had been having sex for several months whenever they could manage the privacy. It had been a refuge from their worries about the possibility of war. The only change in their routine after Dr. Melman's diagnosis was to stop bothering with condoms. Two weeks after moving into their shabby little apartment, Doris missed her period.

When the doctor's office called and said the pregnancy test was positive, she threw her *Theories of Political Science* book at the wall. It left a dark blue scuff on the beige paint, but she was too angry to care. If the news of infertility had been painful, the revelation of pregnancy was disastrous. She had been counting not only on finishing out the semester, but also completing college the next year. Doris started the University of Chicago at age seventeen, having skipped two grades in elementary school. She spent a year after high school attending the American Conservatory of Music. Now she would be a mother at barely twenty. Rob was three years older, working as an electronics technician. They could barely afford their rent, much less a babysitter to allow Doris to attend classes.

She knew better than to ask Sophie for help. Her mother spent her days playing mahjong and canasta or shopping for clothes with her younger daughter, Naomi. Doris had always been daddy's girl, but Samuel was already disappointed in her. She dreaded telling him this news. She thought about trying to find an abortionist, but she had read grisly stories about girls needing hysterectomies after getting infections, or even bleeding to death.

No, she was well and truly trapped. Rob took the news in stride. He was mainly worried about earning enough money to support them. "Last month you were bawling about never having kids," he reminded her.

"I wasn't bawling!" she yelled at him between sobs. "But now I am!"

"Well, just think! We've made a baby! I wonder what he or she will be like."

Rob held her and she calmed down, but every morning when she woke up queasy, reality hit again. She doubled down on her classwork, vowing to get straight A's so she would have the best options for finishing school when she was able.

She also increased her piano practice. She was working on Rachmaninoff's Prelude in C Sharp Minor, but the more hours she spent at the piano, the more her wrists and forearms ached. She soaked them in Epsom salts, but the swelling would not go down. Her teacher took Doris's hands after a run-through. "Doris, your tone is lovely. Your fingering is perfect, and you've almost got the speed, but I think you should give up on this piece."

"But, Sarah, why? You see how hard I'm working and it's only four minutes long."

"Rachmaninoff is known for his huge hands. Not only are yours average at best—but your thumbs are almost an inch shorter than normal. I told you the day would come when a composition with ninths and tenths would defeat you. Look at your poor wrists." Sarah gently squeezed them and Doris winced. "I can see you're in pain."

"Excuse me!" Doris made a dash for the bathroom where she threw up. After she washed her face and came back to the room, she apologized.

"Do you have something to tell me, Doris?"

"Yes, Sarah. I'm expecting."

"Oh, Doris."

"I'm going to have to drop out of school next year. I've ruined everything and disappointed everyone." She slumped on the piano bench.

Sarah rapped her midback, their signal to maintain good posture. "Another Jewish baby in the world is a blessing. Imagine the lovely child you and Rob will make. And frankly, Doris, talented as you are, you'll never be first-rate, or I wouldn't have encouraged you to leave the conservatory and attend college. It's time to stop this quest for perfection. Get some joy out of your music. Play for people you love. Teach piano and earn some extra money."

Doris practiced the prelude at least three hours every day for the next week. On the eighth day, her wrists were so sore that she couldn't chop tomatoes for a dinner salad. She threw down the knife and burst into tears. She went to their scratched, upright piano and tried to rip up the sheet music. Not only did she lack the strength, but the music was already burned into her brain and fingers. When Rob came home, they went out for a burger they could ill afford.

2: August 1942

While Barbara sucked sporadically on her bottle, Doris recalled how she had slogged through the final months of her pregnancy. The University of Chicago granted her an associate degree and an invitation to return for her senior year when she could. She had been by herself in the apartment on a sweltering day in July when a sudden, stabbing cramp took her breath away. A stream of fluid hissed from under her skirt onto the kitchen linoleum. Rob was at work and would be hard to reach. She called her father, who had a car and could drive her to the hospital.

Samuel gave Doris a reassuring pat as a nurse directed him to the waiting room. "Don't worry. I'll phone Rob and tell him to get over here."

"No rush," said the nurse, getting a gurney ready for Doris. "First births usually take quite a while. I'll just take your daughter up to the delivery floor."

Doris had not learned much about childbirth. She thought she would have time yet to prepare. The doctor finally came in after hours of the worst pain she had ever experienced. "Can I have something to make it hurt less?" she gasped.

"I'm sorry, Mrs. Friedman. We can't risk anesthesia because the baby's lungs may not be fully developed." He examined her. "It won't be too long now. Where's your husband?"

"I don't know. He was at work when my water broke. My father was going to call him."

"Nice, deep breaths now."

"It hurts!"

"Time to push," the nurse urged several minutes later.

"Why?" she choked out.

"Because your baby is ready to be born. Didn't you read anything about labor and delivery?"

"I was busy—owww—with my finals!"

Abruptly, the worst pain eased. "It's a girl," they told her. She heard a slap and then a weak cry. "Good, she's pinking up. Just five pounds, Mrs. Friedman."

When Rob came in, they sat him in a chair and put the tiny bundle into his arms. "Have you picked out a name?" asked the nurse. "We need a name within the hour for our records. She's a preemie and we can't guarantee she'll make it."

"Her name is Barbara," Rob said, looking terrified. "That's what we decided, right, honey?"

Doris nodded and closed her eyes. She had never felt so alone.

Although the baby barely gained any weight, the wartime hospital rules meant that Doris and Barbara were discharged after five days. Doris was petrified she would hurt Barbara, who bore no resemblance to a rosy Gerber Baby. She had sores around her mouth from impetigo, a skin infection. The treatment was to paint them with gentian violet. She was also covered with fine hairs that normally would have dropped off before a full-term birth. Even now that she was four weeks old, she still was scrawny and hairy. Her face had purple patches from the medicine.

This afternoon, Doris's friend Annette and several girls still in town from their college bridge club were throwing her a baby shower that had been derailed by Barbara's sudden debut. As she tried unsuccessfully to burp her daughter, Doris made a mental list of things to do before two o'clock. Annette had promised to bring snacks, so Doris would make some lemonade and iced tea. Barbara slept most of the morning, but at one o'clock Doris fed her again and snapped her into pink pajamas that were newborn size but still hung off her small limbs. Doris put on a belted housecoat. She had struggled with her weight before getting pregnant and now was carrying fifteen extra pounds. She pinned back one side of her curly dark blonde hair with a comb that had an artificial flower attached. She swiped on some lipstick. It would have to do.

When Doris heard the buzzer, she answered the door. Four young women filed in, bearing covered dishes and wrapped presents. They wore thin pastel summer dresses, saddle shoes, and bobby socks. "Come in, everyone! Drinks are on the dining table and you can put the food there too."

"Doris!" Annette gave her a hug. "You look . . . a little tired."

"Yes, sorry for the housecoat. I still can't fit into my regular skirts."

"Aren't you breastfeeding?" asked one girl who always drank herbal tea and brought home-baked bread to share at their bridge games. "It uses up lots of calories!"

"I tried, but the baby wasn't gaining enough weight, so the doctor prescribed a special formula instead. It's hideously expensive."

"So where is the baby?"

Doris picked up Barbara from the bassinet in the bedroom and her friends gathered round.

After a brief silence, one said, "She's so tiny."

"Why is her face purple?" asked Annette. "Are those birthmarks?"

"No, don't worry. It's just some medicine for a skin infection that's clearing up. The body hair is falling out too. They told me preemies are sometimes born with it. She'll look like a normal baby soon." She put Barbara over one shoulder and patted her back gently. At that moment, Barbara threw up in an arc, like the Chicago landmark Buckingham Fountain. Some of the spit-up sprayed the dress of the girl standing behind Doris. "Sorry! So sorry. Here's a clean washcloth. I'm afraid she has what the doctor calls projectile vomiting.

Her digestive system isn't quite mature yet." Doris bit her lip to suppress a giggle at her classmate's look of disgust. Barbara started to cry and Doris jiggled her, but not too vigorously, hoping her daughter had nothing left in her stomach. The baby quieted and Doris laid her back down. "Let's sit in the living room. Hopefully, she'll go back to sleep."

Annette passed around a dish of fruit salad and some cookies. Between mouthfuls, one of the girls commented, "You know, when you and Rob married in November and then had the baby in July, I figured you *had* to get hitched. But now I believe you. Barbara was definitely premature."

"Eileen! That was rude," Annette admonished her, but Doris saw by the other girls' sly smiles that they had shared Eileen's suspicions.

"Well, sorry to deprive you of gloating over my shame," Doris said. "You can gloat over my misery instead."

"Doris! We're happy for you! You have a daughter," Annette protested. "I'll cut the cake and you can open your presents."

Doris politely cooed over a lopsided crocheted baby blanket, a plastic rattle shaped like a dachshund, and a yellow sleep sack with a closed bottom. It was supposed to fit a six-month-old, but Barbara would probably swim in it until she was old enough to need pajamas she could walk in. The final gift was a mobile with stars to hang over Barbara's crib, which Rob had not yet assembled since the baby still looked lost in the vastness of the bassinet.

After the women left, Doris changed and fed Barbara again. "I don't expect perfection, kiddo, but do you think you could manage to be a little bit more of a blessing?" She nuzzled the baby's soft forehead. It was difficult to imagine Barbara becoming a person. Right now she seemed like an exacting pixie, sent to punish Doris for her ambitions. Doris waited to feel a rush of motherly love, but was disappointed. When Rob trudged in at 7:30 p.m., Doris and Barbara were both sound asleep. He made scrambled eggs for dinner.

3: February 1943

The February wind cut like a knife, but thankfully it was not snowing. At the kiosk next to the streetcar stop, Doris read the newspaper headline, SOVIET FORCES SECURE VICTORY IN BATTLE OF STALINGRAD. She snuggled into Rob's arms as they waited. "We're shivering," he said, "but without winter, the Nazis would be swilling vodka as they cruised up the Volga."

"That's true, but if the streetcar doesn't come soon, I think my nose will freeze off!"

"Oh no! It's such a cute button nose." Rob rubbed it with his gloved hands. "You could definitely pass for Aryan."

"Shame on you!" Doris punched him lightly in the stomach, her half-hearted gesture muffled by his heavy coat and her own wool gloves.

They were having dinner at the house of Dr. Harrison Hartnell. He wanted to recruit Rob to work on a hush-hush wartime project at the university. Annette's new husband, Joel, a physics undergraduate, had asked Rob to meet with Hartnell. Doris thought it sounded intriguing. Rob was less enthused but accepted the invitation. Doris's parents had even agreed to babysit seven-month-old Barbara for the occasion.

The Hartnell home was only a block from a streetcar stop. Mrs. Hartnell greeted them at the door and took their coats. The air smelled of chicken. Packing crates were stacked in a corner of the living room. "I'm Nora Joy, Harrison's wife," she introduced herself.

"Please excuse the mess. We just moved to Chicago and we're renting this house, so we haven't completely unpacked."

"Thank you," Doris replied. "Dinner smells delicious."

"It's my famous baked chicken. We always served it in Los Angeles when Harrison had students over to dinner."

"And here are our guests! Welcome." A pleasant-looking man entered, probably less than a decade older than Rob.

"Nice to meet you, Dr. Hartnell," said Rob, shaking hands.

"Please, call me Harrison. I'm very informal."

Nora Joy said that dinner was about ready, so the two couples sat at the dining table. They chatted about the differences between Los Angeles, where Hartnell had been teaching chemistry at UCLA, and frigid Chicago.

Harrison asked Rob about his education. "I took a one-year course in electronics. My family couldn't afford to send me to college, like Doris here."

"That's not quite accurate," Doris cut in. "Rob worked as a janitor and gave almost all his salary to his parents before we married. They used it to send his sister to college."

Rob looked uncomfortable.

"You know it's true!" Doris said. "And his sister isn't half as smart as Rob either."

"Well, she got better grades in high school."

Doris snorted. "Rob went to an awful high school. His math teacher wrote the algebra textbook and made a lot of money selling it to the school district. Rob found a bunch of mistakes in the book, and when he pointed them out, the teacher gave him a D!"

"Well, to be fair, I shouldn't have brought it up in front of the whole class. But he was such a puffed-up little toad."

"I can already see you're a man after my own heart. I deplore stuffed shirts," Harrison told him. "You know I work with Enrico Fermi, and despite being a genius, he's one of the nicest, most down-to-earth guys around."

"Gee! I'd love to meet Fermi!"

"Tell them about your Marie Curie biography," Doris urged Rob.

"Marie Curie? You're interested in radiation?" Harrison raised his eyebrows at Nora Joy and offered Rob seconds of the chicken.

"In high school we had to write a biography of a famous scientist. I thought her work was fascinating. I read every book I could find in the library and worked on it for a couple of weeks. I was really proud, but when the teacher handed our papers back, mine had an F and a note to see him after class. He told me I had obviously plagiarized the essay because I could never have written it."

"Can you imagine?" Doris asked.

"I was flaming mad. I brought in every library book I had used and challenged him to find anything I'd copied. I even went to the principal. In the end, my grade was changed—but only to a C minus! So I have mixed feelings about schools. I can learn most things on my own."

"Joel said you belonged on our project, and I agree with him. We'll talk about it after dinner. And, Doris, are you a science type too?"

"Oh no, Harrison. I'm more of a humanities girl. I was in my junior year at U of C last fall when Rob and I eloped. And then we found out we were expecting our daughter, Barbara, and I couldn't finish," Doris said, looking down at her plate. "I hope to go back after the war. I had been thinking about law school."

"Are the two of you much involved in politics?" Harrison asked.

"Not really," Rob replied.

"We're both Democrats. I won't apologize for that," Doris added.

"No need to apologize to me," Harrison said. "I voted for FDR this last time, but before that I preferred the Socialists. I just thought with the war and all, we need Roosevelt's experience."

Nora Joy sighed. "Don't let him lure you into talking politics all night!"

"I don't think we'd disagree much, but Doris isn't too fond of communists. I almost decked her uncle Jacob in December!"

Doris laughed. "Yes, my uncle Jacob is a Bolshevik—the only one in the family. We were having a little discussion and I called Stalin a murdering tyrant. Rob caught Uncle Jacob's arm just before he slugged me!"

After a dessert of chocolate pudding, Harrison took Rob and Doris to the living room, and Nora Joy started to clear the table. Doris offered to help, but Harrison put up a hand to stop her. "No, Doris, you need to hear about this, too, because if Rob joins our team, he'll need your support." She sat back down.

"Now, Rob, I understand you're a good friend of Joel Levitt, who's been working with us as an assistant."

"Yes, Joel and his wife, Annette, were at the university with Doris."

"Annette and I go way back, even before high school," Doris added.

"Did Joel tell you much about our project?"

"No. He said it was secret. But I told him that I'm already doing important war work. I'm designing loudspeakers for battleships so all the men can hear commands."

Harrison lit a cigarette and offered smokes to the young couple. "Well, our project is much more crucial. And with your interests, I think you'll understand. Joel vouched for you, so I'm going to trust you with some extremely confidential information. In December, Fermi and his team created the first nuclear fission chain reaction. They did the experiment right on campus, in a squash court under Stagg Field."

Rob stared. "That's amazing, but it sounds awfully risky."

"It was a small risk, but Fermi was pretty confident it was safe. And the stakes are very high. Doris, do you know what fission is?"

"No, I don't."

"Well, if you bombard the atom of a heavy element with neutrons, you can split its nucleus in two. That's fission."

"Oh! Kind of like breaking the atom's heart?"

"That's one way to think about it! If you split enough atoms, the neutrons keep banging into each other, and a fission chain reaction takes off."

"One broken heart leads to another!"

Harrison smiled at Doris's metaphor. "You're very poetic, like Nora Joy. Before the war, German physicists published work about fission using the element uranium. We've been doing similar research. In peacetime, the goal would be nuclear power for things like electricity. But our mission now is to build an atomic bomb. A fission chain reaction can trigger a tremendous explosion. This bomb will be the most powerful weapon in the history of war. We think the Nazis are also working toward it, so we have to build one first."

Doris clutched Rob's hand. "Oh my God."

"The project needs people like you, Rob, to design new instruments. Things like radiation counters and ion chambers. My group will be creating the first gram of plutonium."

"Plutonium?" Doris had never heard that word. "It can't be from the planet Pluto!"

Harrison chuckled. "Plutonium is a rare, radioactive element. It doesn't occur in nature. We have to make it using uranium. It may be just what we need to fuel the bomb. In several months, my group is going to move to a secret town to continue the project. We'd like you to join us, Rob. Doris would have to stay here for a little while, but the government is building like crazy to get the place up and running. It won't be that long before we get housing for your family. You don't have to give me your answer tonight, but I need to know very soon if we can count on you."

Rob nodded. "Doris and I need to discuss it. It sounds like quite an opportunity."

Nora Joy brought them their coats. They thanked her again for dinner and headed out into the icy street.

When they got home, Doris turned to Rob and asked, "Are you going to take the job?"

"Honey, I don't think I have a choice."

4: February 1943

The next morning, Doris went to her parents' house to pick up Barbara. Her maternal grandmother, Bubbe, answered the door. "Come in before you turn into an icicle," she said in Yiddish, tugging Doris inside. Doris understood Yiddish but spoke it only haltingly. Despite the forty years Bubbe had spent in Chicago, her English was almost nonexistent, but they managed to communicate. Doris heard an angry howl from the living room. Bubbe took her coat and Doris went to find Barbara.

"Oh good, you're here." Sophie gave Doris a pointed look. "Barbara needs her diaper changed. Gevalt. That dress is straining at the waist. When are you going to lose the rest of the baby weight?"

"Bronya can take care of Barbara. Give Doris a minute to get settled." Samuel got up from the couch to hug his daughter and buss her cheek. Plastic slip covers that protected the "good" furniture rustled and clung to his slacks. He was holding Barbara in one arm. Since college, Doris had winced at her mother's taste in furniture. The pink tweed couch and gilt mirrors no longer seemed elegant to Doris, but she would never comment, even to Samuel, and risk a nasty scolding from Sophie. Doris wondered if the decor bothered her father's more artistic eye.

Doris kissed Samuel and Barbara. "Don't worry, I'll take her." She could hear Bronya, the family's Polish maid, rattling dishes in the kitchen sink. Although her parents were far from rich, they always had help.

"The diapers are in your old room," Sophie reminded her. Sophie was not a hands-on grandma. She had declared at Barbara's birth that Doris had made her own bed and Sophie was not about to lie in it with her. Sophie preferred trips to Florida and betting on the horses. She often "complained" about the Cuban bookie at Hialeah who professed to be in love with her. Doris thought he was probably more enamored of the money Sophie placed on the races. Doris's father had never stopped being infatuated with his wife, however, and allowed her free reign over the household.

Barbara quieted as Doris carried her upstairs. Thankfully, Barbara's digestion had calmed down, but she was still a very fussy eater. At every doctor's visit, Doris was scolded for her daughter's failure to meet the weight goals for her age. Sometimes it felt as if the war theater were right there in her kitchen. She gazed down at her daughter. Although Barbara was still small for her age, she had become a pretty baby, with eyes and hair the color of sherry. Doris thought Barbara looked like her. When Rob had brought Doris home to meet his family, his grandfather had refused to believe that Doris was Jewish. Not only had her family anglicized their name from Cohan to Cain, but Doris had a shiksa's hazel eyes, creamy complexion, and rounded features. Rob was handsome in a more classic Jewish way. Although he was skinny, he stood six foot two with dark eyes, bushy black hair, and a Clark Gable mustache.

Doris pulled up Barbara's trousers and took her downstairs. They might as well stay for lunch. She took Barbara into Samuel's office. Samuel made a tidy living retouching catalogues, allowing him to work from home. He was using his air pencil on a photograph of a model wearing pin-striped boxer briefs. He pointed to the drafting table. "The latest in men's underwear. You could order some for Rob."

Doris did not share with her father that Rob only wore jockey shorts. It was too personal to discuss. The pregnancy had dismayed Samuel, but he doted on the baby once she was born. He lifted the air pencil and used its squeaky tones to play a recognizable version of "Mary Had a Little Lamb." Barbara smiled and gave a happy squeal.

"So how did the job interview go?" Samuel inquired.

"Very well. Rob is going to take the position."

"So he'll be working at the university?"

"Yes—for now, at least."

"What kind of work will he be doing?"

"I'm sorry, Papa. I can't talk about it."

"Hmm." He frowned and made a small adjustment to the image before him. "But he still won't be drafted?"

"No, it's wartime work."

Sophie poked her head in. "Will he at least get a raise?"

"I don't know."

"You don't know?"

"We didn't talk about money."

"What kind of job interview doesn't include talk about money?"

"A wartime job interview." Doris glared at her mother.

"I don't know why you couldn't find a nice college boy if you had to marry so young."

"I don't want to hear any more criticism of Rob. He's working tremendously hard." *And he's a lot smarter than you are, Mama.* She restrained herself from saying it aloud.

"Sophie, stop hocking her."

"Anyway, I should know more in a few days. Is Naomi working after school today?"

"Yes, they moved her to junior dresses at Carson's. She works Tuesdays after class and Saturday mornings," Sophie answered. "You should see the beautiful dress she just bought—sweetheart neckline and a full skirt. You should take advantage of her employee discount. Although I don't think that style would look good on you until you slim down."

"I can't really afford new clothes right now."

"Well, you could use some that fit better. You used to be a pretty girl." Sophie shook her head.

"I guess you'll just have to get your *nachas* when you show off Naomi to your friends at shul."

"You know we're proud of you and your family too." Samuel gave his wife a disapproving look.

"Have you had any more letters from Poland?" Doris asked. Her parents had been getting pleading letters for months from cousins near Białystok. The Cains sent what money they could, but it was impossible to bring refugees to the States.

"No. It's been three months now," Sophie answered.

"I'm sorry, Mama."

"From what's in the news, I'm afraid we may not hear anything more," Samuel added.

Doris knew he was probably right. Last December, newspapers had reported the murders of two million European Jews, followed by a trickle of articles describing ongoing atrocities. She wished she could at least tell Papa about the atomic bomb, but she knew she had to remain silent.

5: July 1943

After accepting the job with Hartnell's group in March, Rob had spent three months at the Met Lab and then moved to a place called Oak Ridge. Doris knew only that it was a secret town, carved out of a piece of Tennessee wilderness. Rob's letters over the past six weeks had clearly been censored. Thick black lines were drawn through what looked as if it had been innocuous information. They'd managed a couple of brief phone calls, but Rob said next to nothing about the new lab. Even before he left, Rob had been working long hours, six days a week, leaving Doris to unalloyed motherhood.

The crib was now set up in a corner of the living room. Barbara had pulled herself up to a standing position using the rails and was bouncing on her toes. "Ma! Ma!" she yelled when she saw Doris.

"Yes, you little banshee, I'm going to warm up your bottle," Doris grumbled. "And phew! I can smell you from here!" By now she was a diaper virtuoso. She put the soiled one aside to be rinsed, cleaned Barbara's bottom, applied a swipe of baby powder, and pinned on a clean cloth from the pile by the crib. "There." She kissed the top of the baby's head and pulled a summer dress over her daughter's straight brown hair. "I'm afraid you're in for a life of permanents." She carried Barbara into the kitchenette and deposited her in the high chair. "And happy birthday, Barbara! We're going to a party at Uncle Harry's house later. I bet you'll get some nice presents." Her uncle Harry, the only wealthy person in the extended family, had entered Harvard at age sixteen, despite the strict Jewish quota. Now he was a real estate mogul.

As Doris mashed up a ripe peach, she sang "Happy Birthday" to her daughter, who appeared unimpressed. Barbara drank her bottle but spit out all but a spoonful or two of the peaches. *Well, it's only her first birthday*, Doris reminded herself, sad that Rob could not share the festivities. As Barbara grew, Doris began to feel fascinated by her daughter's developing personality. The toddler was stubborn—even more determined than Doris herself. Soon Barbara would be running around. Doris was not sure that would be an improvement. More mobility would undoubtedly mean more trouble. But in another year, no more diapers, according to the pediatrician. That would be a major relief. It was lucky that her parents had sprung for a diaper service, because she had to do all their laundry by hand.

Later in the day, Doris woke Barbara from her nap and dressed her in a navy-dotted swiss birthday dress with matching Mary Jane shoes. These days Doris got more enjoyment from Barbara's appearance than from her own. "Uncle Harry will take your picture so we can send it to Daddy."

"Dada. Want Dada." Barbara was definitely precocious when it came to her speech.

"I know, sweetie. I miss him too. But there's a war on. Luckily you don't know anything about that, not like the babies over there in Europe and the Far East."

Barbara watched Doris's face and frowned.

"I know you don't understand. None of us understand—not really—what it's like to be in a war. But we're safe here, for now. Let's hope Uncle Harry's cook made a delicious birthday cake for you. If anyone has sugar and eggs, it's Uncle Harry."

"Cake?"

"Yes, a cake just for Barbara! Because it's your birthday."

"Buthday!"

"Yes, happy birthday!"

The buzzer rang and Doris carried Barbara and a large tote bag down the two flights of stairs. Her parents had come to pick them up. Uncle Harry's three-story brick house was in Hyde Park, not far from the place that the Hartnells had been renting. Doris hated the thick carpet that triggered electric shocks if she touched anything. The furniture was heavy, dark wood with somber, woolen upholstery. The decorator had emulated the style beloved by established German Jewish families of Chicago, although Uncle Harry had started out as a *grob yankel* from Belarus. Harry's three adolescent daughters swooped up Barbara, who was happy to show off her tentative walking skills. "The first grandchild in our family," Sophie kvelled to her sister Ida, Harry's wife.

"Well, of course I'm too young to have grandchildren yet," Ida sniffed.

Doris hid a smile. Aunt Ida was actually two years older than Sophie but pretended to be the younger sister since she was also secretly several years Harry's senior. Ida kept her complexion smoother than Sophie's by applying department-store moisturizers morning and night.

Barbara tripped and grabbed Sophie's hem to steady herself.

"Watch out!" her grandmother scolded. "That material creases and I'm not sure your hands are clean."

Barbara whimpered and one of the cousins picked her up and distracted her with a small pile of wrapped presents that would be opened after lunch.

Doris went to greet Harry, who was on the phone in his study. Doris waved and he signaled her to wait. He finished talking and hung up the receiver, then stood to give Doris a hug. "Looking good, Doris! How's the birthday girl?"

"Excited about her cake—or maybe that's me. I'm ready to eat someone else's cooking."

“Well, that’s one thing we can always provide! What do you hear from Rob?”

“He’s very busy. And his letters are censored. But I have a question for you.”

“About censors?”

“No, about making money.”

“Now that I can maybe help with.” He sat back down behind the desk.

Doris took a chair. “I want to find a way to work part-time until the war is over. Rob’s salary is barely enough to keep us afloat. I want to start a savings account.”

“Very admirable, Doris.”

“I can teach piano, but do you have any ideas about other jobs I could do?”

“A wife’s place is in the home, raising good Jewish children. Like your mother and my Ida. Are you keeping kosher?”

“Uncle Harry! We barely have room for one set of dishes and pots in our apartment, much less two.”

“Three—don’t forget the Passover china.”

Doris tried not to roll her eyes. “I promised you I wouldn’t have pork in the house, and I’ve kept my promise. I don’t have a maid and a cook. But women can work too. Just look at all the Rosie the Riveter girls.”

“When do you plan to finish college?”

“I don’t know. We can’t afford a sitter for Barbara.”

“You should have taken me up on my offer to send you to Wellesley.”

“I was only sixteen! I wasn’t ready to go so far from home. And then I might never have met Rob.”

Harry gave her a considering look, leaning back in his desk chair. “Maybe that wouldn’t have been such a tragedy . . . You know I like Rob, but he doesn’t come from a good family. His father drinks and that brother of his would be a gangster by now if he hadn’t gotten drafted.”

"I know, but Rob's not like the rest of them! He's got so much potential."

"And how is he going to reach it, hmm?"

"He's doing important work on this project. And I'm hoping he'll go to college after the war."

"And what are you going to do in Tennessee?"

"The same things I'm doing here, I guess. Take care of Barbara."

Harry stared at the ceiling for a moment. "What if you stayed here for the next year? Move back in with your parents and finish your degree."

"You know Mama and I are like oil and water. And she says she loves Barbara, but she hasn't changed a single diaper as far as I know."

"So let Bronya and Bubbe be the nurserymaids."

"Bubbe's forgetful and has shaky hands. And Bronya holds to some strange Polish customs when it comes to child raising."

"I tell you what. My Barry is only two years older than Barbara. The girl who takes care of him could mind them both during the day. Just drop off Barbara on your way to campus."

Barry had been Ida's unexpected, change-of-life baby. He was overindulged by everyone. Doris had caught him making faces to scare Barbara or snatching her toys.

"That's very generous, Uncle Harry, but what would Rob do without me for a whole year?"

"You said he's knee-deep in work. How is it different than the soldiers at the front? They don't have their wives with them."

"What if he meets another woman?"

"Don't you trust him? If he's that kind of schmuck, better to find out now. This is 1943. People divorce."

"I'll think about it." Doris's heart beat faster. What an impossible choice. Get back on track to her lost future but maybe at the price of her marriage. She'd fallen hard for Rob when he was introduced by a friend. He was so attentive and handsome. He seemed like a grown-up in contrast to the college boys. Rob shared her love of music, although his clarinet playing suffered because he couldn't afford private lessons. They agreed on politics and laughed at the same jokes. But with Barbara's arrival and the demands of the project, she could only dimly recall the delights of cuddling and having sex whenever they wanted. Since Rob's departure, any meaningful exchange had also been prevented by the difficulties of writing or talking by phone. Doris longed for Rob but hadn't realized the sacrifices that marriage and motherhood would entail. She needed time to consider this new option. She changed the subject. "But what about my question? Could I maybe learn to invest in the stock market or real estate?"

Harry narrowed his eyes. "Investing? That's a man's job, Doris."

"Hey, it's 1943, Uncle Harry!"

"Hmm." He drummed his fingers on the desk. "What about accounting? Businesses always need bookkeepers. It isn't hard to learn. You're a smart girl. My accountant taught himself from books. Should I ask him to recommend some?"

"That would be great!"

"I tell you what—I'll do you one better. I'll order some accounting books for you."

"Thank you!" Doris paused. "Do you think I might work in your business if I study hard?"

"I'm sure you'd be an asset, but no. Finish college and take care of Barbara until she's old enough for school. Then maybe we can talk. But you'll probably have more little ones by then. If you go down South, maybe you can help with bookkeeping for a charity. Do they have a synagogue there?"

"I don't know. Probably. A lot of the people working with Rob are Jewish." Doris had not even considered joining a synagogue in Tennessee.

"Well, you can tell the rabbi that your uncle Harry will make a donation if he gives you a part-time job."

Doris flinched. "That seems awful blatant."

"Don't worry. Just tell him you're my niece and leave the rest to me."

Doris knew it was time to drop the subject. The rest of the birthday party was a success. Barbara got more chocolate icing on her face than in her mouth, but Doris managed to ensure that none of it got smeared on the furniture or Sophie. She was exhausted when Samuel dropped them off at home.

6: July 1943

Several days after the party, Doris was snatching a few minutes to study the accounting books that had just been delivered. At least Uncle Harry had been prompt in fulfilling his promise. Doris kept weighing her options for September. She was having a hard time sleeping. Barbara was occupied with a pile of colored wooden blocks. The buzzer rang. It was Annette. Joel was in Oak Ridge, too, although not with Harrison's group. Before Rob left, he said that Joel also knew about the bomb, but Annette had been told only that the men were working on a secret war project.

"Hi, Doris!" Annette breezed in. "I made a tuna casserole and I thought I'd bring some over."

"Oh, thanks!" Doris took the covered dish and put it on the only empty spot on the kitchen counter. "It's nice to have some company, not to mention a free lunch."

"And hello, gorgeous." Annette sat down next to Barbara, who gave her one of the joyful grins she usually bestowed only on Rob. Doris felt a small flare of jealousy. "What are you building?" asked Annette.

"Dada house!"

"Oh, is that your papa's new house in Oak Ridge? Soon you and your mama will move there—and Auntie Annette too!"

"Dada?"

"Yes, we'll see Daddy soon," Doris assured her. Should she tell Annette about Harry's offer?

Annette picked up a fuzz ball from the rug. "Really, Doris, when was the last time you ran the carpet sweeper? You have to keep things clean for the baby."

Doris gritted her teeth. "I did it yesterday." When Doris had been a lonely misfit in high school, Annette had befriended her. They dished on boys they liked and exchanged gossip about the other girls. Annette's mother was kind and welcoming, so her house provided a respite from Sophie's constant carping. Doris knew that even though Annette was two years older, she had envied Doris for being their piano teacher's favorite student and for winning most of their bridge games. Doris also suspected that Annette had a crush on Rob when they all met. But Rob had eyes only for Doris. He said she played piano like an angel. For a while, Doris avoided Annette, put off by her sly digs. However, Annette seemed happier and less critical after her engagement to Joel. The girls' friendship warmed up again. The two couples often shared evenings at the movies or bowling alley, at least until Barbara was born.

Now Annette's efforts to "help" Doris with Barbara felt like opportunities to lord it over her. Doris's homemaking skills were an easy target since her mother had always had a maid. Bubbe also did all the cooking and had banished Doris from the kitchen.

"I'm not sure if I'm going to Oak Ridge."

"What?" Annette exclaimed. Barbara looked up but went back to stacking her blocks.

"Uncle Harry offered babysitting for Barbara if I stay here and finish my degree."

"But Rob is counting on you! I thought you missed him incredibly?"

"I do, but they're awfully busy with their work."

"That's why they need us to make homes for them. Whatever they're doing down there, Joel says it could win the war. I'm applying for a chemistry technician job. They need everyone they can get."

"Good for you. I'd like to work, too, but with Barbara, I don't see how I could."

"Well, you only got a B minus in chemistry."

"I can't believe you still remember my grades! I admit it. Science is not my strong suit."

"Well, maybe you could be a secretary or a schoolteacher. They need those too."

"Maybe." Doris thought those jobs sounded boring. "But who would take care of Barbara?"

"How could you even think of keeping Barbara away from her daddy?"

Doris gave her daughter a quick glance, but she seemed to be absorbed in her play. "Let's not talk about *D-a-d-d-y*."

"Really, Doris."

"All the soldiers and sailors are away from their families."

"But lucky us! We can be with our men. And Joel says that Oak Ridge is filling up with single gals who work in the factories. Do you really want to leave Rob alone there for a whole year?"

"No, but I also want some kind of career. I don't want to pop out four kids like Aunt Ida or spend my life shopping like my mother. I want a job that means something—and to live in a nice house, take Barbara to concerts and the theater."

"Rob will do well. He's smart and he works hard."

"But he's also a people pleaser. He doesn't stand up for himself. He cares more about learning new things than about getting ahead in life. He's not like Joel. I'm sure Joel will end up getting his PhD."

Annette preened a little. "It's true that Joel's a go-getter. But you're lucky Rob fell for you. I think it would be a mistake to stay here."

"Well, I'm going to call him to talk about it." Doris dished out the casserole and sat with Annette at the table.

While they ate, Annette tried to pump Doris about the project.

"Joel said Dr. Hartnell gave you and Rob the rundown."

"Well, as you just said, I don't understand much about the science stuff."

"You sure don't! You're lucky Joel helped you with your classes in college."

"Agreed." Doris kept her expression bland.

"But you must have understood something about what they're doing."

"I don't know much more than you do. And anyway, we shouldn't even be talking about it. If you're so curious, ask Joel, not me."

"He won't tell me anything. Everyone knows the government is monitoring letters and phone calls. But once I'm down there, working in the labs, I bet I can figure it out."

"I'm sure you will. You're a smart cookie."

After Annette left, Doris turned on the radio. The Allies were advancing through Italy and the Russians were holding off the Germans on the Eastern Front. Some tides were turning, but what if the Nazis got the atomic bomb first? She wished she could have shared her worries with Annette. Doris pictured downtown Chicago disappearing in a huge fireball. Surely the Germans would aim for Washington or New York? Could their bombers even fly all the way across the Atlantic? What if the Germans won the war? There were already plenty of pro-German Bund members in America, raring to get rid of the Jews, even if Father Coughlin's anti-Semitic radio show had been canceled.

The next day, Doris called Rob while Barbara was still asleep.

"Operator speaking. How may I assist you?"

"I'd like to place a long-distance call to Oak Ridge, Tennessee."

"Certainly, ma'am. May I have the number you wish to reach in Oak Ridge?"

"The number I have is Clinton-6298."

"Please hold the line while I connect you to our long-distance operator."

After several minutes of silence, the operator came back on the line. "I'm sorry, ma'am, but I cannot find any record of an Oak Ridge, Tennessee."

"But I know it exists. My husband is there. I'm trying to reach him. It's near Knoxville. Maybe you can try the Knoxville exchange?"

Another pause. "I'm sorry, ma'am. That number is not listed in the Knoxville exchange. Maybe you need to check again with your husband." The operator hung up.

Doris tried twice more with the same results. The fourth time she asked to speak to a supervisor. "Hello. My name is Doris Friedman. I've been trying for two hours with three different operators to reach my husband. I've spoken to him twice at the number I gave the long-distance operator, so I know it exists."

"Yes, ma'am, I understand."

"He's working at a new government base in a place called Oak Ridge, near Knoxville, Tennessee." Doris heard her voice wobble. "I really need to talk to him."

"Okay, Mrs. Friedman, calm down now. You say it's a government place?"

"It's a new town with some factories for the war." Doris bit her lip. She didn't want to say too much. Rob had given her the number for Harrison's secretary, since the dormitory had no phone.

"Your husband is working there for the war effort?"

"Yes, ma'am. He told me to call him at this number. It's for the secretary in his unit."

At that moment, Barbara woke and started whining. "Hush, sweetie. Mommy's on the phone. Give Mommy a moment."

"Poor little mite. She sounds hungry. I tell you what, Mrs. Friedman. My name is Audrey. I have your phone number. I promise you I'll find a way to contact your husband before the end of the day. I'm going to start by calling the phone company in Knoxville. You just wait for my call."

"Oh, thank you. I will be right here by the phone."

It took over six hours, but at four thirty the phone rang. "Mrs. Friedman? This is Audrey. I have Mr. Friedman on the line."

"Oh, I don't know how to thank you!"

"We all have to support our boys! Go ahead, please." Doris heard Audrey click off the line.

"Rob?"

"Hi, Doris! Boy, is it good to hear your voice!"

"Oh, Rob, you have no idea. You said it was okay to call you at this number, right?"

"Yes, although I can't tie up Harrison's phone for long."

"It took me all day and four operators to get through."

"Sorry about that. The security here is fierce."

"I can imagine. Listen, Rob, Uncle Harry offered to have Barry's nanny take care of Barbara if I stay here and finish school."

"Stay in Chicago? But they're building our house soon."

"I know, but it would just be until next summer. I have to decide quickly because the fall semester starts in a month."

He paused. "Doris . . . I don't know what to say. I want what's best for you, but I don't know if I can stand to be without you that long. I miss you and Barbara every minute that I'm not working."

"I miss you, too, Rob, but I know you're really busy."

"Not that busy. I'm miserable without you. And do you want Barbara to spend every day with that little stinker? He already bullies her. It will only get worse."

"I know. I just don't know what to do."

"I tell you what . . . get your parents to take Barbara for a couple of weeks and come for a visit."

"But . . ."

"Come on. Barbara will survive and so will your mother. I'll send you a telegram with the train schedule from Chicago. Just let me know the day and time, and I'll meet you at the Knoxville station.

One of the guys at the lab has an old clunker and we get an extra gas ration when family arrives. It will be much easier to talk in person."

"You're right."

"And, honey?"

"Yes?"

"Bring galoshes."

"Galoshes?"

"Yes, the whole place is a big mud patch. If it rains, the mud is like quicksand and it sucks your shoes right off! And when it's dry, the dust gets everywhere."

"Sounds lovely."

"It's not so bad. You'll see. We're going to win this war and then we can worry about colleges and degrees."

7: September 1943

Doris had never taken an overnight train trip. She was grateful that Samuel came with her to Union Station. Together they found the right platform and then the car with her roomette. They had splurged on a private overnight berth since she was nervous about traveling solo surrounded by so many servicemen. It was still a lot cheaper than a Pullman car. The station was full of travelers, many in army or navy uniforms. One tall sailor hefted Doris's battered suitcase into the train. He winked, and she thanked him. Just for a moment she imagined being single and setting out to work at an exciting, wartime job. But even better, she reminded herself, she would see Rob tomorrow and have a break from diaper patrol. Her father hugged her goodbye and she promised to write as soon as she got there.

"Don't worry about Barbara," he said. "We'll watch her like a hawk!"

"Just don't spoil her too much."

"You wait. When you come to get her, she won't want to leave with you."

"That's what I'm afraid of!"

"I'll play her tunes on my air pencil."

"I love you, Papa."

"Take care of yourself. And Rob, too, whatever cockamamie job he has down there in the boonies."

Doris watched out the window for a long time as the train passed the sooty outskirts of Chicago. She had rarely left the city of her birth, except for summer trips to the Indiana dunes. She doubted she would be able to sleep on the train, but when darkness fell, she stripped down to her slip and underpants and climbed into the narrow bed. She pulled up the small rail at the open side to guard against falling out with a sudden stop. To soothe herself, she recalled the night that Rob proposed. After they had been dating for six months, he had taken her to dinner at a candlelit Italian trattoria. Neither of them ordered spaghetti. Doris was unsure of Rob's motives, but she did not want to risk slurping pasta and spattering sauce. A chicken dish might strain Rob's budget, so she settled on eggplant parmesan. They shared a spumoni for dessert and then Rob took her hand. "Doris, you're the only girl for me. I love you."

She was startled by the strength of his declaration. She had felt their relationship deepen, but at the same time, she finally had a group of real friends. She could study and play music in a world outside of her family's tight-knit immigrant community. She was planning on moving into the dorms for her senior year, to escape her parents' strictures. Rob had also introduced her to the pleasures of kissing, caressing, and even orgasms. Sure, she had imagined a future with him, but the image was blurred, like looking at their reflection in moving water. Now, as she gazed at his flushed face across the table, she realized that he was offering to ferry her to the nation of couples, a country whose anthem was "our song." Despite falling short of her mother's criteria for ideal femininity, she was loved as a woman, not just admired for her brains or musical talent. "I . . . I love you too," she stammered.

"I know we're young, and I'm not making much money yet, but I think we're going to be pulled into this war soon. I want to face it with you by my side. Doris, will you marry me? We can wait a while until we can afford an apartment, and you can finish school . . ."

"Yes! Yes, let's get engaged."

Rob grinned. "I can't buy you a ring yet, either, but I'll find a better job soon!"

That night was the first time they had actual intercourse, hushing each other in Rob's narrow, childhood bed to avoid waking his parents. Doris was surprised that she didn't enjoy it as much as all the making out and touching, but with time it got better. Soon, being engaged was no longer enough. Doris wanted all the adult privileges, including seeing Rob daily. A couple of months before Pearl Harbor, Rob got a job that paid just enough to rent a place of their own. They got married. Then her pregnancy burst the bubble of their new life. Despite minor disappointments with Rob, Doris knew she would be devastated if he found someone else.

She must have been exhausted because she woke only to the squeal of the brakes as her car was shunted to the new Louisville and Nashville train that would take her to Knoxville. She dressed quickly and went to the dining car for breakfast. Afterward, she took time to fix her hair and put on some makeup. Her dress was a wrinkled mess, but that couldn't be helped.

The red brick L & N train station teemed like an anthill. Buses were lined up next to the terminal. People, military and civilian, milled around on the platform. Doris wrestled her suitcase to the train stairs and gave a coin to a porter who lifted it down for her. The early September air was still warm and humid, and the trees had not started to turn. She looked for Rob's curly head. It was usually easy to spot him in a crowd because of his height. She saw him and then was being grabbed and heartily kissed.

"Doris! You are a sight for sore eyes!"

"I've missed you so much, Rob!"

He turned to a lanky, sandy-haired man wearing wrinkled khakis. "Sol? Meet my wife, Doris. Honey, this is Dr. Sol Steinberg, one of the chemists at the lab. He drove me here."

"Dr. Steinberg, thanks so much for helping us out!"

"Please, call me Sol. You're in for a treat, Doris. Rob got a pass for the two of you to stay at the Guest House for your first night. But why are we standing around in the heat? Let's get you and your suitcase into the car."

Once they were on the way, Rob explained that everyone had to enter Oak Ridge through one of several guard posts or "gates." "I have a guest pass for you today, and tomorrow we'll get you your own badge. It gets you through the gates, onto the buses, and into some buildings, depending on where you work."

"It may seem strange at first, but you'll get used to it," Sol put in. "My wife never forgets to bring her badge when she leaves the house. She wanted to come today, but we have a son, a little older than your Barbara, I think."

"We'll have several hours to settle in," Rob said, "and then some friends from the lab are going to have a welcome party for us in the Guest House lobby."

"Did Rob tell you that the only alcohol the army allows in Oak Ridge is three-two beer?"

"What kind of beer is that?"

"It only has about sixty percent of the alcohol in normal beer. But your husband is a very popular guy because he's in charge of the alcohol we use at the lab. It has to be pure for our experiments. There's plenty of it and we've developed some pretty creative punch recipes. You'll see tonight."

The breeze through the car windows was only slightly cooling. It took them almost an hour to drive the twenty-five miles to Oak Ridge. The countryside was pretty, with forested hills and a few small farms. They pulled into a line of cars at a gatehouse guarded by several MPs with rifles. Large signs said STOP and MILITARY AREA. When it was their turn, Sol and Rob showed their badges, and Rob presented the guest pass for Doris. The guards opened her suitcase and felt around under the clothes. Beyond the gate, some trees and grassy areas lined the road. However, most of the town was a drab and dusty mess of construction. Roads were an unpaved mixture of mud and gravel. People milled around on wooden boardwalks.

"This is the town center, Jackson Square," Rob said, as they passed a large parking lot surrounded by several grocery stores, gas stations, restaurants and cafeterias, a department store, a drugstore, a bowling alley, a dance hall, and a movie theater. Doris noticed a long queue snaking up to the door of the A&P.

"You see that line?" Rob pointed. "They must have gotten in some cigarettes or nylons."

"My wife always says if you see a line by the store, get in it," Sol told her, "because they're probably waiting for something you want to buy."

They pulled into a lot in front of a large, white wooden building with many windows. A veranda ran the length of the front. In its center was a porch with a peaked roof and four white columns. A sign identified it as the Guest House. Doris thought it looked like a low-budget version of Tara from *Gone with the Wind.* Sol dropped them off and they got the key for their room.

"We even have a private bath," Rob said. "I'm looking forward to it after the dorms."

As soon as they shut the door to their room, they were locked in a sweaty embrace. Doris gave herself over to the familiarity of Rob's strong arms and bony chest against her body. Maybe Oak Ridge would help them recover some romance.

"I feel like I need a shower," she protested in a moment between kisses.

"Afterward."

Rob had learned a fair amount about pleasing Doris in their time together, but today he rushed the foreplay and barely lasted a minute after entering her. "Sorry," he mumbled.

"It's okay. We'll get back into practice. I love you."

They fell asleep, and when they awoke it was almost dinnertime.

"We'll eat in the dining room and then the party is at eight."

"Does the lab always throw a party when one of the wives comes to town?"

"Well . . ." Rob looked sheepish. "The thing is, couples, even married ones, have very little privacy in the dorms. The rules are strict. No opposite-sex visitors. So, when someone gets a pass for a night at the Guest House . . ."

Doris gave him a puzzled look. "What happens?"

"Well, everyone drinks punch in the lobby and couples take turns making the most of the room upstairs."

"Blech! What about our sheets?"

"Don't worry, I brought a clean set so we can remake the bed when the party's over."

"How will I look everyone in the eyes?"

"A couple of glasses of punch will help!"

When Doris tasted the punch, she saw Rob's point. It was a potent, overly sweet mix of ginger ale, apple juice, and alcohol poured over a base of ice cubes. Perhaps twelve people stood around the lobby. She chatted with Sol Steinberg's wife about life in the town. The Steinbergs had moved into their own house just weeks ago. Rochelle told Doris that all houses were prefab, each constructed in a single day using a wood frame covered with panels of "Cemesto," compounded of cement and asbestos. They were called alphabet houses because each layout had a letter denoting its size. Houses were assigned according to the number of people in the family. Rochelle said Doris and Rob would probably get a "B," with two bedrooms, because they had Barbara. The "A" houses had only one bedroom. Each home had a coal furnace, fireplace, and porch. Doris was relieved to hear that a washing machine on the porch was also standard.

"You get coal delivered," Rochelle told her. "There's a box outside, and the coal man fills it. There's a milkman too. You leave him money with the empty bottles in your milk box so he knows how many you need."

"Nobody steals the money?" asked Doris.

"Nope, I never heard of any thefts. The dorms have some problems, though, so keep your things locked up when you're not in your room."

Although everyone knew each other, there was little mention of work. Doris could sense the tension of secrecy. Driving in from the gate, she had seen a huge billboard picturing three monkeys, each covering their eyes, ears, or mouth. The caption read: WHAT YOU SEE HERE, WHAT YOU DO HERE, WHAT YOU HEAR HERE, WHEN YOU LEAVE HERE, LET IT STAY HERE! Another sign pictured Uncle Sam above a drawing of a Nazi soldier collaring an American pilot. The message read: LOOSE TALK HELPS OUR ENEMY. SO LET'S KEEP OUR TRAP SHUT.

8: September 1943

The next morning, the Friedmans left the comparative luxury of the Guest House for the dorms. Doris had only one roommate, a young woman from Memphis who was doing shift work in one of the large factories. Their bunks had metal frames and were made up with sheets and scratchy, plaid blankets. Doris had a small chest of drawers. Several wooden hangers were in the closet for her coat and dresses. As Rob had warned, dust was everywhere, even though the dorms included maid service.

Rob waited downstairs while she dropped off her luggage. Then he took her to an administrative building to get her badge. "I have to get back to the lab, honey, so when you're all through, take one of the buses that says X-10 at that stop across the street. This pass will get you in at the gate to our office building. Tell the guard you're meeting me for lunch and they'll let me know you're there."

Getting a badge involved not only filling out reams of forms, but also sitting through a class on the importance of security. "Report any suspicious activity," their young instructor urged. Most of the women in the class were coming to Oak Ridge for wartime jobs. Doris heard a variety of regional accents, especially the East Tennessee twang. It was obvious that women were badly needed as workers. She felt guilty for not applying to fill a job. However, if she lived in Oak Ridge, she would have Barbara all day.

After several hours, she was given a badge with her picture. She found the bus to the X-10 laboratories and showed her badge to board.

At this time of day, there were a few open seats, which was lucky since the ten-mile trip on rutted roads took about thirty minutes. She had to present her badge and pass at another gate house before arriving at a multistory building with a tall smokestack. She knew it housed the offices and a nuclear reactor that was still under construction. Rob had told her how to spot the correct entrance. A guard sitting at a desk asked Doris to wait on a bench.

As she gazed through a small window in the door that led to the office area, she saw a man in baggy white coveralls walk by with a pole on his shoulder. Then came another ten feet of pole with a small metal pot slung onto it, another ten feet of pole, and finally a second man dressed in identical coveralls. Doris knew the pot must contain a very radioactive source. When she glanced at the guard, however, his face showed mystification and alarm. She felt special because she understood what was going on. She was beginning to realize how rare that was in Oak Ridge. After another few minutes, Rob came bustling out. "Come and say hello to Harrison before we go to lunch."

Harrison wore cotton slacks and an unstarched, open-necked shirt. He rose from behind his desk when he saw them at his office door. "Doris! Welcome to Oak Ridge. Did you have any problems getting here?"

"Not really, other than taking a whole day to find a phone operator who could connect me."

"Oh dear. You're not the only one who had that problem. But I have some good news of my own—Nora Joy is expecting a baby."

"Congratulations! Are you all moved into your house?"

"Yes, she's adjusting to life here, like all the other wives. I'm sure you'll see her soon."

"I'll look forward to it!"

Harrison motioned to them to have a seat and closed the door. "Doris, I just want to caution you—I told you more about the project than I usually do with the wives."

"Yes, I already realized that."

"The vast majority of people working here at Oak Ridge, other than us scientific types at X-10 or the top brass at other buildings, have no earthly idea what their jobs are about. So, please be discreet."

"Of course, Harrison. You didn't even need to mention it. I can see how important secrecy is here."

"You can trust Doris," Rob said.

"Well, it seems I already have!" Harrison smiled. "Go on, kids, enjoy your lunch."

During the next few days, Doris explored Oak Ridge. She walked up to the new streets where their house would be built. The neighborhood was terraced and divided into small lots. Construction equipment and dust was everywhere. She watched the workmen put up frames for houses, hang Cemesto panels, and add windows and roofs. They finished at least thirty homes in a day. Still, it would be weeks before theirs would be ready.

She and Rob ate in the cafeterias, which were adequate, but not the tastiest. Between the limited cuisine and all the walking, Doris was slimming down to her pre-Barbara weight. She heard in the dorm that epidemics of diarrhea sometimes swept through. It wasn't clear if it was the food or the flu. Some evenings, if Rob was not too tired, they saw a movie, roller skated, bowled, or took square-dance classes. Doris also gained a better appreciation for their welcome party. Having time together without Barbara or the pressures of school was a tantalizing reminder of their earlier closeness. And they didn't even have the privacy of a car or a house with absent parents. The frustration was refueling their attraction to each other.

She spent time in the public library, sometimes chatting softly with the librarian. Doris asked her to recommend some books about Tennessee.

"This is one of my favorites," said the librarian. "It's the diary of a schoolteacher who lived through the New Madrid earthquakes."

"I never heard of them."

"Several huge quakes happened in 1811 and 1812. So big they rang church bells in Boston. The Mississippi ran backwards for a few hours, and Reelfoot Lake was created in northwest Tennessee. The earth kept opening up, so people would cut down trees to bridge the rifts."

"That's terrifying! Are there earthquakes here now?" asked Doris, thinking about the nuclear reactor.

"No, I'm from Knoxville and we've never had one. It was all centered pretty far from here, near the border with Missouri."

"I'll definitely read it. Sounds fascinating. I'd like to learn more about the hill people around here. I know so little about their history. I've never felt more like a city girl."

"Not many books written about them, but you can learn by watching and listening! Although they aren't real fond of Oak Ridgers. You know, the government forced them to sell their land for a song to build this place."

"I can imagine they feel resentful." Another reason to feel like an interloper. Doris had already discovered that Oak Ridge residents were unpopular in Knoxville, where the locals believed that people working on the base got special privileges and extra ration cards. The salespeople in Knoxville stores often identified Oak Ridge customers by the mud on their shoes or hems, serving them only after everyone else.

A week after her arrival, Rob suggested that Doris go to a grocery store in Jackson Square for picnic supplies. The next day they would drive up into the woods with two other couples from the lab. Doris had not yet ventured into one of the food stores. She picked a time during the day when she thought the store would be less crowded, although stores were never empty. Oak Ridge plants had shifts working around the clock.

She put six Coca-Colas, some cold cuts, bread, and mustard in her cart. When she got to the cash register, a man with a weathered face and wearing a flannel shirt under his apron asked, "Where's your empties, young lady?"

"Empties?"

"For your Co'Cola. Can't give you new bottles without empties." He gestured to a rack of empty Coke bottles at the end of the aisle.

"I'm sorry, but I just got here. We don't have any empties."

He frowned. "Another Yankee."

"Yes, sir, I'm afraid so."

"Well, I'm going to turn mah back." He dramatically turned so he was facing away from the empty bottles, tapping his foot.

Doris stood still, unsure what to do. The man faced her again.

"Little lady, I'm turning mah back!" For good measure, he gestured toward the empty bottles and again turned around, his arms folded. Doris finally understood that he meant her to take some. She picked up six empties and put them on the counter.

"Here are my empties, mister!"

He smiled, showing teeth that had probably never been viewed by an oral hygienist. He put the empties back on the pile and rang up her groceries. Then he asked, "You want 'em in a poke?"

"Pardon?"

"I asked you, little lady, you want your things in a poke?"

"A poke?"

He picked up a brown paper bag. "This here's a poke."

"Oh! Yes, please. Please put everything in a poke."

She entertained their friends at the picnic with the story of her first Oak Ridge food shopping expedition. That night in her bunk bed, however, she was swept by a powerful wave of homesickness. She wanted her old Chicago life—Barbara, her friends, her piano, Rob sleeping next to her. A letter from Samuel had just arrived with some snapshots of Barbara sitting on a blanket in Lincoln Park with Aunt Naomi. Doris vowed to appreciate Barbara more when they were reunited. She wanted to sob, but she let the tears trickle silently so that her roommate would not hear.

9: September 1943

News from the war was grim. The Allies had landed in Italy, but the Germans quickly countered with their own invasion and Italy surrendered to the Nazis. Americans were bombing German cities, with heavy losses on both sides. The Germans had promised to murder four million more Jews before the end of 1943. The Allies were fighting the Japanese in the Solomon Islands and New Guinea.

Rob and Doris wanted an escape. On a Friday afternoon they took a special weekend tourist bus to Gatlinburg, a small resort at the edge of the Great Smoky Mountains National Park. People from Oak Ridge were offered discount hotel rates, so it was a favorite destination for a short trip. They would eat at restaurants and hike into the lush, wooded foothills.

When they arrived, they saw a one-street town with a few parked cars, cabin-style motels, restaurants, and a craft store. All around Gatlinburg were ridges. The trees on the lower slopes were just beginning to turn gold, red, and orange. As the sun started to set, the hills faded to a hazy blue. Swaths of creamy fog gathered in the hollows between them. It reminded Doris of Japanese woodblock prints she'd seen at the Art Institute. Except now Japan had been reduced to the enemy rather than a distant land of beauty. After a dinner of locally caught trout, Doris and Rob took advantage of the precious refuge of their cabin. It was cooler than Oak Ridge, so Rob lit a small blaze in the fireplace.

"How's this for romance?" He gestured at the logs.

"It's good, but I'm still a little chilly. Let's get under the covers."

After a satisfying interlude and a rest in each other's arms, Rob asked, "Want me to warm you up again?"

Doris yawned. "How about in the morning? I'm exhausted."

"You think you're tired? In case you haven't noticed, I've been working twelve-hour days, six days a week." He lowered his voice although their cabin was yards away from its neighbors. "The reactor will go critical soon."

"Rob, are you in danger, like from radiation?"

"Nah. I'm careful. And most of the time I'm just working on the instruments."

"How would you know if there was a problem? It's scary that you can't see or feel it."

"I wear three different badges that measure the dose I get every day. The radiation safety guys from DuPont run these annoying weekly meetings. Harrison hates it, but he says the best way to keep the bastards away is to do everything right. Some of the SED guys—you know, the men from the army Special Engineer Detachment—also do safety inspections. I have to admit, though, some guys don't take things too seriously."

"No?"

"In the lab, DuPont hung a glass case on the wall with a sign: WATCH OUT FOR DANGEROUS TOOLS! It had things in it like a saw with a broken tooth and a battery with a frayed wire . . . Well, last week we came to work and somebody had put a giant sausage in the case!"

Doris giggled.

"And that's not all. We have a hotshot chemist who was in Chicago with us at Met Lab, Jim MacDonald. Everyone knows that when you're working with a radioactive liquid, you use a vacuum bulb to suck it into the pipette."

"What's that?"

"A pipette? It's a glass measuring tube for mixing chemicals. The setup is kind of like a turkey baster. Well, Jim ignored the rule. He sucked right on the pipette and got a mouthful of radioactive isotope! He had to run to the radiation safety people and rinse his mouth out for about an hour. They made him do it in public, too, as a warning to everyone. Now we call that solution 'the MacDonald cocktail!'"

"I guess he learned his lesson."

"Nope. At the last safety meeting, the DuPont guys announced that MacDonald had the lowest radiation exposure on his badge for the month. They asked him to give a little lecture on how he kept his lab so clean. So, he got up in front of everyone. He was wearing his white coat and he showed us his badges clipped to the collar. Then he said, 'Every day I put on my white coat, clip on my radiation badges, and go to the door of my lab. And every day I take off my white coat and hang it right next to the door.' And he takes off his coat with the badges. 'And then I walk into my lab and start to work.' Everyone howled, except for the DuPont guys!"

"At least it sounds like you're having some fun at work."

"Not really. A Nazi bomb is never far from our minds. All the scientists and most of the research techs know why we're in Oak Ridge."

"I think about it a lot too. I'm glad we can talk now, because I've felt really alone."

Rob drew her close. "I'm sorry, Doris. I know this is hard on you. I'm not sure why Harrison told you everything. Like he said, most of the other wives don't know what we're doing. I hope you're being careful about what you say."

"Of course I am, but I feel so out of place and useless here, Rob! I love you but . . . I want to go home."

"When we have a house, and Barbara's with us, things will be better."

"Will they? What will I do all day? I miss my friends. You're working hard, but you have a purpose. I want one too—more than changing diapers."

"Annette's coming very soon."

"I'm not sure if that will be an improvement."

Rob drew back and frowned. "I thought you girls were best friends."

"She's always criticizing me. She says the nastiest things in that sweet voice of hers."

"I think she's just jealous of you."

"Yeah, but that doesn't make it easier to be around her."

"Come on, Doris. I know you love Annette, even if she annoys you. And you'll make other friends. You can play the piano."

Doris stretched, enjoying being in a roomier bed than her bunk in the dorms. The fireplace was also a nice touch. "I could give lessons. A lot of people here love music."

"That could be good for you."

"And I could make a little extra money without leaving Barbara with a babysitter. I'm studying the accounting books too. Someone around here must need a bookkeeper."

"Can we just enjoy this weekend? Tomorrow we'll hike up to a beautiful waterfall. And there are wildflowers."

"And bears!"

"Honey, they're more afraid of you than vice versa."

"If you say so." She tucked herself along Rob's body and soon was fast asleep.

The hike the next day was even more scenic than Doris expected.

"You see?" Rob said, as they sat next to a burbling stream and ate the sandwiches they had brought. "The South isn't all moonshine and segregation."

"No? Look at how they treat the colored workers at Oak Ridge. I hear they live in plywood huts with wooden shutters instead of glass. And all over town they have to use 'colored' bathrooms and cafeterias."

"Yes, it's bad, but they're also making much more money than they did before the war."

"You know where the Nazis got their ideas about inferior races?"

Rob shook his head.

"From us, Rob! From the United States of America! We read about eugenics in our anthropology class."

"Well, of course it should change, but look around the world. Where are things better? Not in Europe and not in Stalin's Russia for sure. At least we have freedom of speech!"

"I don't exactly feel free to speak in Oak Ridge."

"Well, there's a war on, Doris. And if the project works, we have a much better chance of winning it. Harrison says I'm doing a good job, but the stress and the hours are brutal. I need you here, and I thought you needed me too."

"You know I love you, Rob. But it's hard to stop short of a degree when I only have a year to go."

"Can't you wait until we get home? By then, Barbara could be in preschool or kindergarten, so you'd have more time. The university said you could always come back and finish."

"I worry that something else will get in the way by then."

"What about our promises when we got married? I said I'd take care of you, and you would take care of our family."

Doris did not recall those exact words. "What if I want more than that? I thought we said we'd be partners."

"Exactly. Our family is our partnership."

"Yes, but you also have a job that fascinates you."

"You'll have time to find the right kind of work after the war."

Doris sighed and put the remains of their lunch back in the tote. She still hadn't made a decision about Harry's offer, although it was getting harder to contemplate leaving Rob alone in Oak Ridge. "Come on, let's go back down."

After dinner, Rob asked the man at the motel desk what would be fun to do.

"Do you folks square dance?" the man asked.

"Yes, we've recently learned some steps in our town."

The man must have known they were from Oak Ridge because of their tourist discount but did not comment. He pointed out the dance hall where a square dance was being held.

Rob and Doris joined a line of locals and paid a small entry fee at the door. Doris had packed a full skirt that she wore at square dances in Oak Ridge. They noticed only a few younger men among the Gatlinburg people. Most were fighting in the war or had gone to cities to work. However, a number of older men, dressed like farmers, accompanied their wives and daughters. Doris felt conspicuously like a city girl.

A large bin just inside the door was labeled GUNS AND KNIVES. As each man passed it, he dropped in a shotgun, pocket knife, or hunting knife. The crowd was silent. Few even exchanged greetings. In the corner, the band stood, including a fiddler, a bass player, a guitar player, and a caller with a microphone. Doris worried that she and Rob would be chased out, or at least shunned, but as couples formed squares, the others beckoned to them. Doris was excited to have a Tennessee adventure.

The lively music began. The caller started chanting instructions. Many were familiar: *Grand right and left, then meet your partner with an elbow swing. Keep on swinging around the ring!* Others were new and Doris and Rob watched the other couples carefully: *Couple do that four-leaf clover—back-to-back and elbows over.* Doris loved being swung off her feet by her partners at intervals, and Rob, too, got the hang of his part. Doris smiled at him over their partners' heads, proud to be his wife. The songs had names like "Golden Slippers," "Bile Them Cabbage Down," "Sally Johnson," and "Shoot That Turkey Buzzard."

When the dance was over, everyone filed out, the men recovering their weapons. Doris did not see any hesitation as they picked out the correct rifle or knife. Despite their busy day, she and Rob made the most of their cabin and comfy bed. She had almost resolved to move to Oak Ridge when they rode the return bus.

"I feel like we're traveling forward in time," she told Rob.

"Yes, back to all our worries."

10: September 1943

"So, have you decided?" Rob asked Doris. They were taking a walk in Jackson Square to get ice cream after seeing a movie.

She sighed. "I want to be here with you . . . And I know it would be better for Barbara. I worry about leaving her with Barry and the nanny. She's used to having all my attention. And here she'd have both of us. She's really been missing you."

"How about you, Doris? Have you been missing me?" He pulled her closer.

"You know I have!" She put her arm around his waist as they strolled. "Even if I stayed in Chicago, it would only be until next summer." She leaned into her husband and his unique scent, and the warmth of his body flooded her senses. If only life could be simple, without having to give up one dream for another. But, she reminded herself, she and Rob were lucky compared to so many couples separated by the war.

"Right now we're on the waiting list for a house. I'm afraid if you don't move down here, we'll lose our place. You've seen the shortage of housing in Oak Ridge. Harrison really stuck out his neck for all of us in the lab. There's no guarantee we could still get our own house if you wait to come until next year."

"That's a good point."

"And it would be expensive for you to pay rent in Chicago."

"But living in the dorms here is cheap for you."

"Cheap but uncomfortable."

"True . . ."

"Doris—sometimes I worry that your family is trying to split us up."

"No, Rob. My father really likes you. And you know Uncle Harry. He can be cutthroat when he wants something—and he just thinks I should finish college. Anyway, I'm not going to let anyone come between us. I love you."

"Then let's be a family like we planned."

"Promise that, after the war, you'll do your best to help me finish my degree?"

"Of course I promise."

She slurped the rest of her ice cream. "Okay, then I'll come back when our house is ready."

"You won't regret it, honey!" Rob gave a little hop of joy and planted a lingering kiss on Doris's lips, earning them some smiles and even a wolf whistle from people around them.

"Did you just propose?" asked a woman sitting on a nearby bench.

"Naw, we're an old married couple," Rob replied.

The day before Doris's return to Chicago, Rochelle invited her over. Her two-year-old, Benjamin, was a sunny child, content to look through picture books and play with stuffed animals while the women chatted.

"Try to keep things like flour and sugar in canisters," Rochelle advised, taking a loaf of bread out of her pantry, "because it's hard to avoid bugs and mice."

"Ugh! Well, we had a few cockroaches in Chicago no matter what I did."

"By the way, we don't keep kosher. Is that a problem for lunch?"

"Not at all."

"We tried when we first married, but we were living near Caltech in Pasadena, so getting the meat was especially difficult. Here, it would be next to impossible. I think the nearest kosher butcher is in Atlanta!"

"My parents keep kosher, but it's easy on the South Side of Chicago. When Rob and I married, my uncle Harry asked us not to have pork in the house. Rob loves bacon, though, and I do buy it when I can. What Uncle Harry doesn't know won't hurt him!"

"Why is Uncle Harry the authority rather than your father?"

"Oh, Papa is easygoing. He loves music and art. Religion isn't important to him—or me, either, if I'm honest. Harry is married to my mother's sister. He owns a bunch of hotels and office buildings and is a big *macher* in the synagogue. Everyone looks up to him. He offered to send me to Wellesley for college, but I was scared to go so far away." She sighed.

"Sounds like you're kind of hard on yourself, Doris. Look at how far you've traveled now!"

"Not to any place I expected. But it's good to be here with Rob, even though I worry about Barbara. I'm starting to feel like myself again. Our marriage didn't have a lot of time to grow, what with the war and the baby. What about you, Rochelle? How did you and Sol meet each other?"

"He was the best man at my cousin's wedding."

"Classic!"

"When we started to talk, we discovered we had a lot in common. And, of course, I thought he was handsome." Rochelle bent down to give Benjamin a squeeze. "And you look just like your daddy!"

Benjamin smiled. "Can I have a cookie, please?"

"What good manners!" Doris marveled.

Rochelle handed her son a cookie and he thanked her. "Eat it here at the table." Rochelle sat him on a chair.

Doris sat next to Benjamin. "He's darling! Barbara is so contrary. She's also a really picky eater. She adores Rob, but sometimes I'm not sure she likes me. She ignores me half the time, even though she wants attention from everyone else. I wish I could take a motherhood course. I feel like I was thrown into it headfirst."

"It can't have been easy being so young. I'm almost thirty and I got my master's degree and had a couple of years under my belt of working before Ben came along." Rochelle set the table with plates of sandwiches and fruit.

"It has been rough. I wouldn't give Barbara up for anything, but I worry that I don't know how to be a good mother. My own mother did so many things that I don't want to repeat with Barbara. She used to pinch me, hard, if I did something she didn't like. When I was little she told me that if I swallowed an apple seed, a tree would grow in my stomach. It took me years to bite into an apple again."

Benjamin gave Doris a wide-eyed look and Rochelle shook her head. "All those old wives' tales."

"Yes! Don't worry, Benjamin. Apples are very healthy and the seeds only grow in the ground. My mother and Bubbe also always said that if I didn't wash out my ears carefully, potatoes would grow in them."

Benjamin giggled and Rochelle said, "Now that would make medical history!"

"And there was my uncle Michael. He died from a heart defect when he was in his early twenties. My grandparents stopped in Vilna on the way to the steamship to America to see Bubbe's brother-in-law, who was a rabbi. According to the family legend, he cursed the baby in her womb who would be born in a godless land. I think my mother actually blames Michael's death on that curse."

Rochelle tsked. "My family has stories like that too. Sometimes I can almost see the shadow of the shtetls reaching out over the Atlantic, like in an animated newsreel. The shtetls and the Nazis both." She sat down to eat. "Well, I'm glad you're enjoying this little interlude with Rob. Sol says he's really helpful on the project."

"Yes, he seems to have a talent for electronics. You know, he doesn't have a college degree."

"Sometimes practical know-how is better than book learning."

"That's just what Rob says. He's working so hard. He's exhausted and sometimes he gets short with me."

"Whatever they're doing, it's a lot of pressure."

Doris assumed that Rochelle did not know about the bomb, so she simply agreed. "Can I ask your advice about Oak Ridge?"

"Of course."

"My uncle Harry offered me a way to stay in Chicago and finish college. He said I could leave Barbara at his house with his son and the nanny while I go to classes. I came down here to visit to try to make a decision before school starts. I ended up telling Rob I'd move to Oak Ridge to be with him."

"That sounds like a hard choice."

"I love Rob and it's been wonderful to be together again, but I'm afraid that now I'll just be a housewife forever."

"I don't think delaying your degree in the middle of a war means you'll never have a career. Living in a place like Oak Ridge could even open up some doors."

"You said you're a social worker? How did you decide on that?"

"Both my parents are doctors. My older brother also went to medical school. I knew I wanted a family and I like to help children, so I took a different route. Since we're stuck here, I'm taking advantage of the extra time with Benjamin. I'm actually happy to have a break."

"I'm thinking about giving piano lessons. And I've been learning accounting from some books."

"I'm impressed! You don't give up on your goals."

Doris took a bite of her chicken sandwich. "Mm! Much better than the cafeteria."

"I should hope so!"

"Well, thanks for the encouragement. Uncle Harry sent me the books. He thinks I could do bookkeeping to make a little extra money—but really I'd like to learn how to invest, like in stocks."

"Smart girls like us have big dreams. But you found a good man. That's important too. The best job can't make you happy without people you love. And you could end up as a single mother. I've counseled plenty of those, and it's no picnic."

"Yes, I'm pretty sure I'm doing the right thing." Doris took her empty plate and glass to the sink.

"And, Doris—no marriage is perfect. Sol is a real slob."

Doris was glad she had taken the initiative to help clear the table. She really wanted Rochelle to like her.

"You can just pile those next to the sink," Rochelle said from her seat at the table. "About all Sol does at home is take out the garbage and fix the furnace. Sometimes when I pick up his dirty underwear, I want to wipe his face with it. He doesn't like to talk about problems either. But the things I love about him make it worthwhile. I'll look forward to your coming back here, even though Oak Ridge is like a goldfish bowl, with everyone watching us swim. Just try not to let the stress get to you."

"I bet you're right. It's a town full of strangers, but people in the lab all know each other. I hope you won't mind if I ask you a question now and then about how to take care of Barbara."

"Any time! And maybe she and Benjamin will be buddies when they get a little older."

The Friedmans' parting at the train station was more hopeful than sad. *See you soon!* Doris mouthed, waving to Rob from the train car's doorway.

11: November 1943

In mid-November, Rob called and said their house was ready. The government provided a small allowance for the move. They would ship their somewhat battered piano and the deluxe English baby carriage that Uncle Harry had given them. Its large wheels should be able to navigate the boardwalks. Doris couldn't imagine dragging a toddler with her on foot when she did errands. Winter was looming and it sometimes snowed in Oak Ridge. Doris packed up the Chicago apartment and got train tickets for just after Thanksgiving.

Annette was already working as a technician in X-10. She and Joel would feed Rob whatever passed for a turkey dinner in Oak Ridge. If they could not find their own turkey to roast, they might just eat in the cafeteria. In any case, Rob said the work never really stopped, even for a holiday.

Doris brought Barbara to her parents' house. They would all go together to Uncle Harry's for Thanksgiving dinner.

"I offered to have Thanksgiving here," Samuel told her, "but Harry's got the cook and the maid."

"So do we! Bubbe and Bronya."

"Not in the same league, according to your mother."

"After you-know-where, this seems like the lap of luxury."

Barbara sat on the living room floor, scribbling with some crayons on a pad of paper. "Look, Grampa, dog!" The picture was a brown blob with four stick legs. Curving lines suggested a sidewalk and a red square appeared to be a house.

"Barbara, that's beautiful!" Doris praised. "Can I keep it?"

"No! Mine."

"Okay." Doris could see that the advent of language was unlikely to ease her maternal struggles. She longed to pick up Barbara and cuddle her, but she was afraid her daughter would just wriggle away. "She's pretty advanced for her age, isn't she?" she commented to Samuel.

Her father picked up the drawing and examined it. "You know, I've seen three-year-olds who can't draw like this. See how the house is smaller, in the distance? The kid already draws in perspective. You'll need to get her art lessons, Doris."

Doris was proud of Barbara, but also worried about doing a good job with such a smart child. "She must get it directly from you. Drawing skipped my generation."

"You have other talents, *mamaleh*. But Barbara's pretty attached to me. I'm going to miss the two of you."

"I'll miss you too. I got homesick during that visit."

"You're the one who was so eager to tie the knot."

"I know. But Rob's worth it. We just need to get through this war, and then we can pick up our lives again."

"I don't think the war is ending any time soon. Even if the Red Army has the Wehrmacht in retreat in Russia, Europe is still crawling with Nazis."

"I know, Papa."

"And in the South Pacific, the navy is fighting inch by inch for the Gilbert Islands."

"Well, I can't tell you anything, except that the work in Oak Ridge could be the key to winning the war."

Samuel looked skeptical. "Really?"

"Really. You just have to trust me for now."

He shrugged. "If you say so."

Doris watched Barbara add a yellow sun blob to her drawing.

"Still, Papa, I didn't bargain for living in Dogpatch! There's a little downtown with shops and a grocery. One of the local women likes to walk around there. She must live in town because she wears a badge. Everyone in Oak Ridge wears a security badge, except for little kids. She has long, wild red hair and her clothes look like she sewed them herself. She has twin babies and she breastfeeds the two of them right there in public! And the way the local people talk—you can hardly understand them."

"But Rob can't be the only science type working there."

"Oh, no, lots of educated people have come."

"So they must be bringing their wives and families too."

"Yes. Now that we'll have our house, I hope to make some friends. Rob is doing well. The men in his group seem to respect his skills."

"I have confidence in you, Doris. You'll figure it out. I should have pushed you to go to Wellesley when Harry wanted to send you. I was selfish to keep you here a little longer."

Doris gave him a hug. "I wasn't ready to go. But now I have to take care of Rob and Barbara. Papa, do you think I'm foolish to want a career?"

"Of course not! Maybe the war will give you some opportunities."

"I hope so. I want Barbara to have all the same choices a boy would have. Barbara, what other animals can you draw?"

Barbara scribbled and another four-legged blob emerged. Lines at its feet in green crayon suggested grass. "Cow!"

"Yes! What does a cow say?"

"Moo!"

"You sound just like your daddy. Papa, did you ever hear Rob's story about being an announcer?"

"No, I don't think so."

"You know, I love Rob's crazy sense of humor. Before I met him, he was working in Milwaukee as a radio engineer. One day the station manager said Rob had a nice, deep voice. He asked if Rob would like to try out as an announcer. Rob said sure, and they told him to read the call sign on the air. So Rob said, 'This is WMLK, the voice of America's dairyland . . . Moo-oo!' He was banned from the airwaves."

Barbara laughed with them. "Moo! Moo-oo!" She even sat in Doris's lap for a few precious moments.

The rest of the visit passed all too quickly. Thanksgiving dinner at Uncle Harry's was a prewar dream of fine china, shining crystal, and abundant platters of turkey and side dishes. Barbara sat contentedly in her high chair for longer than Doris would have predicted and then fell asleep in a makeshift playpen.

Before the Cains left, Uncle Harry took Doris aside. "So you rejected my offer—again!"

"I'm sorry. I was very tempted, and I so appreciate your generosity. But being there with Rob . . . I realized I have to put family first."

"Just like a woman to think with your knish instead of your brain."

"Isn't it usually men who think with their you-know-whats?"

"Don't be vulgar, Doris!"

"Just following your example, Uncle Harry."

He shook his head. "Thank God you're my niece, not my daughter."

12: November 1943

This time, Doris knew how to find the train and her reserved roomette. She tipped the porter who stowed their luggage, but she kept a valise handy with picture books, crayons, and a pad of paper, as well as snacks for the trip. All went smoothly until she took Barbara to the dining car for breakfast. They managed the meal with little trouble, although Barbara ate almost none of her oatmeal. However, when Doris took Barbara back to their compartment, holding her daughter by the hand, the last car before theirs had become so crowded with soldiers that she could barely get through the aisle.

"What a pretty little gal!" a red-faced, thickset man declared, patting Barbara's head. "Want to sit on my lap, sugar?"

Barbara smiled at him and tugged at Doris's hand.

"I'm sorry, sir," Doris said as she pulled her daughter closer. "We have to get back to our seats and get ready for the next stop."

"Hell, you can come sit on my lap, mama! I like me a woman with some curves," a blond private on the other side of the aisle called out.

Doris tried to push by him but felt a pinch on her behind.

"Don't you touch me! I'm a married woman."

"Don't see no hubby here," her tormentor answered.

His friends laughed. Doris felt another hand on her thigh. She picked up Barbara in one arm and faced the group of men. She swung her handbag hard, hitting the nose of the man who had grabbed her.

"Damn!" He cradled his nose.

The others guffawed. Doris could smell their sweat and beery breath.

"Fucking bitch!"

Doris struggled to pull away and her dress ripped at the waist.

Barbara started to scream. "Grampa! Want Grampa!"

A man with sergeant's stripes shoved his way to Doris. She saw he had a pistol in a holster at his waist. "Get away from her! What kind of soldiers are you?"

"Horny ones!"

"One more word, and you'll be enjoying the stockade when we get to base." The sergeant turned to Doris and tipped his cap. "Sorry, ma'am. These SOBs have had a little too much Thanksgiving cheer."

"Thank you." Doris practically ran with Barbara in her arms. As she crossed over the clacking joints between cars, she heard several more shouts of "bitch." She shut and latched their compartment door behind them and distracted herself by soothing Barbara. "We're going to see Daddy very soon. No more bad men will bother us."

She was glad Rob hadn't been there. He might have been beaten up defending her. Even though he was tall, Rob was skinny, nearsighted, and flat-footed. If he hadn't had an essential wartime job, he might still have been exempted from the draft. She knew he compared himself unfavorably to his tough-guy brother. Of course, if Rob had been there, the men would probably have left Doris alone. She was proud she had kept herself and Barbara safe. To her shame, she was also glad she did not look Jewish. That might have further inflamed those yokels.

Sol Steinberg had again brought Rob in his jalopy to meet the train. Doris started to apologize for her limp hair and torn dress. Barbara immediately ran to Rob to be picked up. He held his daughter at arm's length so he could look his fill. "Wow, I think you grew six inches! You're a little heavier too. Did you like Bubbe's cooking, Barbara?"

"Pisgetti! Bubbe makes pisgetti."

Rob kissed Barbara's forehead and held her close. He gave Doris a worried glance. "Are you okay, honey? You look frazzled."

"We had a little incident with some drunken GIs on the way back from the dining car this morning."

"Did they hurt you?" Sol asked.

"Only my pride. I walloped one of them in the nose with my purse when he groped me."

Sol clapped. "Good for you, Doris! We should send you to liberate Italy."

"Was Barbara scared?" asked Rob.

"One man was admiring her and she was kind of flirting with him at first. You know, the way that babies flirt. But then a couple of others ganged up on me and I got pretty upset. She got scared then too. Luckily a sergeant was in the car and he told them off. He had a gun."

"I should teach you how to shoot my CO_2 pistol," said Rob as they loaded the car.

Doris and Barbara settled themselves in the back seat and Sol turned the key in the ignition. "A BB gun is limited when it comes to self-defense."

"Yeah, but it looks like a real gun, so Doris could use it to scare a guy."

"How did you get one of those past the guards?" Civilians were not allowed to have guns in Oak Ridge.

"I bought it when we were in Gatlinburg and Doris hid it in a Kotex box in our suitcase. There were a lot of people getting off the bus on a Sunday night, so they were mainly looking for splo." *Splo* was the local term for moonshine whiskey. "I thought maybe I could get a rabbit on our next picnic."

"Ugh! Only if you clean and cook it yourself." Doris shuddered.

"I could."

"You're a real big-game hunter, Rob!" Sol pulled out of the parking lot.

"I've never gutted a bunny, but I do know some kitchen basics," Rob responded. "Hey, who taught you how to roast a chicken, Doris?"

"Actually, Rochelle gave me her chicken recipe," Doris reminded him. "She's a good cook! I hope she'll have some ideas for me on how to entertain children at Oak Ridge."

"I'm sure she would be glad to help. We're just a few streets over from your house. She got the mothers in the neighborhood to start a little play group."

"Maybe don't tell her about my problem on the train. I feel kind of ashamed."

"Why? I'm sure you didn't do anything to deserve it!" Sol replied.

"I didn't, but you know how people talk."

"If it makes you feel better, I won't say a word."

A few snow flurries had begun, but the precipitation just made the boardwalks slippery without being deep enough to hide the ever-present mud. Their one-story Cemesto B, on a brand-new street called West Malta Road, looked much like the surrounding houses. The siding was a dull cream color with darker bands over and under the row of windows. All the houses had standard interior paint colors, but the hardwood floors were nice. Doris was relieved that their furniture and goods from Chicago had already been moved in by a crew from the company, Roane-Anderson, that ran Oak Ridge for the army. She had heard horror stories of furniture left at the wrong address. Rob had even put sheets on the small cot for Barbara, who was too big for a crib at seventeen months. The carriage was parked just inside the door to the porch.

That first night, after singing endless lullabies to settle Barbara in her new room, Doris told Rob she was too tired for sex. "They called me a fucking bitch," she told him.

"I'm so sorry I wasn't there," Rob said. "It's okay. I'm exhausted too." They snuggled together in their bed.

"Did you get any time off for the holiday?"

"A half-day. Better than nothing."

"Did you get some turkey?"

"We ate at the cafeteria. They claimed it was turkey. At least it wasn't Spam."

"I hate to tell you this, but Uncle Harry's cook made a nice, moist bird. And cranberry sauce from scratch with orange juice in it."

"Doris, you're a sadist." Rob gave her behind a light pinch.

"Stop it! Did you see I smuggled a bottle of scotch in my suitcase? I hid it in one of my galoshes."

"I wondered why you weren't wearing them when we picked you up. Okay, I forgive you for enjoying Harry's dinner. Now we can be a family again, with a little scotch to warm up a Saturday night."

13: December 1943

Doris settled into a routine. There was the ever-present mud to mop or dust to sweep, depending on the weather. The town center was almost a mile away and she was glad to have the big-wheeled baby carriage. It didn't roll well on their unpaved street, but it could navigate the wooden sidewalks. With rationing, she needed to go to the grocery several times a week to find adequate food. Barbara enjoyed the "bumpety-bumps" and was fascinated by the construction equipment. She loved to stop and watch the Caterpillars and bulldozers in the endless race to create enough Cemestos for the growing population. Barbara always waved gaily to the coal delivery men and the milkman.

With so many college-educated people and the limited range of entertainment, musical groups were springing up, including a small symphony, chamber ensembles, and amateur jazz bands. Doris started to give several piano lessons a week. It was against army policy to do any business in your home, so Doris used only word of mouth to alert people to her services. She taught several army engineers from the SED. Other students came from the families of project scientists.

One morning a woman knocked on the door. She looked vaguely familiar. Her platinum-blonde hair was arranged on top of her head in perfect victory sausage rolls. Her face was a bit round, and her eyebrows were plucked to thin arches above her gray eyes. Her scarlet lipstick looked freshly applied. She wore a soft, aqua-blue wool coat and short white gloves. Her only concession to Oak Ridge appeared to be her rubber boots.

"Hi, I'm Betty," she drawled, "from three houses over. I'm inviting you to a bridge party tomorrow." She handed Doris an actual, handwritten invitation. "Don't worry, you can bring your baby. We have a sitter to watch the children. You do play bridge, don't you?"

"I love bridge. I played all the time in college."

"Where was that?"

"The University of Chicago."

"Oh, you're one of the Chicago people."

"Yes." Doris knew that the wives exchanged information about their hometowns but avoided sharing details of their husbands' jobs. "I'm sorry, I'm forgetting my manners. It's chilly out. Would you like to come in?"

"Oh, not today." Betty waved a gloved hand. "Just delivering the invitations. I'm a Sweet Briar woman myself. My husband, Will, is a manager at DuPont. We came here from Richmond."

"How nice! Thanks so much for the invitation. I'll look forward to tomorrow."

"Have a blessed day."

Doris had never heard that particular phrase but just nodded. Betty clomped down the boardwalk to complete her list.

That evening, Annette dropped by after dinner. "Have you ever heard of a college called Sweet Briar?" Doris asked her.

"Yes, it's in Virginia. A fancy school for Southern belles who don't want to be corrupted by the Seven Sisters. I've met several women in Oak Ridge who went there. Debutante types."

"Oh boy. One of my neighbors invited me to a bridge party at her house. She said she's a Sweet Briar woman."

"Just be yourself, Doris. You're a killer bridge player. I just think it's a shame you can't work here. It makes life much more interesting."

"I have eight piano students now."

"I meant a job to help the war effort."

"Music helps everyone's morale."

Annette snorted and sat on the couch. She leaned forward. "Hartnell told you about the project. Now I know about it too."

"How nice. But we can't talk about it, even here." She went into the kitchen and brought Annette a glass of lemonade.

"Thanks." Annette took a sip. "Don't you think the men in X-10 talk about it? They're careful about the words they use, and who's in the room, but I can assure you they do."

"But we're not in X-10 now. I hear security people are everywhere. I guess you'll just have to discuss it at work or with Joel."

"Well, don't get intimidated by a bunch of housewives."

"Thanks, Annette. I wonder if that's all I'll ever be—a mindless homemaker who reads recipes and cleaning tips in the *Ladies' Home Journal*."

"Doris! I'm sure you'll find your niche. But you have to admit—you were the one who got pregnant."

"Thanks to my mother's incompetent gynecologist! His ideas on a tipped uterus were way behind the times."

"Uh, I think someone else was involved."

"Okay, Miss Priss, you're no better than me."

"I'm more careful."

"Or luckier. Even rubbers break sometimes."

The women listened to Bob Hope's *Pepsodent* radio show and then Annette went home. Doris wondered if Annette would have been harassed on the train. She hadn't told her about it, fearing that Annette would blame Doris's appearance or attitude for attracting unwanted male attention. The memory was still interfering with her desire when Rob made advances. She shivered, hearing the echoes. *Sit on my lap, mama. Bitch.* Even though her daily life felt uneventful, the constant broadcasts about battles and civilian atrocities lent tension to everything.

The only woman Doris knew at the bridge party was Rochelle—and now Betty. The other five players lived in neighboring streets. One was a colonel's wife. Other husbands either worked at Roane-Anderson, DuPont, or one of the project sites. Doris had curled Barbara's hair and dressed her in a pink pinafore over a white blouse. Everyone said she looked adorable. A babysitter who worked an evening shift at one of the factories took Barbara, Benjamin, and a smaller baby into another room. "Clementine will take excellent care of them," Betty assured the mothers. "We haven't yet been blessed with children, but we were lucky to be assigned this 'C' Cemesto so we can be ready." DuPont was known for giving their employees lavish moving allowances. Doris noted the expensive furniture and oriental rugs that graced the living room, but even Betty had the standard paint colors on her walls.

Doris partnered with Betty and the two of them won the game. Doris got a prize of a pair of nylons, but Betty gave the second party favor to one of the other women rather than keeping it for herself. Betty set out a frosted layer cake and Doris went to check on Barbara, who had fallen asleep on a blanket on the floor. "You should be putting her on the potty," Clementine whispered. Her accent identified her as a local. "She's a great big girl to still be in diapers and rubber pants."

"She's not even eighteen months yet. Our pediatrician said to start around now."

"You have some different ways up North."

"I guess we do." Doris had trouble thinking of undersized Barbara as a great big girl. "What is the age for potty-training around here?"

"In my family, all the children are out of diapers by the time they turn a year."

"Gee! Thanks, Clementine. I may ask you to teach me your methods." But Doris was just being polite. She dreaded the thought of trying to persuade her stubborn daughter to use the potty. It could wait a few more months. She went back to the living room to have a slice of cake. "This is delicious, Betty! I can tell it's not made with molasses."

"I brought some extra sugar from home. Well, girls, let's have a rematch next Friday here at my house. But, Doris, it will be your turn to bring the cake."

Doris hoped her flash of panic was not visible, but Betty asked her to stay a moment after the others left. "Is a smart girl like you worried about baking a cake?"

"Betty, I have to confess I am. My grandmother does most of the cooking at my parents' house and she refused to teach me to cook. She claims all her recipes are secrets from the old country."

Betty shook her head. "Here, we'll just put the dishes in the kitchen. Clementine helps out with some housework, so she'll wash them. We also had a cook growing up, but my mother made sure I learned how to bake. And how to put together a nice dinner."

"Well, I'll tell you the story of my first cake." The two women sat back down in the living room. "In Chicago, we had an awful, tiny apartment. I knew nothing about cooking, as I said. To give you an idea, my husband, Rob, loves shrimp, so when I was pregnant, I bought some at the store. I swear I never knew shrimp had shells, and ugh—legs and heads. I cried while I cleaned them, and I had to go and throw up at least twice. But at least they came out well."

Betty snorted. "You are a caution."

"My next project was the cake. It was really hard to get sugar, even if you had ration coupons, so I clipped out a recipe from the newspaper to make a victory loaf cake with molasses. I mixed it all up and poured it into the pan. I was so proud. But when I put it in the oven I realized the door didn't fit tightly. I knew cakes needed an even temperature, so I took the rest of the newspaper and crumpled it up to stuff in the cracks."

Betty put her hand over her mouth, her eyes wide.

"Yes, it caught on fire. So I splashed it with water and put the fire out and just kept baking the loaf. When the time was up, it looked nice and brown, though the pan seemed awfully heavy. So, I waited a couple of minutes, used a knife to get the cake out of the pan, and put the loaf on a plate. I thought some orange icing would go well with it, so I mixed up a batch and spread it over the top. I went off to do some chores. When I came back to admire my cake, the icing was gone! So I mixed up another batch, spread it on, and went back to my cleaning."

Betty tittered. "Nobody told you to let a cake cool before you ice it?"

"You got it. When I looked again, the second batch of icing had melted and was pooling around the bottom of the cake, so I made a third batch. By then, the cake had cooled enough so the icing stuck. After our dinner, I gave Rob a slice. He took one bite and spit it across the room! He said he was sorry, but I cried for an hour. I haven't tried baking a cake since."

"I'll tell you what, Doris. We'll bake one together next week so you get the hang of it."

"I would love that. I should get Barbara and let you relax."

"Don't you worry. I have nothing but time. Can I ask you something?"

"Sure."

"Friedman—that's a Jewish name, isn't it?"

"Yes."

"I've seen your Rob. He's tall and handsome, but he's dark, like I expected a Jew to look. You don't look like a Jew. And pardon me, but neither of you have horns."

"Horns?"

"In Sunday school they taught us that Jews have horns."

"You're joking, right?"

Betty leaned back and waved a hand. "No, I thought all you people would have little horns—maybe just under your hair?"

"Like Michelangelo's Moses?"

Betty looked blank.

"You do know who Michelangelo is?"

"Some French or Italian artist, as I recall."

"What the heck do they teach you at Sweet Briar?"

"Oh, you know. Literature, some math, a little history—especially of the South . . ."

"Weren't there any Jewish girls there?"

"Not as far as I know."

"There must be Jewish people in a big city like Richmond."

"I suppose, but not in our circle."

Doris felt herself getting tense. "So what other 'facts' do you know about Jews?"

"Well, you killed our Lord Jesus."

"Nope. The Romans did that."

Betty shrugged. "I can see you're upset, Doris. I'm sorry if I insulted you. I honestly just wondered—"

"Betty, are you aware that the Nazis are murdering all the Jews in Europe? They've already killed several million, including a bunch of my relatives."

Betty looked taken aback. "I do read the papers, but everyone says those stories are exaggerations. And maybe the Germans got mad because the Jews are so rich and control the movies and the news."

"Oh my God! Do they teach *The Protocols of the Elders of Zion* at Sweet Briar?"

"I never heard of that."

"It's a forged book that claims Jews run the world. Betty, you are . . . an ignoramus. Don't expect me next week at your little club." Doris retrieved Barbara from the bedroom and left without a backward glance.

At dinner, Doris told Rob about the confrontation.

"I'm glad I'm around a bunch of scientists and engineers all day." Rob sliced into his baked potato. "Your cooking is definitely improving, Doris. This potato is cooked all the way through. Now if we just had some butter instead of this oleo . . ." He chewed and then went on, "At least half the guys in the lab are Jewish. I can imagine what Betty thinks about colored people. You're right about the slum where the colored workers have to live in Oak Ridge. I went by there on the bus when I had an errand. Those hutments look like they're made out of cardboard."

"I didn't even bring up the topic of race. It sounds like her family in Richmond is well off. Did I tell you she has a Cemesto C even though they don't have children yet? I guess her husband's being a manager at DuPont has its advantages."

"Harrison thinks DuPont spends too much on fancy digs for their people and doesn't understand research. Though he admits their engineers are efficient. But Harrison likes scientists better than engineers. I think he just tolerates me because they need help with the electronics." He paused. "Maybe being at the bridge club is like how I feel working with all these guys who have college degrees and even PhDs. They treat me like one of the bunch, but I always worry I'm not at their level. You and Joel are natural eggheads. I just work hard."

"You're just as smart as they are. And I certainly don't feel inferior to Betty!"

"No, I didn't mean that. But it sounds like those women are stuck up."

Doris recalled her conversation with Harry. "I blame your family for discouraging you. What kind of mother sees a boy reading advanced math books and says, 'Oh, Robby, why don't you go play baseball like your brother?'"

"I guess she wanted me to get some fresh air."

"Fresh air! Your big brother ran around with the local mobsters."

Rob shrugged. "I think that's an exaggeration. People looked up to him in the neighborhood. And you've never liked him, or my sister."

"I just worry that they take advantage of you. Oak Ridge could give you a real boost. When the war is over, you can go to college and have a job that uses your potential."

"I'm using my potential now."

"It's a start. But once the war is over, you should get your degree."

"You know, sometimes, Doris . . . Your father never finished high school and your mother told me she almost fainted when her first-grade teacher came into the bathroom to pee. She didn't think teachers needed to. So don't treat me like some greenhorn. You're the one who thought plutonium came from Pluto."

"I was just making a joke!"

"Yeah, right." He threw his crumpled napkin on the table. "I'm doing my part for this family and the war. I think I deserve a little respect."

"I do respect you. That's exactly what I was saying. Anyway, if it weren't for you, I'd be graduating next semester."

"Why is your degree so important anyway? I'm taking good care of us."

"What happened to all your talk about equal partners? Now I'm supposed to just be the little woman? Lie back, spread my legs, and keep my mouth shut?"

"Damn it, Doris! You came home whining how you could never have a baby. Don't blame me for not using rubbers."

Doris's chair shrieked against the floor as she stood up. "No, I don't blame you, Rob. I blame myself for letting sex get in the way of my better judgment. I hate this place!" She went outside and sat on the porch, smoking, until Rob turned out the lights. It was the worst argument they'd ever had, but she refused to let Rob see her cry.

14: December 1943

The following afternoon, the telephone rang. The Friedmans had just had one installed. Only a minority of people in Oak Ridge were granted a home phone, but Harrison wanted to be able to contact Rob if he was urgently needed. When Doris picked up the receiver, Rob was on the line. His voice sounded strained.

"Hi, honey, I wanted you to know I won't be home tonight."

Doris was still upset. They had barely mumbled good morning to each other at breakfast. "Can I ask why?"

"I'm at the hospital. There was a kind of accident at the lab today. I don't think I should explain over the phone."

"Rob! Are you okay?"

"I feel fine. And they say I'm going to be fine."

"Was it something like the MacDonald cocktail?"

"Kind of, but it wasn't my fault."

"Will they let me see you?" She heard Rob ask someone if his wife could visit him.

"The nurse says yes, but what about Barbara? I don't want you to bring her to the hospital."

"I'll see if Rochelle can watch her for a couple of hours."

"Okay."

"I'll be there as soon as I can." Doris's annoyance at Rob evaporated in the face of her fear that he could be injured.

When she burst into the hospital lobby and asked for her husband, a nurse came out and escorted her, unlocking an unlabeled door. They entered a corridor with several rooms and a nursing desk.

"Mr. Friedman's in that room." The nurse pointed. "Your husband says you know what he's working on. Don't worry—radiation just passes through a person, so it's safe to be close to him."

When Doris entered the room, Rob was dressed in a hospital gown, lying on a bed and reading an engineering journal.

"Rob! What happened? The nurse said radiation."

"Yeah, I got a little overdose. It was so stupid. This morning a couple of health officers from the SED came in. They said my badges had been completely exposed two days in a row."

"Oh no!" She sat on the edge of his bed. "Couldn't they have told you yesterday?"

"They called yesterday, but I'm not working on anything hot so we thought it must be a mistake. Today they were angry and asked me what the hell I was doing. I told them I'm running the counting lab. No radioactive samples allowed. So they turned on their Geiger counter—you know to measure radiation? It started to click and they walked toward my desk. The closer they got, the faster it clicked. The thing was going crazy! But I showed them I had nothing on my desk to set it off. So they went next door. The guys there had a hot source and they had shielded it carefully with lead bricks—on three sides and the top. They didn't think about putting bricks on the side next to the wall between the container and my desk!"

"Those idiots!"

"What the health safety guys did next was almost as dumb. They took me over here and made me take a shower and scrub myself for half an hour. I didn't get any radioactive liquid or powder on myself. I just got radiated!"

"Do you feel sick?"

"No."

"Are you scared?"

"A little. They don't expect anything much to happen, but they told me to watch out for nausea, headaches, and diarrhea. I might also lose some hair, just temporarily."

"At least you have a lot of hair! But what about getting cancer, like Marie Curie?"

"I don't think they know. Not many people have worked with radiation until now."

A doctor came in and repeated much the same information that Rob had just told her. "We'll keep him overnight for observation, but we think he'll be fine."

A man in an SED uniform knocked on the frame of the open door to announce his presence. "How's he doing?"

"So far, so good," Rob replied.

The doctor agreed and left.

The SED man turned to Doris. "And who's this dish? Maybe I need to get some gamma so you'll visit me?"

Rob frowned. "This is my wife, Doris. Doris, this is Dave Sokol, one of the radiation safety officers."

Dave saluted Doris with a mocking smile. "Sorry, no offense meant, Mrs. Friedman."

"None taken."

Dave's uniform was neatly pressed. He was a little shorter than Rob but built like an athlete, muscled and with broad shoulders. Brown hair crowned a high forehead. He wore horn-rimmed glasses over dark eyes.

"Do you think Rob will get sick?" Doris asked him.

"Probably not. Those badges aren't very accurate, but it's a good sign that he's not throwing up. Where do the two of you hail from?"

"Chicago," said Rob.

"Oh, fellow Midwesterners. I grew up in Kansas City. Not a great place for a Jew."

"Neither is Oak Ridge," said Doris.

"Come on, Doris. You just had one bad experience," Rob said.

"Yes, I met a neighbor who asked about my missing Yid horns."

"You're kidding!"

"I wish I were." Doris sat on the edge of Rob's bed.

"That's worse than having to mail-order matzoh for Pesach. Not to mention the Kansas Ku Klux Klan shutting down the city with their parades every Sunday. I've only been here a couple of weeks, but it seems like there are plenty of us."

"There are," Rob confirmed. "How did you wind up in the SED?"

Dave struck a pose. "We're special GIs. The chosen few. Selected for knowledge and high IQ."

Rob blew a raspberry.

"Actually, I have a degree in electrical engineering. It looks like you've been designing some nifty new instruments."

"Yeah, when my friends aren't beaming death rays through the wall."

"Pretty careless—but I've been hearing some wild stories about MacDonald, and that guy Louis Slotin too."

"Yeah, I never figured this would happen to little old me."

"So, what do you normally do all day?" Dave asked Doris.

"How about taking care of a toddler?"

"You don't look old enough to be a mama!"

"That's the story of my life."

"No hobbies?"

"Doris is a terrific pianist. It's one of the reasons I fell in love with her." Rob put his arm around her waist.

Doris managed a tight smile but she hated Rob's relegating her music to a hobby.

"Is there much chance to play here?"

"We have an old upright piano. But at least it's in tune. I've been giving some lessons."

"Hey, I might be your next pupil. I've been noodling on the piano since I was a kid. Some jazz but mostly classical. I'm out of practice though."

"Sure, I'll give you our phone number." Doris found a grocery receipt in her purse and wrote on the back.

Rob gave Dave a searching look. "I wouldn't think you'd have time for piano lessons."

"Oh, they don't work us as hard as you civilians. And they assigned me a jeep, so I don't have to wait around for the buses all the time. But if you don't approve . . ."

"No, no. It's fine. I totally trust Doris."

"Then I'll give you a call soon to set up a time." Dave waved with the hand that held a folder, presumably his report on the incident, and left.

Rob gazed after him with a peeved expression. "He was flirting with you!"

"Maybe a little. Men like that don't mean anything by it. Do you want me to say I can't give him lessons? He'll probably never call anyway."

"I hope he doesn't, but it's up to you."

By the next week, Rob had developed a miserable sore throat and was hardly able to swallow. The doctor diagnosed strep throat and told Rob he was lucky, because the hospital had a supply of the brand-new miracle drug penicillin.

"Is this related to the radiation overdose?" asked Doris.

"Frankly, Mrs. Friedman, we aren't sure. We're just learning about the different ways radiation affects the body. But we're going to fix your hubby right up."

"At least I don't glow in the dark," Rob choked out when they got home.

"I'm glad, because that would make it hard to sleep! I wish I had Bubbe's recipe for chicken soup. Good for whatever ails you."

"Do you think she would give it to you over the phone?"

"No way! And the few times I've seen her cook, if I ask her how much salt or spice, she says, 'You just shit a little in.'"

Rob's sore throat gradually improved, but his weight dropped to 140 pounds, just short of skeletal for his frame. Doris stuffed him with as much decent food as she could, given the limits of ration coupons and stock at the stores. His hair did not fall out, which seemed like a good sign. Doris tried to put the accident out of her mind, but when he was at work, she jumped if the phone rang. Rob seemed less concerned. He resumed his long hours at the lab. Doris did not mention Rob's radiation exposure to anyone but only alluded to his strep throat. They also did not bring up their argument with each other, but Doris was aware of the tension between them. She felt lucky if they had sex once a week.

"Aren't you angry at the guys at work for being so careless?" she asked Rob one night as they were getting ready for bed.

"Not really. Everything we're doing is so new, we're bound to make mistakes sometimes. I think they learned their lesson. The radiation safety guys read them the riot act and so did Harrison." Rob pulled the blanket up around them. "It's true that some of them, like MacDonald, act like cowboys. Maybe it's their way of dealing with being afraid. A lot of the stuff we handle is pretty dangerous. But it's not as bad as being on a battlefield."

"On a battlefield you can see the enemy."

"Not always. Or even if you see something coming, like a shell or a bomb, it may be too late. I just wish we knew more about radiation. But I think I'll be fine."

"I hope so."

"The doctor said I might have trouble having more kids because radiation can make men sterile."

"You didn't mention that." Doris was exasperated. It was so typical of Rob to gloss over negative news.

"I didn't want to upset you."

She sighed. "Well, for now, Barbara is plenty. We'll worry about more kids after the war. I have to say, though, I'm still upset with those guys in the next lab. It could have been much worse. You need to stand up for yourself, Rob."

"What good would that do now? I'd just make them feel bad."

"Maybe they would be more careful next time."

"I'm sure they will. And it was just bad luck that my desk happened to be next to that wall. Harrison is lobbying the army to build us a special hot lab for working with highly radioactive stuff. Let it go, Doris."

"I guess you're right. Maybe I hold on to things too much."

"That's why we make a good team. Come on, let's lie like two spoons in a drawer."

15: January 1944

On a chilly, gray day, Doris dressed Barbara in a wool hat, jacket, and mittens and tucked a blanket around her in her pram for a journey to Jackson Square. Since the pram was too wide to fit through the door of the pharmacy, Doris parked Barbara next to the entrance and ran in to get some cough syrup. Rob, like many others, had the "Oak Ridge croup" from the dust and damp. For once there was no line, but when Doris came back out, Barbara and the carriage were gone. She looked wildly all over, shrieking Barbara's name. Few others were on the street. After what felt like an hour, but was probably less than five minutes, someone tapped Doris on the shoulder.

"Missus?" It was the red-haired hill woman, although today she did not have her twins.

"I went into the drugstore for just a minute, and my baby is gone!"

"I seen that guard wheel the buggy into the bank."

"Oh, thank you!"

Doris ran down the block and tore open the glass door to the bank. Just inside, a middle-aged guard and one of the female tellers were admiring Barbara, who was sucking on a small green lollipop with evident enjoyment. "That's my daughter! I was in the drugstore for just a minute! Why on earth did you take her?"

The guard straightened up and frowned. The teller crossed her arms and glared at Doris.

"The baby was cold! What's wrong with you Northerners!"

"What's wrong with me? What's wrong with you! You don't move someone's child without permission. She's all bundled up and she would have been colder if I took her inside with me without her blanket."

"Well, I'm sorry if I frighted you," said the guard. "She's just a little doll. What's your name, sweetie-pie?"

"Barbara." She gave Doris a smirk and put the lollipop back in place. Doris tried not to imagine how she was going to deal with Barbara as a teenager, especially if she continued to be so pretty.

"She talks an awful lot for her age," the teller said.

"I like caterpills 'n' dozers," Barbara informed them.

"Yes, we watch the construction machines almost every day."

"Hain't much else to look at around here!" agreed the guard.

Doris was vastly relieved, but she'd be damned if she'd apologize for being angry. "Well, we need to finish our shopping. Don't worry, I'll take her with me into the A&P."

"You do that, ma'am."

Outside the bank, the red-haired woman was waiting.

"Thank you so much for helping me find Barbara," Doris said. "Where are your beautiful twins today?"

"My sister is watching them back at the farm."

"I admire your strength, carrying the two of them around."

"Yes, missus. Would be nice to have a buggy like yours."

"I know. I don't know what I'd do without it."

"Sure is a fancy one."

"It is. We could never have afforded it. It was a present from my uncle when Barbara was born. Is your farm inside Oak Ridge?"

"Yep. We have a little bit of land. We raise chickens. Tastier than the ones you get in the stores. You need a hen, come by our place just before you get to the Edgemoor gate."

"I'll definitely keep that in mind. Um, would I have to kill it and pluck it?"

“Oh, you Yankee gals! Pay a little extra and we’ll clean it up nice for you.”

“Great! I’m Doris, by the way.”

“Alice.” They shook hands and then each went about their business.

When they got home, Doris put away the groceries and put Barbara down for a nap. She heard a tentative knock on the door. It was Betty, carrying a plate that appeared to hold a loaf cake.

“Hi, Doris, can I come in?”

“Okay, but let’s talk quietly. Barbara’s asleep. Here, come into the living room.” Doris gently shut the door to her daughter’s room. “Can I get you something to drink? A Coca-Cola?”

“That would be nice, thanks. Here, this spice cake is for you and your husband.”

“Thank you.” Doris sat down with her own soda. She knew she should break the silence, but she was inwardly relishing Betty’s discomfort.

“I came to apologize,” Betty began. “I really don’t know what I was thinking.”

“What you were taught to think, I guess.”

“I’ve been doing some reading, about the Nazis and all. I talked to my husband, Will, about it too. You’re right, I was an ignoramus.”

“I shouldn’t have called you that. I’m sorry too.”

“It wasn’t very polite, you know . . . And I still don’t think you look Jewish.”

Doris took a deep breath. Okay, maybe History of the Hebrews 101 would help. “Betty, Jews have been around for five thousand years. We got thrown out of our homeland, and Spain and Portugal, and England too. Wherever Jews lived, we’ve mixed some with non-Jews. Not always voluntarily.”

“Oh. I didn’t think about that.”

“My family came from Russia and Poland, where there are a lot of blonds. I don't know if a Cossack raped one of my ancestors, but my grandfather had very fair hair and blue eyes, a lot like yours."

"In the South, it's usually the darker complexions that bring out a family secret." Betty unbuttoned her coat.

Doris reached out to take it from her. "Here, I'll hang up your pretty jacket." She stroked the sleeve. "This wool is so soft." She sat back down. "Humans prey on each other all over the world."

"Or just break the rules. People do fall in love. Sometimes because they're so different . . . Well, the thing is . . . I like you, Doris. And you're the best bridge partner I've ever had. Do you think you could come back to the bridge club?"

"I guess I'm willing to give you the benefit of the doubt. It took guts to come over here today."

"It did. I've been working up to it."

"You know, for me, college was the first time I really got to know people who weren't Jewish. My parents came to America as young children, and all their friends have similar backgrounds. I can understand that you'd have some misconceptions if you've never known any Jews. In fact, Oak Ridge has been kind of a shock for me. You won't believe what happened this morning." She told Betty about the "kidnapping."

"Your Barbara is a charmer."

"She drives me crazy sometimes. We didn't plan to have a child yet, but I went to a quack doctor who told me I was infertile, so we stopped taking precautions."

"The doctor was wrong?"

"Well, Barbara was born not even eight months after we married." Betty teared up and Doris hoped she had not shocked her with such frankness. "Hey, it was a little upsetting, but of course I love her."

"Oh, Doris, what I wouldn't give for a baby." Betty's shoulders shook with sobs. "We've been trying for two years, and nobody knows how to help us. I get terrible cramps every month, but they come like clockwork." Betty took a pristine handkerchief out of her handbag. "We try all the time, and I even lie on my back with my legs in the air afterwards for a whole ten minutes . . ."

Doris tried to banish the mental image Betty's words conjured, but she wondered if Betty used the same scarlet nail polish on her toes as on her fingers. "I'm so sorry, Betty. That sounds rough."

"I can't talk to my friends back home. Some already have a second child. And my mother-in-law barely speaks to me anymore. Though just between you, me, and the wallpaper, that's a blessing!"

"Have they tested Will?"

"Yes, and the doctor says everything's okay on his side. It must be me." Betty wiped her eyes again. "They all tell me to relax. I even saw a psychiatrist in Richmond, and he said I had"—Betty lowered her voice—"penis envy. That I had to learn how to be a real woman."

"That sounds ridiculous. How do you know if you're a real woman?"

"When you . . . when you have a you-know-what, a climax, with your husband inside you. And I never do that."

"I hardly ever do either. Other ways . . . yes. And obviously I got pregnant. Does Will pressure you?"

"No, he's very sweet to me. He says if it doesn't happen soon, we can adopt. I can just imagine how his mother would react to that. She's president of the Richmond chapter of the United Daughters of the Confederacy."

"That does sound like a burden." Doris decided not to say anything about the merits of glorifying the Civil War.

"Do Jewish people worry about having children?"

"Betty, haven't you read your Bible?"

"Of course I have. I had to go to Bible study every week for years and years."

"Did it include the Old Testament or just the New?"

"Well . . . mostly the New."

"Did you ever hear the stories of Sarah and Abraham, or Rebecca, or Rachel?"

"Sure, now that you mention it."

"Think about it, Betty. They all were upset because they wanted to get pregnant. Not that I think praying or offering sacrifices is the answer. It's got to be a medical problem. Both of us know that gynecologists can make mistakes."

"Or psychiatrists. By the way, I'm pretty sure mine was Jewish."

"I thought you didn't know any Jews in Richmond?"

"He was the exception, now that we're bringing this all up."

"Penis envy. That was Freud. I read about him in college. Of course, Freud was Jewish too. But only a man would come up with that idea."

"Well, it might be convenient to pee standing up."

"Betty! I'm surprised at you." They giggled.

"I know, right? Can I bum a cigarette?"

"Of course."

"Will doesn't like me to smoke. I'll use a breath mint before I go home."

"Well, thanks for telling me about the baby problem. I hope you have better luck soon. Let me know if you want to talk more about it."

"Thanks, Doris."

"I feel kind of guilty that it was so easy for me. Too easy."

"Just enjoy having Barbara."

"I try to. She's so much more affectionate to Rob though. Sometimes I want to ask her, 'What am I? Chopped liver?'"

Betty looked puzzled.

"Oh. I guess that's a Jewish expression. It means 'Why don't you appreciate me?' Because chopped liver isn't exactly gourmet cuisine. Maybe you might say, 'What am I? Grits?'"

"Hey, grits are delicious!"

Doris made a face. "I've only had the ones in the cafeteria."

"You wait! I'm going to introduce you to Southern cooking."

"Anyway, Barbara makes me feel rejected."

"Rejected? She's not even two years old. Maybe that's the problem. She's a smart little thing. Maybe she's just having the terrible twos a little early."

They laughed and finished their cigarettes.

16 January 1944

Doris was sweeping the floors when she heard the doorbell ring. "Mommy, door!" Barbara called, running over to see who their unexpected guest might be. Doris swiped her forehead with the back of her hand and opened the door a crack. It was Dave Sokol. She let the door open fully.

"Why, hello. Aren't you AWOL from work?"

"I'm on my lunch break. I was at Harrison's lab this morning and I asked Rob if you'd be home. I was hoping we could have a piano lesson."

"Oh, come in. Let me hang up your coat. I thought about taking Barbara to the playground, but they said we might have snow flurries this afternoon."

"Hi, Mr. Soldier!" Barbara piped up. "What's that?" She pointed to a small package that Dave was holding.

"Barbara! It's not polite to ask guests about presents. And what do you say when you meet a new grown-up?"

Barbara giggled and saluted. "Hello, sir! Reporting for doodie."

"I'm sorry. Toddler humor," Doris explained. "She learned that from some older kids. Try again, Barbara. Remember, it starts with 'how do you do?'"

"Umm . . . How do? I'm Barbara."

Dave bent down and solemnly shook Barbara's hand. "Hello, young lady. My name is David Sokol, and you can ask your mother if you could have one of these chocolates."

"Ooh, can I, Mommy?"

"Yes, you may have one. And what do you say now?"

"Thank you, Mr. Soldier."

Doris rolled her eyes and helped Barbara choose a vanilla cream. Her daughter crammed the whole candy into her mouth and went back to leafing through picture books.

"You didn't have to bring anything, but thanks very much."

"I know you civilians can't buy things at the PX, so I thought you might enjoy them."

"I never refuse chocolate—although I should."

"Nonsense. Food is one of life's great pleasures, along with wine and women."

"You forgot song."

"I'm here for some song."

"Good, because that's all that's on offer. I should tell you that I charge $1.50 for a half-hour lesson."

"A little pricey, but I suspect you're worth it."

Doris had to admit to herself that she enjoyed the banter, but she knew she should shut it down. She went over to the piano. "It would help me to hear you so I know more about your skill level. Do you want to look through my sheet music and see if there's something familiar?"

He flipped through a few books. "Oh, I used to play these pieces for children by Kabalevsky." He sat down at the piano and pounded out creditable versions of a slow waltz and a march, although his performance was rather mechanical.

"Very nice. My teacher always stressed the importance of sitting up straight and taking a deep breath before you start."

"Are you accusing me of being a schlump?"

"Just giving some general advice."

"Perhaps you could show me the correct posture? Are my shoulders in the right position now?" He puffed out his chest and gave her a cocky smile.

"I think you know what I mean. Do you have any particular goals for our lessons?"

He looked her up and down. "Well, for starters . . ."

"Musical goals, of course."

"Sweet harmony?"

"I was thinking more about a particular composer or composition that you want to work on."

"I like Tchaikovsky, even if he was a queer."

Doris winced. "I hate that word."

"Okay, even if he was a homosexual."

"And so what?"

"So nothing. I like his music. How about something from the *Nutcracker Suite*?"

Doris thought of telling him she'd cheerfully crack his nuts but bit her lip. "You do gravitate to the Russians. I hope you're not a communist?"

"Who, me? I'm a Republican."

"That's almost as bad."

"I think the government shouldn't interfere too much in people's lives."

"You know Tchaikovsky hated the *Nutcracker*."

"Really?"

"And you're too late for Christmas season."

"It's not our holiday, anyway."

She searched through a pile of music. "You're in luck. Here's the 'Dance of the Sugar-Plum Fairy.' You're welcome to borrow it. It should be just your speed, but remember, it needs a delicate touch. Is this same time next week good for you?"

"I'm more concerned if it's good for you."

"It's fine. I'll get your coat."

"Bye-bye, Mr. Soldier!" Barbara waved as Dave exited the front door.

Doris snickered and put the $1.50 in her cashbox. She had to admit, it was fun to get a little extramarital admiration.

17: January 1944

Doris listened to the evening news on the radio. Eisenhower had arrived in London to take charge of the Allied invasion force, but a few days later, Britain was bombed by almost five hundred Nazi planes. In the Pacific, American troops were taking the Marshall Islands, "leap-frogging" one by one. Still, the death toll was devastating.

She had the volume turned down because Rob was singing Barbara to sleep. It was amusing that her daughter's favorite was the Irish "Too-Ra-Loo-Ra-Loo-Ral," though another Bing Crosby standard, "Down by the Old Mill Stream," was also in the top ten on the Friedman lullaby list. When it was one of Doris's nights, she sang "Oyfn Pripetchik," the old Yiddish song about children learning their alphabet by the fireside. She had happy memories of her own father singing it to her at night. She didn't think Rob ever had that much attention and care from his own parents, but it warmed Doris's heart to see how affectionate he was with Barbara. She prized the times when the three of them could just enjoy each other as a family. Since her fight with Rob, they had avoided discussing plans for after the war. Daily life was tough enough.

Rob's working hours continued to be merciless. If anything, it seemed as if the pace was increasing. Doris was glad she knew as much as she did. At least they could talk about what he was doing. She sensed it was a safety valve for Rob to be able to confide in her. It also made her feel closer to him. Not only did she understand a little, but she knew he trusted her to keep his secrets.

Rob emerged from Barbara's bedroom and closed the door. She rarely woke if her parents talked quietly in the living room.

"Tough day?" Doris asked.

"Yeah, busy. The hot lab is up and running now, but we're still working out some bugs."

"What is the lab like?"

"It's got four small rooms, each with thick concrete walls. But that's not all—each room is lined with four inches of lead. All the mixing and pouring in the lab has to be done by remote control. Actually, I worked on that part."

"Really?"

"Yeah, I put together circuits and we made special switches so the guys can control the arm's direction—right or left, up or down—and make the claw open and close to pick up a container."

"That kind of sounds like fun."

"Someday robots will do stuff like that."

"Do you think so? Isn't that science fiction?"

"Science fiction is just stories about the future. Did you know that H. G. Wells published a novel about atomic bombs in 1914?"

"You're kidding."

"He did. It's called *The World Set Free* and it even mentions uranium and dropping bombs from airplanes. Sol lent it to me when we first got here."

"I bet General Groves would love to ban that book!" General Groves was in charge of the Manhattan Project and was famous for his toughness.

"If he tried, it would probably just draw unwanted attention. It isn't much fun to read, anyway. I liked *The Time Machine* and *War of the Worlds* a lot better."

"Yes, both of those were good." Rob had introduced Doris to some of his favorite authors.

"Of course, some of it is way off base. The trigger for the bomb is a stud. You have to bite through it with your teeth, before you throw the bomb over the side of a little plane. But still . . ." They contemplated art anticipating reality.

"So, in the hot lab, I was wondering how you can see what you're doing. Wouldn't windows let the radiation through?"

"You're right. Doris, I may make you a science maven yet."

"I may not be an engineer, but I'm not a total idiot."

"The rooms in the hot labs have special periscopes so you can see inside them."

"Periscopes?"

"Yeah, like they use on submarines to see above the sea surface. The tubes go through the walls of the labs. Harrison got his hands on some plastic lenses that were designed for a new warplane but never got used. They're curved, so you can see almost 180 degrees around—a half circle. It turns out Harrison had a lot of foresight to push for the hot lab. Los Alamos really needs what we're making. I'm not sure why, but they say Oppenheimer wants it as fast as possible. He keeps calling Harrison to nag him. The army even sent us another bunch of engineers and chemists to speed things up."

"Is the hot lab mostly for making more plutonium?"

"No, once we figured out how to make plutonium, they built factories to mass-produce it. You've heard the guys mention Hanford, right?"

Doris nodded. "In Washington State."

"This stuff we're making is another radioactive chemical."

"There's so much going on in this place! Those huge factory buildings, the reactor, the labs, the thousands of people working here . . . Do you think the Nazis have their own Oak Ridge?"

"That's the million-dollar question. But one good thing is that Hitler thinks physics is 'Jewish science,' so hopefully he'll overlook how important it is."

"How can you overlook Einstein?"

"It's not Einstein. He's not actively involved in the project. But a lot of Jewish physicists fled from Europe and now they're on our team, especially in Los Alamos. Joel has some friends there from Chicago, so he hears news now and then."

"I wish I could help, like Annette does."

"You're helping me a lot. Not that I'm anything but a tiny cog in all the wheels. But having a home and a family makes everything worthwhile. I know it's hard for you to be here. After the war, we'll have our time."

"If we win the war."

"We will. We have to." Rob put his arm around Doris.

"Rob?"

"What?"

"If you could magically see your future, what would you most want to know?"

"For the world, or just for me?"

"Just for you."

"Will you keep loving me."

"Oh, Rob. It makes me sad that you doubt me."

"I bet you thought I'd want to know whether I invented something."

"I wasn't sure what you'd say."

"You and Barbara are the most important things in my life. I always wanted my own, happy family." Rob hugged her closer. "We both have parents who don't really understand us. I think that drew us together. Did I ever tell you about my dog Tippy?"

"No."

"He was a collie pup. A neighbor gave him to me. Dad said I could keep him if I worked in the store after school. I think I was twelve. Tippy would jump up and lick my face to greet me and he slept by my bed—or on it, when my mother wasn't looking."

"Rob, are you crying?"

He sniffed. "One day my sister let Tippy run out the door. I was just getting home from school. He loved to chase things, and the streetcar was coming. I called him but he didn't stop, and it hit him . . . His body just flew through the air. By the time I got to him, he was dead. We didn't have a yard, so I had no place to bury him. I had to just wrap him up and put him in the garbage."

Doris wiped a tear from Rob's cheek. "That's awful. Well, you have us now."

"Maybe we'll get a dog one day."

"I like dogs too. After the war, I hope we can manage to buy a house and then we'll have a yard for a dog."

"We could get a small dog and it could live in the house. I bet Barbara would love to have a puppy."

"She would. By then she'll be out of diapers and I'll have more patience for housetraining."

"Well, at least I have someone to cuddle with in bed." He put his arm around Doris.

"Are you saying I'm almost as good as a dog?"

"You know that's not what I meant."

They sat in silence, each lost in their own worries, until it was time to go to sleep.

18 February 1944

On a Friday night a couple of weeks later, Rob was annoyed that Doris did not have dinner ready when he walked in at six thirty. Barbara was recovering from a cold and had been whiny and demanding all day. The furnace had run out of coal and the temperature in the house started to drop. Rob normally filled a bucket from their coal box and refilled the heater, but their delivery arrived only after he left for the lab. Doris ventured outside. Rob had absentmindedly left the shovel in the coal box and it was buried under a foot of new coal. By the time Doris freed it and filled the bucket, a layer of black grit covered her gloves, sleeves, and the front of her winter coat. She brushed off as much dust as she could on the front porch, but still left a trail of footprints from the door to the furnace. After she finished mopping the floor, she realized it was time for Dave's piano lesson. Mercifully, Barbara had fallen into a fitful sleep.

Dave gave her a curt greeting and sat at the piano. He played a technically correct but emotionless "Dance of the Sugar Plum Fairy."

"I'd call that the dance of the sugar plum robot," Doris remarked.

"Hey, it took a lot of moxie to assign that piece to me. You think I'm some kind of schnook?"

"You asked for something from the *Nutcracker.* If you don't like music with so much feeling, maybe we should try some Bach. How about 'Jesu Joy of Man's Desiring'?"

"So either I have to be a fairy or a goy?"

"Puh-leez. Here it goes like this." She played the beginning.

"Oh yeah, I've heard that one. I'm willing to give it a try."

After the lesson, Dave asked if she could make him some coffee. "I'm afraid otherwise I'll fall asleep at work."

"Sure, it will just take a few minutes." Doris put coffee and water in the percolator.

"You know, you have something black on your cheek."

He moved forward as if to wipe it away but Doris forestalled him, mopping her face with the dish towel. "Coal dust, I'm afraid."

"Gone. How old are you, anyway?" Dave asked, lounging against the counter.

"Twenty-one."

"Wow, you're just a baby!"

"I'm so sick of men telling me how young I am! I finished high school when I was sixteen. I was always younger than everyone else."

"I beat you. I graduated at fifteen. But it didn't bother me."

"No?"

"I liked being the smartest."

"You didn't care that all the girls were older?"

"Naw. I wasn't interested in girls until later."

"So how old are you now?"

"Thirty-two." He slurped his coffee.

"And how come you're not married, old geezer?"

"Having too much fun."

Doris scoffed, rinsing her own cup in the sink. "I bet. Lots of single girls in Oak Ridge, especially for a guy with a big . . . jeep."

"But the best girls are already taken. You like older men?"

"Rob seemed a lot older than me when we met."

"He's a baby too."

"You should be more respectful about my husband."

"Rob's a nice guy. But it takes men a while to learn their way around a woman." He eyed her above his coffee.

"Don't you need to get back to work?"

He checked his watch. "I've still got some time. So what have you been doing besides Barbara and piano?"

"Believe me, that's enough to fill my days! But I've been studying accounting. I was thinking about law school before the war, but now I think maybe business or investing would be interesting."

"Good for you. More women should join the workforce, even once this war is over."

"Rob thinks it's his job to support the family."

"Nothing wrong with both contributing."

"You always come across so cool. Are you passionate about anything?"

He pondered. "If I were, would I tell you?"

"Probably not. I sure don't hear much emotion in your music. And you claim you're a Republican. Personally, I think you're a secret Red."

He choked on a mouthful of coffee. "That's ridiculous."

"You remind me of my uncle Jacob. He says he's the champion of the proletariat, but I notice he enjoys the finer things. And you have too much of a sense of humor to be a Republican."

"I'm wounded!" He thumped his chest with a fist.

"Yeah, right."

"I'm passionate about how things work. New inventions."

"Now that, I believe."

"I have to say, Rob's an ace in that department."

"I'm not a very good judge, but I think his group is happy with him."

"That sounds a little lukewarm."

"I'm very proud of Rob. I just sometimes wish . . . he would stand up for himself."

"It would be hard to stand up to you, even young as you are. You're gonna be a real ballbuster when you get older."

"Gee, thanks a lot!"

"But you're also a good teacher. I respect that. Well—gotta go. Next week same time?"

"Okay." Doris looked out the door as Dave jumped into his jeep. She half expected him to make a grand exit by accelerating away, but nobody risked their tires on the icy, potholed roads.

After Barbara woke, Doris read her a couple of stories, then sat on the couch while her daughter drew pictures. She put on the radio and "Chattanooga Choo Choo" came on. Who would have predicted she'd end up in Tennessee? Though she'd still never been to Chattanooga. The last time she had heard that song was on Lenny Stein's car radio when he gave her a ride home from a dance, freshman year of college. She had arrived at the campus venue with Annette, who quickly joined a group of other first-year students. Doris was standing in a corner nibbling on a cube of cheese and feeling like she did not belong. Redheaded Lenny introduced himself. He was a graduate student in the business school. He dazzled Doris with his descriptions of Manhattan night clubs and his quotes from John Maynard Keynes. When Annette came up and asked if Doris wanted to join their group to go to a movie on campus, Lenny suggested that he drive her home instead. He parked a few doors down from her parents' house and they kissed for a few minutes. He was clearly more experienced than her previous dates. He made Doris feel desirable. She began to hope that life would bring many more moments like this.

"Do you want to say goodbye here?" he asked, "or we could drop in at the Blue Note and listen to jazz?"

"I'm afraid I can't drink yet," she confessed.

"Really? You seem so with it, Doris. Just how old are you?"

"Seventeen."

"Oh jeez, jailbait!"

"I'm afraid so."

"Well, it was great meeting you, cutie. Look me up in about four years."

As the song's horn section faded away, Doris remembered how her heart had fallen. After meeting Rob, Doris had all but forgotten about the incident with Lenny. Now, it seemed emblematic of the limitations of her life. She was so tired of men belittling or even dismissing her. And if she defended herself, she was a bitch or a ballbuster. Rob talked a good game, but he clearly thought his work was more important than her future career. Doris also worried that his recent disinterest in sex was somehow her fault. She missed Papa, and the war seemed endless. She knew it was time to put the chicken in the oven but could not muster the energy to get up off the sofa. She did manage to turn on the lights when the sun went down, so Rob did not find her and Barbara sitting in the dark.

"Doris, what's up?"

"Nothing, just tired out."

"Well, I'm starving!"

"Sorry. Why don't you make yourself some bacon and eggs."

"What happened to dinner?"

"I told you! Barbara's still feeling lousy and I'm exhausted."

"From what? All you have to do all day is a little cleaning and cooking. Can't you even manage that?"

"A little cleaning and cooking! How about digging for the coal shovel under a ton of new coal, filling up the furnace, cleaning up the mess, wiping Barbara's snotty nose every ten minutes, giving piano lessons, trying to get some food into Barbara, and changing her diaper every couple of hours . . ."

"Sounds a lot easier than having everyone hounding me because the ion chamber isn't calibrated accurately!"

"Boys and their toys."

"Oh yeah? If these toys break, get ready to say 'Heil Hitler'!"

"I won't have to. We'll all be dead."

"You're so goddamn dramatic."

"Look who's talking."

"Didn't you make anything for dinner?"

"There's a chicken ready to roast, but it will take too long now. We can have it tomorrow. I'm sure you can find something to stuff your face. I'm going to bed."

Barbara woke up from her nap on the couch and started to sneeze.

"My throat hurts, Mommy."

Doris sighed heavily and carried Barbara into the bathroom to get her ready for bed.

19: March 1944

By March, Doris noticed that winter in Oak Ridge was easing. Blizzards would still be in the forecast in Chicago, but in Tennessee some of the trees were getting greenish buds. The red mud sucked at her boots like quicksand if she strayed from the boardwalk. Gravel was routinely spread on the roads but could not prevent ruts. Most of the time, she and Rob rubbed along together, but Doris was aware that she was being less affectionate than usual. One morning the phone rang. Doris jumped, hoping it was not news of some disaster at the lab.

The operator asked, "Am I speaking with Mrs. Doris Friedman?"

"Yes."

"Please hold for Colonel Barton."

Doris groaned inwardly. She had never heard of a Colonel Barton but suspected he was calling to bust her for giving unsanctioned piano lessons. She had not breathed a word about the project to anyone, so it couldn't be about security. Besides, everyone knew that security men showed up at your house if you were suspected of anything.

"Is this Mrs. Friedman?"

"Yes? How can I help you, Colonel?"

"I understand you're quite the pianist. One of my lieutenants has been taking lessons with you."

Doris's heart sank. "Well, Colonel, sir, I just love the piano and I thought it could help morale if I—"

"Yes, yes. I'm not calling to complain about a few piano lessons. Teach to your little heart's content. I need your help picking out a piano for the Officer's Recreation Hall."

"Oh! Of course, I'd be delighted to help."

"Excellent. Meet me in front of the Guest House on Thursday at 0900 hours sharp. My driver will take us into Knoxville."

Doris arranged a babysitter for Barbara and dressed in a gray tweed suit and jaunty hat. She made sure to be in front of the Guest House at the appointed time. She wore boots and carried her heels so that she could change them in the car and avoid muddy shoes.

A large olive green sedan with an army star stopped in the road. It had been raining daily, so the ruts were filled with water. Luckily Doris was standing back far enough to avoid being splashed. The driver rolled down his window and leaned out.

"Mrs. Friedman?"

She waved and he hopped out and opened the back door. Doris avoided the puddles and scooted in, making sure to keep her knees covered by her skirt. A burly man in a colonel's khaki uniform was already seated in the back seat, leafing through some papers. His salt-and-pepper hair was cut short and mostly covered by his cap. He turned and pumped her hand.

"Mrs. Friedman. Thanks for joining us."

"Nice to meet you, sir."

"Hmph. Your husband works at X-10, I understand?"

"Yes. He helps with electronic instruments."

"On the project."

"The project, yes." Doris was not going to say anything out of turn.

"Where are you from?"

"Chicago. He started out working at the university."

"Yes, good bunch there from Chicago."

"I also was a student at the University of Chicago."

He frowned at her. "I don't hold much with college for women.

Guess you went there to get an MRS degree? Waste of resources. My wife was my high school sweetheart."

"How nice."

"Been married thirty-four years now. Excuse me, little lady, but I've got to look over these building plans while we drive."

"Of course." After a few minutes, Doris saw that they were coming to a hill where road construction was still in progress.

"Colonel, sir, this road is about to end. We have to turn around to catch the road to the Edgemoor gate to get to Route 25."

The colonel did not look up. "This is the shortest way. Drive on!"

"But, sir . . ."

"Drive on, I said! The road is at the bottom of this hill."

The driver tried to edge down the hill, but the car slid sideways. He pumped the brakes and the car skidded to a stop. When Doris opened her window and looked out, the wheels were half buried in mud. The driver tried to rock the car forward and back, as you might to escape a snow drift, but they were stuck fast.

"If Marshal Zhukov had a driver like you, the Nazis would be sitting pretty in Moscow!"

"Sorry, sir." The driver saluted.

"Don't tell me you're sorry! Get out of this frigging car and go get those construction workers to pull us out! Pardon my French, little lady."

The driver trudged over to the construction crew, who turned a small excavator in their direction. Doris began to open the door to get out of the car.

"Stay put, Mrs. Friedman. They can pull the car out with us in it."

Doris sat back. She wished she had brought a book, but she got sick if she tried to read in a moving car. The construction crew hooked chains to the front of the sedan and managed to pull it back up to the end of the completed dirt and gravel road. The driver thanked them and got in. Doris waved and gave them a high sign, but the colonel ignored everyone. Doris felt sorry for Mrs. Barton and any offspring the couple had.

It took another hour to arrive in Knoxville. They found a parking space in front of the Clark Piano Company. When she walked in with the colonel, Doris was pleased to see three Steinway grand pianos on display. Within moments, a man in a dark suit introduced himself as the owner of the store.

"Colonel, it's an honor. How may I help you and your lovely wife?"

"She's not my wife. Young enough to be my daughter. This lady is a pianist, or so I hear. We're here to buy a piano for the Oak Ridge Officer's Recreation Hall."

"Of course. Of course. Do you have a particular type of piano in mind?"

"It's up to the colonel," Doris answered, "but I always prefer a Steinway grand. I'm surprised you have three. I heard they were hardly making any since the war started."

"Well, madam . . ."

"It's Doris. Doris Friedman." They shook hands.

"You may not know that Steinway buys most all of its wood from the Vestal Lumber Company, right here in Knoxville. So we have more stock than many other showrooms. Were you here for Rachmaninoff's concert in February?"

"I wish I had been. I didn't arrive until September though."

"Of course he played a Steinway."

"If only I could have heard him. Was that his last concert before he died?"

"Yes, it was. A great loss to the music world."

Doris thought of the prelude and glanced down at her thumbs. "May I take a few minutes to try each of these three?" Doris included the colonel in her query.

He gestured a yes and sat on an armchair, still perusing his papers.

Doris played all the keys of the first piano, tried out the pedals, and examined the soundboard for cracks. Then she played the opening of a Schubert Impromptu and a few bars of Chopin's *Grande Valse Brillante*. She repeated the procedure with the other two pianos. The final time, she played the entire waltz because she couldn't resist the beautiful instrument. After she finished, the owner applauded softly. Even Colonel Barton was watching.

"This one, I think," she said.

"Well, little lady, we have ourselves a piano. Would you like to come and play it sometimes?"

"I would love that! I've just been playing our old upright at home."

The colonel signed an invoice and promised to have his secretary call the next day to arrange payment and delivery. When they got back in the car, Colonel Barton reminded the driver that they had one last stop in Knoxville. They pulled up to a shuttered restaurant and the driver went around to a side door. He came back almost immediately with a cardboard box. Doris heard the clink of bottles as the driver gently deposited it in the trunk. She was amused. Obviously, Colonel Barton had his own way around the local liquor prohibitions. She would bet the contents of the bottles were not just "splo," either.

He glanced at her. "For the officers."

"Of course."

When they arrived at the gate to Oak Ridge, the guards omitted their usual inspection of the car interior and trunk, waving them through.

Doris told Rob about her day. "Would you play the waltz for me now?" he asked.

"Okay, though it's kind of a comedown to play it on this piano after the Steinway." She sat down and began the piece. Doris lost herself in the bright notes, picturing whirling couples, the women in colorful ball gowns with full skirts. Barbara twirled in the middle of the living room and Rob picked her up, waltzing her while she giggled. Doris glanced behind her and called out, "Dance on!"

20: April 1944

As spring progressed, pale green leaves and dogwoods softened the Oak Ridge landscape, although nothing could disguise the muddy roads. A tornado struck Lebanon, Tennessee, a military training zone about 130 miles to the west, flipping a fighter plane and killing a soldier. On a Sunday with better weather, friends from the lab carpooled to a picnic near Norris Dam. The grass was interspersed with Jack-in-the-pulpit, bluebells, and Indian paintbrush. Barbara picked small bouquets and gave them to Rob. She usually ignored Doris when they were with other people and continued to be inconsistent with the potty. When it came to motherhood, Doris would grade herself a C minus.

"Would you like some apple?" she asked her daughter.

"No! Annette, play patty-cake."

"Are you giving her enough attention at home?" Annette asked, holding Barbara on her lap. "I know how much you love reading or practicing piano. She's probably sitting in a corner amusing herself."

"Doris is a great mother. She spends all her time with Barbara," Rob said, defending her.

"I don't know how much you see, Rob. We're all so busy at the lab." Annette's tone was saccharine.

"I spend hours with Barbara every day," Doris retorted. "She can already count to ten and knows some alphabet letters. And when she naps I study my accounting books or do housework. I wish I knew why she says no to everything—at least if I suggest it."

"Well, Doris, I remember your mother said you were reading chapter books when you were four. She's probably just smart."

"I'm a smart girl! One-two-three-four-five!" Barbara bounced on Annette's lap.

Doris offered her hand to Barbara. "Come on, sweetie, let's go look at the lake."

"No. I stay with Annette."

Doris tried not to show her hurt. "Okay, Daddy and I will take a walk." Rob got up and took Doris's hand.

Barbara scrambled up. "I come too!"

As the family strolled to the lake, Rob said, "I don't like the war news, even if the Brits are bombing the hell out of Germany. I think my brother's tank unit is somewhere in Italy."

"Has your mother heard anything?"

"Just a couple of postcards. And you never know what could have happened after he sent them."

"I don't blame you for worrying. But those tanks have a lot of armor."

"Yeah, and they spend more time fixing them than fighting in them!"

Doris lowered her voice. "I hope work is coming along."

"Slowly but surely. I think we'll get there. The big plants have a lot of problems, though. Enough that I hear they're on the lookout for a German saboteur. It's probably just snafus with all the new technology." He paused. "Don't let Annette get to you."

"She sounds so concerned, but she knows where to stick the knife."

"I think she still feels inferior to you."

"She really bugs me sometimes. But don't worry, I've been dealing with her for years. And Joel is a dear. There's something to be said for old friends who really know you. Let's invite people for dinner next Saturday night. We can pool ration coupons and I can try out a new recipe or two. We could have a few people from the lab."

"Sounds great. I know how much the single guys appreciate a home-cooked meal instead of cafeteria food."

"Even my cooking?"

"Your cooking really is getting better, honey."

"Should we invite Dave Sokol? His piano lessons are coming along." Doris knew she looked forward too much to Dave's sessions. "Tell him he's welcome to bring a date."

Rob's main concern for the party was finding a way to make the pure alcohol drinkable, since the Thanksgiving scotch was long gone.

The Steinbergs were the first to arrive. Sol suggested a recipe that was usually a winter holiday staple in Harrisburg, Pennsylvania, where he had grown up.

"The coal miners call it Boilo. You take some orange and lemon juice, honey, and cinnamon and boil it for about a half hour. Then you can mix it with the alcohol."

"I have the ingredients, but I don't have a very big pot," Doris fretted, "and I'd hate for most of it to evaporate."

"Hey, I'm a chemist. We'll figure it out." Sol looked through the kitchen shelves. "Here!" He picked up their large coffee percolator. "Heat up the juice mix in this."

"I'm not sure how much of each thing to use."

"Yeah," said Rob. "Don't ask Doris about recipes or numbers."

"Damn it, Rob! I do just fine with math and you said my cooking is much improved."

"Sorry, honey." Rob retreated, his hands in the air. "I didn't mean anything by it."

"Now you're in the doghouse," Sol commented. "We'd better mix this up ourselves."

After putting the Boilo together, the men went into the living room and Rochelle kept Doris company as she finished making dinner.

"Guys!" Rochelle mouthed. "Just ignore them."

Dave was one of the last to arrive, bringing a quiet young brunette who said she worked at one of the factory buildings.

"My job is to keep adjusting a dial so that it stays in the right zone," she told them. "It's a pretty boring way to spend a whole shift, but none of us girls ask any questions."

The roasted chickens, bought from Alice's farm with the help of a ride from Rochelle, were more tender than usual. Potatoes and green beans were also a success.

"We're lucky to be in Oak Ridge, with a supply of fresh food," said Joel.

"I don't know," Dave said, grinning at Rob. "Do you feel lucky after how we met?"

"Lucky they had penicillin to cure his strep throat," Doris said, before Rob could respond and possibly mention radiation. She wondered if Dave was working with security. Everyone knew that some people reported anyone who said too much about their work. Sometimes the stoolies deliberately tried to provoke indiscretions. One of the engineers in X-10 had abruptly been drafted and sent to Alaska a few weeks ago. It was rumored that he had revealed communist leanings. Rob loved to feel like one of the guys. He would not be on the lookout for an informer, so Doris resolved to keep an eye on Dave.

"Would anyone like seconds?" The remaining food was passed around the table.

Doris had even baked a cake with pink frosting the night before. The dessert had almost been derailed when she spied a small brown mouse in the pantry. She shrieked and Rob came running. He was wearing only his jockey briefs since he was about to take a shower. He got out his air pistol and surveyed the pantry while Doris stood in the kitchen yelling, "Don't shoot the sugar! Don't shoot the sugar! I only have enough for the cake." After several minutes she heard a loud *pffft* and Rob came out, holding a dead mouse triumphantly by the tail. The rest of the baking was uneventful and Doris waited until morning to frost the layers.

Passing out dessert to their guests, she saved a small piece of cake for Barbara, who had conveniently fallen asleep soon after the party started. While washing some dishes, she overheard Dave and Rob talking in the hallway.

"I don't see why I couldn't take a look at the circuit diagrams," Dave was grousing. "You know I have the security clearance."

"If Harrison says it's okay, it would be fine with me."

"Do you need his permission for everything?"

"If it has to do with security, yes."

"Such a good *boychik*."

"Quit it, Sokol. Or maybe I'll mention to Harrison that you're snooping around."

"Geez. Let's just drop it."

"Fine with me." They both went into the living room where the other guests were chatting. Doris was upset with Dave. Was he deliberately trying to get Rob in trouble? She resolved to bring it up with him at his next lesson.

They brought out the Boilo. Arthur, a chemist who had been one of Harrison's students at UCLA, poured himself a generous amount in a coffee cup. He tasted it and pronounced it delicious, gulping the rest. Within a few minutes, he started slurring his words. He slumped down on the couch, and his wife, Susan, poked him. "Hey, he's out cold," she said.

They could not wake him, so they laid him full length on the couch—not an easy feat since Arthur was as tall as Rob and built like a linebacker. By midnight they could still not fully rouse him, so they decided to let him sleep it off on the couch until morning.

"Do you think we should call the hospital?" Doris asked.

"Nah," Sol replied. "He isn't in a coma. He's just plastered."

Arthur's wife, Susan, seemed more annoyed than alarmed.

"My dad used to have a liquor store," Rob remarked. "On the South Side of Chicago. After I finished high school, I helped him out in the evenings. I got held up three times."

"What did you do?" asked Sol.

"The first two times, I just put my hands up and let them empty the cash register. Then I insisted that we get a gun—a .45—and I hid it under the counter. The third time, I was ready, but there were two guys. Each of them had a pistol and they told me to get inside the walk-in fridge. I wanted to pull out the gun, but I have to admit, I was too scared. After they left, I called the police. When the detective came, I told him what had happened. I really felt ashamed. He said, 'You only made one mistake—having the gun in the store to begin with.'"

"I was so glad that the store had failed by the time I met Rob," Doris put in. "So he didn't have to work there."

Rob shrugged. "I still would like to be a good shot. That's why I got the air pistol."

"You going to shoot you some rabbit stew?" teased Dave.

"He shot a mouse in our pantry last night!" Doris announced.

"My hero!" Dave said in falsetto.

Doris shot him a dirty look.

"Anyone hear what happened last month with the guards?" asked Joel.

Nobody had heard any story. Doris knew that guards patrolled the borders of Oak Ridge, especially along the barbed wire by the Clinch River. "Two of them were riding their horses by the fence and they saw a big, fat bunny. One of them told the other, 'I'm gonna shoot me some dinner!' So he aimed his pistol, but as he pulled the trigger his horse saw the rabbit and shied. Darned if he didn't shoot the horse right through its head. The guards were scared because those horses belong to the army. They decided to get rid of the corpse and claim the horse had run away. So, they got some kerosene and poured it over the horse and set fire to it. By the time they were through, they had started a big brush fire and had to call in the fire department. I guess they aren't guards anymore. At least I hope not." The end of the story was greeted with drunken laughter.

The conscious guests departed, including Susan. Doris noticed with a pang that Dave had his arm around his date as he handed her into the jeep. Well, what did she expect?

Doris and Rob got ready for bed.

"I left a big bowl next to Arthur in case he needs it when he wakes up," Doris whispered.

But the next morning, their friend went home with only a mild headache. They decided not to risk serving Boilo again.

21: May 1944

In May, after one of the bridge club meetings, Betty took Doris aside. "I have some wonderful news, Doris—I'm pregnant!"

"I'm so happy for you. How far along are you?"

"It's early yet. Just over two months. I notice I'm getting a little bigger up top, but I haven't had morning sickness."

"Not everyone does, I hear. I sure did though. It was miserable trying to keep up with my classes at college. Is Will happy?"

"He's over the moon! He and my mother-in-law are trying to keep me practically on bed rest."

"Well, if you need lessons on diapering, you can practice on Barbara."

"That great, girl! She's almost two, isn't she?"

"She's very stubborn. She says it feels good to wet her pants. The pediatrician told me to take away her diaper and rubber pants and let her stay in her wet, cold panties. I think it's working, but I'm getting tired of mopping the floor."

"Poor Doris. You really should have some help around the house."

"We just can't afford it, Betty. And what else do I have to do? I've turned into a drudge. Shopping and cleaning and cleaning and shopping. And then throw in Barbara's picky eating and daily tantrums. I wanted to go to law school."

"Really! Well, you're smart enough for it. But not many girls get that far."

"We'll see after the war. If this war ever ends."

"We just have to pray hard."

Doris was silent. She respected Betty's religious feelings, even if she did not share them. But she sometimes wondered how much Betty actually believed, or if she had just been raised to drop pious phrases.

"Do you want to see the darling baby clothes my mother-in-law sent me?"

Doris admired the white baby layette with yellow ducklings. It looked as if it would need to be ironed each time it was washed. "My sister in Chicago is working in a department store. She mailed me a couple of ruffled pink panties for Barbara. I told the little stinker she can wear them when she's gone a whole week without an accident. I'm hoping that will be the straw that breaks the camel's back."

"Fashion is always a good bribe. Girls are more fun that way."

"I'm not sure I'd call raising Barbara fun. You know the last time I took her for a checkup, I'm ashamed to admit it, but I ended up in tears when they told me again that she's way underweight. It's such a struggle between her picky eating, the toilet training, and her pushing me away half the time . . . Oh, just listen to me! You're so happy to be pregnant, and here I am, complaining about motherhood."

"Complain away. I'm looking forward to everything, even the diapers."

"Oh, Betty, enjoy those crazy dreams! Just wait until your baby spits up, or worse, all over that lovely little outfit. Tell your mother-in-law to send you lots of spares so you don't have to do laundry three times a day."

"I am perfectly sane. In fact, I feel like I'm walking on air."

"Well, I'm glad one of us is still sane. The pediatrician obviously thought I needed help. He told me that they had just added a psychiatrist to the hospital staff. He had me take Barbara in for an evaluation. A nurse asked me about a hundred and one questions about her development. Then she had me leave the room and she gave Barbara some special tests, disguised as games. The next week I had a meeting with the psychiatrist himself. He told me they didn't find anything wrong with Barbara."

"See?"

"He said, and I quote"—Doris mimicked the doctor's Boston accent—"'She's quite advanced for her age, especially with speech, drawing, and symbol recognition. Basically, we think she's just too smart for you.' How dare he imply that I'm no match for a manipulative toddler! So I asked if he had any suggestions about how I can get her toilet trained, or improve her eating habits. Or understand why she seems to love everyone but me.

"He just puffed on his damn pipe and said, 'Patience, Mrs. Friedman. Patience, consistency, and gentle limits. I think raising Barbara is going to continue to be a challenge.' Well, golly, tell me something I don't already know! So I stood up and looked down my nose at him."

"You don't have very much nose, Doris!"

"I know, but I did my best. And I thought about you, actually. I said, 'It could be worse. At least you didn't tell me I had penis envy.'"

"You didn't! You really said it?"

"Yep! You should have seen his face. But he just said, 'Feel free to make another appointment if you have more problems with your daughter, or for yourself.' Now I'm sure I have 'psychotic mother' as a diagnosis in my chart!"

22: June 1944

Doris now had fifteen piano students and was putting her savings into a special bank account. She had been following newspaper columns about the stock market. She purchased a few shares that were touted as good values, careful never to repeat her father's Depression-era mistake of buying on margin. Dave continued his lessons every couple of weeks. She tried to keep their interactions businesslike, but he often threw in double entendres. She hesitated to bring up her suspicions that he was working for security until one day he asked, "How much does Rob tell you about the lab?"

"Why do you want to know?"

"He told me Hartnell informed you both about the project. That was a little unusual."

"I don't know why he told you that story. Rob is too trusting." She paused. "Tell me the truth, Dave—are you in security?"

"Me? That's a laugh."

"No, it's not. You're military and you keep mentioning things we aren't supposed to talk about."

"I am not in security, Doris. But I do have a security clearance since I inspect the labs for radiation safety."

"Then why are you asking me about Rob's work? He's just Harrison's 'electronics boy.'" Doris had heard Harrison refer to Rob that way several times and it annoyed her, although she knew he called all his team members boys.

"I like instruments and Rob has been designing some interesting new tools. I don't really have a chance to look at them close up."

"So ask Rob, not me. I only understand about half of what he tells me anyway."

"People in the lab don't like it when an outsider gets interested."

"Because we all know, 'Loose lips sink ships.'"

"I don't think I'd get very far as a Nazi spy."

"Joel says the commies are interested in the project too."

"The Soviets are our allies."

"For now. Would you want to live in Stalin's Russia?"

Dave shrugged. "From each according to his ability. To each according to his needs. Not a bad philosophy."

"Marx was a dreamer. I thought you were more pragmatic."

"That's why I'm a Republican, doll. Win the war quicker with Dewey and Bricker! But there's no place that really lets Jews feel at home. America, Russia, they're both filled with anti-Semites."

"Where are your family now? Still in Kansas City?"

"They're all gone."

"Gone?"

"Dead." He gave Doris a quelling look. "Now I'm going to play my piece so you can earn your $1.50."

One of the biochemists in X-10, Ronald Loeb, was a violinist. He put together a small orchestra, the Oak Ridge Symphonette. Doris and Rob attended the first concert, held in the high school auditorium. Dr. Loeb conducted. Although Doris's critical ear detected a few flaws, she was impressed that people so involved in the project, including about ten SED men, had taken the time to rehearse and give a creditable performance. Rob had auditioned to be a clarinetist but was gently told he was not ready. The symphonette did not include a pianist, but after the concert, Doris went up to compliment Dr. Loeb.

"Oh yes, I've heard about you—Rob's wife." Dr. Loeb shook Rob's hand. "You give piano lessons. He told me about your wild ride to Knoxville to buy the Steinway."

"Yes, 'Drive on!' I was wondering if I could help you out somehow. I have a two-year-old daughter at home, but sometimes I could bring her with me, or maybe do a job from my house."

"Definitely! We need all the help we can get. We're just starting the music library, and we need volunteers to do publicity or fundraising."

"I have an idea for a fundraiser. When I was twelve, I won a piano contest in Chicago and my prize was to play several pieces with the symphony orchestra in a youth concert. Because of the Depression, it didn't happen until I was sixteen, but I've never forgotten that day. I have several teenage students with talent. Maybe we could have a youth music competition and sell tickets to a concert with the winners."

"Very nice. Would you write up a proposal and give it to me? Roane-Anderson has given us some funding, but we could certainly use more. We need sheet music for everyone and better instruments."

"Sure. I'm also trying to learn some accounting, so maybe I could help you set up a bookkeeping system."

"That sounds fantastic, Doris. You'll definitely be hearing from me."

"You were great, honey," Rob commented after they'd moved away from the group around the conductor. "You're a good organizer. I know you've been feeling a little down. Maybe working with the symphonette would be something you'd enjoy."

"Yes, even if I can't be a performer, I would like a job that involved music. I can only do a limited amount here, with Barbara, but it could give me some experience."

"I know you like having some extra pocket money."

"We need more than pocket money, Rob!"

"We could go to Knoxville and have a night on the town."

"I'm saving that money for our future."

He shrugged. "Okay, Doris, whatever you say."

Doris and Rob had not had any major blowups, but by dinnertime they were usually too exhausted to do much talking. They were having sex even less frequently and it seemed to become more routine. On a Monday night Rob told her that one of their friends, a physicist named Louis Slotin, had deliberately exposed himself to radiation. "He was running an experiment on the floor of the water tank next to the reactor. You know, Doris, that water is there as a shield, to absorb radiation. On Friday, Louis needed to fix something, so he asked to have the reactor shut down. They told him he'd have to wait until after the weekend. When everyone had gone home for the day, he stripped down and dived into the tank and adjusted his instruments, under six feet of water. He probably got more radiation than I did at my desk that time. But he did it on purpose."

"That's insane! Louis has a great sense of humor. I wouldn't have pegged him for being that driven."

"Oh, he is."

"I don't care how urgent the project is. It could have waited a couple of days. Is he okay?"

"Seems to be."

"I wonder how many people in the lab will live long and healthy lives after this."

Rob sighed. "Well, don't worry. I'm being careful."

One morning a week, the neighborhood mothers took turns babysitting their young children, including Barbara. When it wasn't Doris's turn to watch the kids, she went to the symphonette office. She was proud of the systems she set up for filing and keeping track of funds. Sometimes she took work home with her, finishing it during Barbara's naps. She told her younger piano students about the plans for the contest and suggested pieces they could play. Some started to practice more, although a few were clearly taking lessons only because of parental pressure.

Every now and then she played chamber music informally with Ronald and a couple of symphonette members. Some of her happiest hours were spent forgetting about the war and losing herself in the intertwining melodies.

23: July 1944

Doris dreaded listening to the radio broadcasts. D-Day gave her hope but the casualties were terrible. It seemed like the Allies had to fight for each mile of territory. Although she felt guilty for her calm life in rural Tennessee, nobody at Oak Ridge could forget that they lived in a secret wartime base. One afternoon the announcer said that Hitler was touting new Nazi *Wunderwaffe*—wonder weapons. Doris felt unsettled all the rest of the day.

"Do you think they mean the bomb?" she asked Rob that evening after dinner.

"Nobody knows. All we can do is work as fast as we can."

"I wish we could warn our families."

"Yeah, Sol and I were talking about that today. But you know how important it is to keep everything secret."

"Right, like that new billboard says, 'Your pen and tongue can be enemy weapons.' Speaking of tongues, are you too tired for a little romance?"

Rob gave her a kiss. "I guess it's been a while, huh?"

"Sixteen days, but who's counting?"

"I'm sorry, honey. These long hours really take it out of me. I'm always scrambling to measure something new that hasn't been measured before."

"Are you sure it's just that you're tired? Sometimes I worry that you're tired of me."

"No way, honey. Hey, are you upset?"

Doris turned her head away. “I get lonely. And I feel like we’re acting like old folks. Remember when we couldn’t keep our hands off each other?” She recalled how they’d laughed softly and shushed each other in Rob’s narrow bed so his parents wouldn’t overhear.

Rob took her in his arms. “I’m really sorry. It’s definitely not you. You’re still my best girl. Come on, let’s go to bed.”

Afterward, Doris reflected that the uninspired sex made her feel like the old gray mare who knows her way home rather than a sleek filly gamboling around a green pasture. She had a hard time falling asleep, noticing Rob’s soft snores and fidgets more than usual.

The next morning, Doris watched Benjamin at her house while Rochelle went to a doctor’s appointment. Barbara was not old enough to play games with Benjamin, but both of them enjoyed drawing pictures and singing songs with Doris. She also read them picture books. After the third story, Doris could see that the kids were getting restless. Rochelle had suggested she take them to the park that was just several blocks away. It had swings and a small slide. It would be more pleasant before the midday heat.

“Who wants to go to the park?” she asked.

“Me!” shouted Benjamin.

“Me too!” echoed Barbara.

Doris filled a thermos with ice cubes and apple juice and put it in a tote bag, leaving a hand free for each child. Being responsible for both children’s safety made her anxious. Benjamin was unusually well-behaved for his age and Barbara tended to follow his lead when they were together, but what if one of them ran into the street or fell on the playground? “You’re a twenty-two-year-old woman,” she told herself. “You’re certainly competent enough to take two children to the park.”

As she opened the screen door, Benjamin hopped onto the porch. Just next to the washing machine, Doris spotted something that did not belong—a large, coiled bronze snake sunning itself. She grabbed

Benjamin's hand. "Oh my God!" she whispered. "It's a copperhead! Benjamin, stay still and quiet." She hoisted him into the air and slowly backed through the doorway. Luckily, Barbara was still inside. She slammed the screen and front doors shut. "Barbara, Benjamin, we can't go outside. There's a big snake."

Barbara looked scared but peered out the window. Benjamin crowded in next to her to get the best possible view. Doris was never more grateful that they had a phone in the house. The operator connected her with the military police, and within half an hour a jeep pulled up. The snake had not moved. An officer motioned them to get away from the windows. He shot the snake in the head. "You can come out now, ma'am," he said, putting the dead reptile in a cloth bag. "He probably would have just slithered away, but it's best to be careful."

"I know their bites don't kill adults, but I was taking my daughter and her friend to the park when I spotted it."

"Yep, snake bites are more serious for little ones. And that chunkhead was a big sucker. We don't see many in town. They tend to hide out in the woody areas. Be careful if you go hiking or camping. And, kiddies, if you see a snake that funny brown color, with patches shaped like an hourglass, stay away. A copperhead will bite you soon as look at you."

"Another thing to worry about in this place," sighed Doris.

"You done good, ma'am. Everyone's safe."

"Thank you."

"Mister policeman, can I see your gun?" asked Benjamin.

"Well, little man, I'll hold it up to show you, but you cain't touch. This here's my Colt 1911."

Benjamin admired the pistol and Doris thanked the MP again.

"Can we go to the park now?" asked Barbara.

"Well, I'm feeling a little shook up. How about if we drink our apple juice here and I'll play you some more songs on the piano?" She looked at the clock. "Anyway, Benjamin's mommy will probably be back in a half hour."

When Rochelle rang the doorbell, Benjamin opened the door for her. "Mommy, Mommy! We saw a big chunkhead snake and the nice policeman shot it with his giant black gun!"

Doris saw Rochelle's eyes widen and hastened to assure her that everyone was fine. She told her what had happened.

"Quick thinking, Doris!" Rochelle hugged her. "Thanks for keeping Benjamin safe!"

"I was worried you'd be mad at me."

"For what? I suggested you take the kids to the park. And picking up Benjamin and getting him back in the house was very brave."

"I'd never forgive myself if anything happened to him."

"Doris, if I didn't trust you, I wouldn't leave Benjamin here."

"Would you like a Coke before you take him home?"

"That would be nice. I'm thirsty after the bus."

Rochelle followed Doris into the kitchen. While she filled the glass, Doris told her, "I know I shouldn't be so insecure. Annette always implies I'm not a good mother—and it gets to me. Like I said, my own mother wasn't a good example."

"That's a shame."

"It's not just my mothering skills. I was a plump child, and when Mama was mad she called me fatso. Even though I know Barbara is too skinny, I'm glad she doesn't take after me."

"Doris! You're very pretty. You have the kind of curvy figure men like. And Barbara does look like you. Annette can criticize all she wants, but she doesn't have any children yet herself, so how does she get to be such an expert? I see the effort you make with Barbara—and I think she's growing out of some of her moods. Remember that preemies sometimes take longer to develop."

"Thanks, Rochelle. Your opinion means a lot to me." She handed the glass to Rochelle. "My mother really is a piece of work. She and her sister lie about their ages, especially since my aunt married a man three years younger."

"Would that be your famous uncle Harry?"

"Exactly! But one time I got the better of my mother. Some woman at shul asked her how old she was. My mother gave her a glare that could have stopped a charging buffalo, but before she could say a word I said, 'She doesn't know because her birth certificate burned up in the Great Chicago Fire!'"

"That was in what—1870?"

"1871, thanks to Mrs. O'Leary's cow! And my mother was born in 1898. She was so furious with me."

Both women laughed.

"After *Gone with the Wind* came out, my younger sister asked our grandmother if she ever wore hoop skirts," said Rochelle. "She was not amused—but I was. Honestly, can you imagine hoop skirts on the Lower East Side?"

"Would make it hard to navigate between the push carts! *Zie gezunt*, Miz Scarlett, vould you like a pastrami sandwich?"

"Oh fie, sir"—Rochelle gave her head a toss—"I cannot abide the smell of pickle juice!"

That evening, Doris told Rob about the copperhead. She kept a close eye on the dusty boardwalks. She saw a few rats and squirrels, but nothing more threatening. Still, she stayed vigilant.

24: August 1944

Three weeks later, Clementine, the bridge club babysitter, knocked on the Friedmans' door.

"Doris, can you meet Betty at the hospital? She started bleeding and cramping. I think she's losing the baby. I can stay with Barbara."

"Oh no! Is Will with her?"

"He drove us there, but I think another woman would be a comfort."

"Of course I'll go. Do you have a room number for her?"

"When I left she was still in emergency. I'm sure you'll find her."

Doris showed Clementine where she kept things for Barbara and headed for the hospital, trying not to think of the last time she'd gotten an urgent summons. When she arrived, Betty had been assigned a room. She did not want to intrude on a visit from Will, but a nurse in the corridor said Betty was alone. Doris knocked gently. When there was no answer, she pushed the door open slightly. Betty was lying in the bed, hooked up to an IV bottle. Her eyes were closed.

"Betty? It's Doris."

Betty's eyes opened, but she gazed at the ceiling.

"May I come in?"

"Yes." Betty's words sounded a little slurred. "The baby is gone."

Doris entered and took a chair next to the bed. She put her hand on top of Betty's. "Betty, I'm so sorry. I know how much you were looking forward to being a mother."

Betty said nothing, but tears dripped down the sides of her face.

Doris saw a box of tissues on the table next to her. She took one and gently wiped Betty's cheeks. The two women sat in silence for a while.

"Where is Will?"

She cleared her throat, still staring at the ceiling. "He had to go back to work."

"Do the doctors know what went wrong?"

"Not really. They said some pregnancies just miscarry. They said it wasn't my fault. I keep thinking and thinking . . . what did I do wrong?"

"Betty, you were so careful. Sometimes the baby just doesn't develop right."

"You didn't even want a baby. It's not fair! And I doubt you prayed for it, either."

"Life isn't fair. But now that I have Barbara, I wouldn't want to have missed it. Rubber pants and all. Betty, you need time to cry and be sad. But I bet you that before this war is over, you'll be diapering your own baby and cursing every safety pin."

Betty smiled just a little. "You forget—I'll hire a nanny to take care of that."

"Well, la-di-da! I wouldn't want you to chip a nail, Miz Scarlett."

"Just don't pick out another bridge partner while I'm in here, Chicago girl."

"I promise I'll wait for you. None of the others are on our level."

"Doris?"

"Yes?"

"I can't see."

"What do you mean you can't see?"

"Everything is foggy, except I see lightning flashes now and then."

"It's probably the drugs. Did they put you out?"

"They gave me shots for the pain, and to calm me down."

"That could explain it. I bet by tomorrow your vision will be back to normal."

"No, I think I'm going blind."

"Have you told the nurse?"

"Yes, and the doctor came in and shined a light in each eye. I could see that much. He said something about my pupils working right."

"That sounds promising. Why don't you try to get some sleep, Betty."

"Maybe I could go deaf instead. Then I wouldn't have to have a call with my mother-in-law."

"Tell your husband you're not ready to talk to her yet."

"Huh. One, he wouldn't dare tell her, and two, she wouldn't listen if he did."

"If she gets on the phone, just cry a lot."

"That might work for a couple of days, but eventually I'll get 'the talk' about my duty to carry on the family line."

"That's so much less important than what you want for yourself, Betty. What about your mother? Could she come visit?"

"My mama died three years ago. Some kind of women's cancer."

"Oh, Betty, I'm sorry." Doris took her friend's hand. "Do you miss her a lot?"

"All the time, especially now."

Tears streamed down Betty's cheeks. Doris took another tissue and gently wiped them.

"My daddy's already moved on. He met a new woman at the country club. A bottle blonde. He gave her my mother's diamond earrings. I can't stand the bitch."

"Well, she probably takes care of him, so at least you don't have to worry."

"I suppose. You're a good friend, Doris. I'm going to try to sleep. You come back now, you hear?"

"I promise."

When Doris got home, the babysitter was watching Barbara fill in a coloring book. Although her crayons sometimes strayed outside the lines, she picked the right colors—brown for a dog, green for grass, blue for the sky.

"Those pictures are really pretty," Doris told her, and was rewarded with a rare smile. She kissed the top of Barbara's head. "I love you, Barbara."

"I never saw a child this young color so well," said Clementine.

"My father is an artist, so maybe she gets it from him. Although he mostly touches up pictures. I wish he'd paint some of his own. I'd like to give you something for watching Barbara."

"You don't need to. I have the evening shift today and I wanted Betty to have a friend with her."

"No, please." Doris handed her fifty cents. "Go see a new movie or something."

"Thank you kindly. How is Betty?"

"A little groggy, and of course very sad. She said she was having trouble with her vision. I imagine it's the drugs. I'll come visit her again as soon as she gets home. Thanks again for coming to get me."

"Us girls have to stick together. I'll see you and Barbara when Betty feels up to having the bridge parties again."

25: September 1944

When Betty came home from the hospital, Doris went to visit. She found Betty lying on the couch in a pink chenille bathrobe, with a cloth over her eyes.

"Are your eyes still bothering you?" Doris asked.

"They don't hurt, but I can barely see. Thank goodness Clementine has been coming for a few hours every day. The doctors say there's nothing wrong with me though. They told my husband I have hysterical blindness."

"Is that a complication of penis envy?"

"Doris, don't make me laugh! I still hurt down there."

"Are you just lying here all day?"

"I listen to the radio. At least Paris is free now. We went there for our honeymoon."

"You lucky duck! You need to get your vision back so you can see it again. And I hate to tell you this—but your nail polish needs a touch-up."

"That psychiatrist at the hospital said if my eyesight doesn't come back, they might have to give me electric shock treatments."

"That sounds pretty drastic."

"You know, Doris, there are things I don't want to see. But I see them anyway, in my mind's eye."

"Like what?"

"Like . . . all the blood that came out of me when I lost the baby."

"Are you scared of blood?"

"Well, I don't like it. Who does? But it wasn't just blood." Tears dripped down Betty's cheeks. "I was four months along, and there was a tiny baby. It had skinny little arms and legs like a . . . like a frog." She sobbed. "They tried to hide it from me. They took my baby away in a metal pan with a towel over it, like a bedpan!"

"That's so sad. Move over, Betty." Doris put her arms around her friend's shoulders and made space for herself on the couch with Betty's head in her lap. "I'm sure your mama is looking down on you, wishing she could be here."

Betty's sobs got louder. "I miss her so."

"You have yourself a good cry. I'm here." After a few minutes, Betty was calmer. Doris took the cloth and wiped her friend's face.

"I must look a fright. Can you get me my compact? It's in my purse on the table by the door."

Doris found the compact and brought it to Betty. Betty fumbled with it as if she couldn't see but managed to open the catch. She held the mirror up to her face and gazed into it. "You know, it's still fuzzy, but I can see myself. And I do look just awful!"

Doris laughed. "I'd say that's progress. I bet if you let yourself cry, your eyesight will clear up a little more each day."

"Maybe. And I did manage to convince my mother-in-law that a visit to Oak Ridge would be too inconvenient for her."

"Are you going to have a funeral for the baby?"

"No, they said it was too early to call him a baby."

"It was a boy?"

"That's what they told me."

"That's tough. Well, maybe you could do something special to remember. Do you go to church here?"

"Sometimes. They have a Baptist service on Sundays at the chapel."

"Do you like the minister?"

"We call him a pastor, Doris."

"At least I didn't call him a rabbi! So, is he kind and compassionate? Or is he one of those hellfire types?"

"Doris!" Betty frowned at her. "Maybe you should pay a little more attention to hellfire. But the pastor here seems kind."

"Maybe you could ask him to pray with you for the baby."

"I'll consider it." Betty was silent for a moment. "Do you believe in heaven and hell?"

"Not really. Jews worry more about what we do while we're alive. I think you Christians care more about an afterlife. Is that something that bothers you?"

"Not too often, but I do wonder sometimes if I'll end up in hell."

"What kind of sin would damn a Sweet Briar woman?"

Betty put the cloth back over her eyes. "Promise you won't tell anyone?"

"Cross my heart and hope to die. Besides, who would I tell? The girls at bridge?"

She uncovered one eye to give Doris a gimlet stare. "Don't you even think about it!" The cloth went back on. "The thing is, I wasn't pure when I got married. I had a boyfriend the summer before college and we . . . got carried away. Only one time! Will doesn't know. I told him I rode horses a lot, so I didn't bleed on our wedding night. Don't look like that, Doris! Sweet Briar is known for its equestrienne competitions. I even went fox hunting."

"Tallyho!"

"Exactly. But with a Virginia accent!"

"Betty, Rob and I had sex before we got married. So do most people, I think. With all the evil in the world, do you really believe you'll go to hell for having sex one time?"

"When you put it like that . . . But maybe God is punishing me by not letting me have a baby."

"Then why did God—if there is a God . . ."

"Doris!"

"Well, you asked me what I believe! Then why did God give me a baby when I had sex before marriage? Though I didn't actually get pregnant until afterwards." Doris tried not to think about Rob's news about potential radiation side effects.

"Hmph. I'll have to think on that one . . . Maybe it doesn't count for Jews."

"Right! Only you Christians are supposed to be virgins at the altar."

"Well, you could be going to hell if you don't accept Jesus as your personal savior."

"I'll take my chances."

Betty took the cloth off again. "Doris, why don't you wear one of those necklaces with the special star?"

"I'm surprised you know about those. We call it the Star of David, as in King David from the Old Testament."

"You're never going to let me live down the horns, are you?"

"Betty, I'll be telling that story for the rest of my life!"

"You are a mean girl. Rochelle wears a star."

"That's true. I don't know, Betty. I'm just not that religious. And wearing a star can sometimes get you nasty looks or negative remarks. It's hard enough down here being a Yankee!"

"In Oak Ridge? This place is swarming with Yankees!"

Doris thought about the soldiers on the train. "You know the Nazis make Jews wear a big yellow star sewn to their clothes. So, I guess the right thing to do would be to wear a star necklace to show I'm proud to be a Jew . . . maybe I'm just chicken."

"You are!"

"And I'm not even a kosher chicken."

Betty chuckled. "You know, I hope when we all go home that I can make some Jewish friends. I wouldn't have wanted to miss knowing you."

"I feel the same way about you. I'll have to look for some Sweet Briar women in Chicago. There must be one or two!"

"And wherever we end up, let's try to keep in touch."

Doris went home, hoping her friend had turned a corner.

26: September 1944

In mid-September, Rob got an urgent call at ten in the evening to report to X-10. Sol even came in his car to pick him up. Doris kissed her husband goodbye and tried to get back to sleep. She had woken up and fed Barbara breakfast by the time Rob walked in at about nine in the morning and collapsed onto the couch. "Well, it's done."

"What's donc?"

"You can't tell anyone."

"You know I wouldn't."

"Tonight we finished making a batch of that isotope they need at Los Alamos, to test something—I don't know what. The bigwigs have been dogging Harrison all week. He's been working around the clock. This new stuff is super radioactive, so they've been making it in the hot lab, using the remote controls."

"I'm glad to hear that—instead of keeping it next to your desk!"

"Harrison took a break to have dinner with Nora Joy last night because it was her birthday. While he was gone, the guys combined all the stuff in glass tubes and started measuring it. They were sure they had enough to satisfy Oppie. A truck and a couple of army cars were waiting to take it to New Mexico. But you know what?"

"What?"

"They could actually see the radioactive glow inside the glass, but when they poured the solution into a special metal cone, there was only a fraction of what should have been in there. A couple of the guys went to Harrison's house and waited until he got home. They brought him back to the lab. That's when they came to get me. I was able to put together an ion chamber to measure the radioactivity. Meanwhile, they sent cars to pick up MacDonald and several other guys. MacDonald was at the movies in Jackson Square with a date! He was the one who figured out that the radioactive sample was still lining the glass tubes. Water hadn't dissolved it. They had to wash the tubes out with an acid solution. When they poured the liquid into the container again, everyone heaved a sigh of relief, because it was all there."

Doris could see that Rob's eyes were starting to close, but he woke up enough to finish the story. "So they put the cone with this glowing sample into a concrete box with a lead door about a foot thick. They pulled a flatbed truck up to the loading dock next to the hot lab. They had a crane ready. Slowly and *ve-e-ry* carefully, the crane picked up the box and lowered it into an even bigger lead vault on the truck. They're driving it in an armed convoy all the way to Los Alamos."

"If people knew what's merrily rolling along . . ."

"I'm sure they'll be careful. But hopefully things will slow down a little at the lab. You know what happened to the first, tiny amount of this stuff that we sent to Los Alamos?"

"What?"

"MacDonald was telling us that the physics guys there don't have a remote-control setup like ours. They rigged up a way to handle the stuff from a distance with pulleys and strings, but they dropped the glass tubing. It broke and the isotope spilled out. There was no way to clean it up, so they had to tear out the whole floor of the building and bury it in a canyon somewhere!"

"It sounds like Los Alamos is even more dangerous than Oak Ridge."

"I'm sure they'll be more careful with this big batch. Otherwise, they may have to evacuate the whole town! We don't hear a lot about what they're doing. I'd love to understand more. I wish I could go up there." He yawned. "I think I'll just take a quick nap before I go back to work. I can't afford to be useless all day."

27: October 1944

Rob asked Doris if they could host a small dinner the next weekend.

"Sure, I don't mind. Could be fun."

Doris made beef stew, cooking the tough meat for several hours over low heat to tenderize it. Annette and Joel contributed a bottle of Chianti they had smuggled in from their last trip to Chicago. Rochelle brought a macaroni casserole. Dave, as usual, brought chocolate from the PX. His date was one of the chemistry technicians who worked with Annette. She was a blonde from Alabama and clearly not Jewish. Her tight skirt accentuated her small waist. Doris was angry at herself for feeling a stirring of envy.

When they sat down to eat, the conversation turned to the news that the Germans had started to target London and other areas of England with V-2 rockets.

"I guess that was their new wonder weapon," Dave said. "It's bad, but it could have been something a lot worse, couldn't it?"

Everyone looked at him, but nobody responded. Doris was certainly not going to mention German atomic bombs in front of a stranger, even if the girl worked at X-10.

"I feel so bad for people in London," Annette put in. "They don't even get a warning that a V-2 is coming!"

"And there's no way to really shoot one down," Joel added.

"I agree, it's horrifying," said Doris.

The friends sat in silence for a moment.

"Would anyone like seconds?" Doris asked. The remaining food was passed around the table.

After dinner, Rob asked if everyone would like to hear the arrangement of "Für Elise" for piano and clarinet that he'd been rehearsing with Doris.

"Do you think we're ready?" Doris asked him, her heart sinking a little.

Rob practiced his clarinet earnestly, but their musical skills were simply not on the same level. However, he managed to get through the piece with only one mistake. Their performance was greeted with polite applause. Rob raised an eyebrow at Doris.

"That was great," she praised. "Keep on like that, and maybe you'll be drafted for the symphonette. Annette, would you like to play?" Doris knew the invitation would please Annette, who was an excellent pianist.

"Sure. But I'll let you in on something," Annette said to the group. "That duet showed how much Doris loves Rob."

Doris gave her a warning look, thinking that Annette was going to criticize Rob's playing, but Annette continued, "Doris is the only person I know who hates Beethoven! So this is for you, my old friend."

Annette played the first movement of the *Moonlight Sonata*. Dave got a dreamy look on his face and clapped loudly when she got to the end. Annette took a mock bow.

"That was lovely, Annette. I don't hate Beethoven. He's just not my favorite."

"Would you also play for us, Doris?" asked Dave.

"Okay." She sat down at the piano. "How about the Gershwin Prelude no. 3?" It was modern, kind of flashy with the syncopation, and also short. She wished she could play it on the Steinway in the officer's club, but at least her piano was recently tuned. The humid Oak Ridge weather was tough on musical instruments.

It was getting late for a Sunday night, so the party broke up. Dave came into the kitchen to thank Doris for dinner.

"I'd like to learn that Gershwin piece."

"Sure. It's fast and a little tricky with the jazz rhythm. And you'd have to put some real feeling into it."

"I have real feelings."

"I don't doubt it." Doris rinsed a plate and put it in the dish rack. "But they don't show up much in your piano playing. Your date is pretty."

"Yeah, nothing serious."

"You never seem to bring the same girl twice."

"Maybe I would if I found someone like you."

Doris tried not to show her gratification at his words. What was wrong with her?

Rob had walked quietly up behind Dave. "Oh yeah? Well, I found her first!"

"Just expressing my appreciation." Dave winked and went to collect his date.

"Does he talk to you like that when you give him piano lessons?" Rob asked when everyone had left.

"Not really. We focus on the music. I think he likes to rile you up. Though he told me he admires your work."

"Yeah, sometimes I think he's a little too curious about what we're doing in the lab."

"Well, he has to understand it for safety purposes, doesn't he?"

Rob shrugged. "I don't see the rationale for some of his questions. I told Harrison. He said to just be careful around him. He's the army's responsibility."

"Well, anyway, I'm not interested in anyone but you," Doris reassured him, giving him a soft kiss on the mouth. She wished her emotions were really that simple.

28: November 1944–January 1945

As the weather grew cold again, Doris took Barbara to the children's corner in the library. She let Barbara pick out several picture books and then read them to her daughter quietly. Now that Barbara was almost two and a half, her toilet training was finally improving, with only an occasional lapse. Still, Doris felt that life was a monotonous round of housework, motherhood, and worry about the war. Her college days seemed so carefree in retrospect, even though she had complained about studying and exams at the time. She even envied the women lining up for their shifts at the various Oak Ridge plants. At least they had a purpose.

She visited with Betty a couple of times a week. Betty's vision had returned to normal and the bridge club met regularly. Betty was dreading a trip to her in-laws' in Richmond for Thanksgiving but wanted to take the opportunity to see her obstetrician back home. She confided that she was taking several months off from trying to get pregnant. "I hope giving those parts a rest will help with the next try."

"Do you mean no sex?"

"Heck no! A girl's got to keep her husband happy. Just using, you know, some precautions and not worrying about all the fuss afterwards." Betty took a drag on her cigarette and then tapped off the ash into the bowl she was using as an ashtray. Doris knew she would open the windows and hide the evidence before Will got home. "Is Rob all better?" Betty was only aware that Rob had been ill from strep throat.

"That was almost a year ago now. Time goes so fast. He seems just fine. He's back to his normal, skinny weight. It isn't fair that men can eat whatever they want and not gain much." Doris was constantly struggling with her weight. Her father told her she was just zaftig, the Yiddish word for buxom. Smoking seemed to help keep her weight under some control. Almost everyone she knew smoked. She had resisted as a teenager, but every time she rode the El train to school, she got motion sickness from the tobacco smell. She asked her doctor what to do and he told her, "Just start smoking." It worked like a charm, except now she had to negotiate the endless lines to buy cigarettes.

At the end of November, the newspapers interviewed two escapees from Nazi camps called Auschwitz and Dachau. Doris read about the gas chambers and ovens. Sometimes, her heart pounded and she swore she could feel the ground shaking under the house. She would pick up Barbara and sit with her on the porch, remembering the vivid account she read of the New Madrid earthquakes. She had visions of the earth splitting open to swallow the house. Barbara would quickly get restless sitting on Doris's lap. It was chilly, too, so they always ended up back inside. Doris wondered if there would be a decent world left by the time Barbara grew up.

Rob was only getting home at eight or nine in the evening. He confided that they were creating another, triple-sized radioactive sample to send to Los Alamos. "The glass tubing we used to make the first batch got so radioactive that it turned black. You couldn't see through it at all. It was inside a metal vat that we needed to reuse, but first we had to break up the old tubing and replace it with new glass. There was no way to do it by remote control. Harrison had about ten guys each get close enough for a minute or two to scoop some glass out of the container and throw it into a lead box. He did his turn too. He said whatever dose his 'boys' got, he would take twice as much. Everyone's badges were completely exposed."

"Did you take a turn with the glass?"

"Not this time. Harrison said I already took my dose for the team."

"I'm relieved."

"I felt bad. I didn't want to be a special case."

"But what about us? We need you alive and healthy."

"This project has to succeed so we don't have Auschwitz in Chicago. Can you imagine if the Germans get the bomb before we do? Goodbye, London or Paris."

"Do you think one bomb could do that much damage?"

"I don't know, but if it's our bomb, I hope so."

"I don't see how Germany can fight much longer anyway."

Thanksgiving dinner was a small gathering at Rochelle and Sol's house. They had chicken because few turkeys were available. This was not a year when Doris felt she could relax and be grateful. Besides, she always had trouble feeling enthused about the original Thanksgiving feast. Far from being pilgrims to the new world, her ancestors had been eking out a meager existence and getting thrown out of country after country in Europe. She did feel very thankful, however, that they had eventually managed to flee to America.

In mid-December, everyone at Oak Ridge was talking about the Battle of the Bulge. The fight between US troops and the German army in Belgium cost over nineteen thousand American lives, although the Allies won in the end.

On a gray day in January, Rob came home and pulled off his work boots to avoid tracking mud and slush into the house.

"Do we have anything alcoholic to drink?" he asked Doris.

"There's a couple of beers in the fridge."

"Nothing stronger?"

"Nope. I guess you could call a taxi." Taxis in Oak Ridge did a thriving business delivering local moonshine, despite the official prohibitions.

"Not worth the money."

"Is something wrong? You look upset."

"I tried to enlist today."

"What?" Doris sat down abruptly in one of the armchairs.

"You heard me. I tried to enlist. I should be over there fighting our enemies. With guns like my brother." Rob threw himself on the couch and lit a cigarette.

"But they need you here! Don't you think what you're doing is more important than shooting at Germans from a tank? Why do men think it's glorious to be cannon fodder? Or were you hoping to be assigned to the SED and get GI benefits?"

"No, I want to be in combat. I'm tired of people looking at me like I'm some kind of coward."

"When does that happen?"

"Every time we leave Oak Ridge and it's obvious that I'm not in uniform. You just don't notice. And my parents' letters always have news about my brother. They hardly even ask what I'm doing. But don't worry—the recruiter told me to scram. He said I knew too much. If I signed up, they'd just send me to Alaska where I could never be captured."

"I'm glad somebody has some brains."

"Doris, I'm sick of you looking down on me."

"How could I look down on you? You're half a foot taller than I am."

Rob stubbed out his cigarette. "You think I need to go to college and that my family is low-class. I don't have good taste. I'm too much of a Mr. Nice Guy. I even smell bad."

"Not anymore, now that you use deodorant."

"Right, thanks to your nagging. Do you think I don't notice your little digs?" He stood up.

"Where are you going?"

"Out."

"Rob, I love you. I always tell you how smart you are. Am I wrong to try to help you get ahead?" Her voice choked. "I married you, didn't I?"

"Maybe you regret that. I see how you look at Sokol."

"Now you're imagining things! I don't regret marrying you. Except when you go and try to enlist without even talking to me first."

"I knew you'd be against it."

"Yes, I'm against it! You're doing a crucial war job. We depend on your salary. Even the SED guys only earn fifty dollars a month, and you get two hundred. And I want you alive and at home. I came to this godforsaken place to be with you."

"Oh, you're such a martyr! You like it here now. You're having a good old time, teaching piano, playing bridge, hosting bachelor Dave at dinner parties."

"If I've learned to like it here, is that a reason to make me leave? What do you think would happen to Barbara and me if you went overseas to one of the fronts?"

"You'd go and live with your parents. That's what you wanted to do, anyway."

"No, I didn't! I would have stayed in our apartment. Do you honestly think I could go back to living in the same house with my mother?"

"I don't know."

"Well, I do! I don't want to live apart from you. We've made our own family. We belong together. That's what you told me. You're so self-centered, Rob. Look around you at the real world."

"You're the one ignoring the real world. I'm going for a walk." He left the house.

Doris sat and stared into space. How could you want to kiss a man one moment and feel like slugging him the next? It felt as if her heart were splitting into its constituent molecules, like fission. She pictured the shards whizzing around like so many neutrons, but they just bounced off Rob's heart, fizzling instead of setting off a chain reaction. She didn't really want to trigger an explosion between them, no matter how angry she felt, but at least she wanted to register on him, like clicks on a Geiger counter.

29: January 1945

The holidays, such as they were, had passed. Germany and the Allies battled fiercely in the Ardennes. Finally, the Allies won several victories and advanced into Eastern Europe, only to experience the horror of liberating Auschwitz and the other concentration camps. Doris showed Rob a front-page photo of a group of surviving children. A young teen held out her forearm, palm up, to show the numbers tattooed on it.

"She looks so much like Harry's youngest daughter."

"At least most of them have scarves and jackets."

"Probably from our soldiers. You don't think the Nazis provided them, do you?"

Rob shook his head. "And that's one of the only pictures I can stand to look at." He turned to the newspaper's second page. "Oh, my mother called yesterday. My brother is still doing okay."

"That's good to hear." Doris knew that Rob did not like to dwell on the negative, but sometimes it left her feeling lonely.

As pressure grew on the project, many of the wives complained that tempers were short at home. Rob had been quieter than usual since their blowup over his attempted enlistment. Doris felt the tension but did not comment on it.

One evening when they were having dessert at Sol and Rochelle's, the phone rang. Sol answered it. He listened and then narrowed his eyes.

"Are you sure? I remember locking it. Okay, okay." He put down the receiver. “That was some guard at the office. He claims I didn’t lock my file cabinet.”

“But you remember locking it before you left?” asked Rob.

“I thought I did. But I’m going to have to go in and check.”

Rochelle groaned. “We’re trying to save our gas ration, so that means riding the bus ten miles at this time of night.”

“You could take a taxi,” Doris suggested.

“It’s too expensive. And it would take too long to get here. If someone got into those files, I need to check them and make sure everything’s safe . . . Damn! I’m going to have to pull out every file and inventory it against my list. How could this have happened?”

“I could go with you,” Rob volunteered. “If someone got into the files, you shouldn’t go to that building all alone. It’s already after nine.”

“He can bring his air pistol,” Doris joked.

“That’s not a bad idea. Sol, come by the house with us. I’ll walk Doris home and get the pistol, and then we can catch the bus at Jackson Square.”

Doris was already getting on her coat, but she put her hands on her hips. “The guards will be there, so I don’t see why you need to be armed. Besides, you aren’t going to disable any spies with an air pistol!”

Rob and Sol were determined, however, so Doris went along with the plan. She managed to fall asleep and did not wake up until it was time to get breakfast ready. Rob was snoring gently next to her in the bed. She tried to give him a few extra minutes of rest, but when his eggs were on the table, she shook him awake.

“Rob, honey, it’s time for breakfast.”

He dragged himself out of bed and quickly got dressed. “I’ll shave afterwards, so everything doesn’t get cold.”

When he was seated at the table, Doris asked what had happened at the lab the night before.

“It was the strangest thing! Sol’s file cabinet was locked and none of the guards had made that phone call. We did the inventory anyway, just in case we overlooked something. It took the two of us about an hour and a half. Nothing was missing or looked disturbed. We can't figure it out."

When Rob got home that evening, the mystery had been solved. Arthur Thompson, the Boilo-loving chemist, was a practical joker. After several sly digs at Sol, he admitted that he had made the prank call that sent the two men to the lab. "If Arthur weren't so damn huge, I think Sol would have punched out his lights! Joel says Arthur is a poor, deluded fool who thinks he's Dick Feynman."

"Who's that?"

"He's a genius young physicist at Los Alamos. He came here last year to help with the Y-12 uranium plant. He has a hobby of picking locks to show how easy it is to break into top-secret files. He won a bet with one of our colonels that he could open his safe in less than thirty minutes. But he does it to tweak security about their weaknesses, not to torture his friends!"

"You and Sol need to get some revenge!"

"Yeah, but it can't be something that would hurt the project."

"I have an idea! I'm good at doing the Tennessee twang, right?"

"You are! You wan' it in a poke, little lady?" Rob drawled.

"Not quite—but I can do it better. How about if tonight we get together with Sol and Rochelle, so they can share the fun. I'm going to call Arthur and pretend to be from Roane-Anderson. I'll tell him he didn't pay his bill and they're coming tomorrow to take out his phone." The scientists and engineers at X-10 were among the minority at Oak Ridge who had phones installed in their homes, for just such potential emergencies as the one Arthur had faked. Losing your phone was a fate to be dreaded.

"That's brilliant! But don't you think he'll recognize your voice?"

"He's only met me a couple of times. For one of them, he was sloshed on Boilo. I think I can pull it off. I'll give Rochelle a call."

When they got to Sol and Rochelle's, Annette and Joel were also there. The phone was in the living room. Everyone sat around, trying not to make any noise. It was around 7:00 p.m., but Oak Ridge offices stayed open late with shift workers toiling around the clock. Doris got Arthur on the line. "Hello, Dr. Thompson?" She pitched her voice a little lower than normal.

They could just make out Arthur's booming response. "Yes, this is he."

Doris used her best Tennessee accent. "I am calling you from Roane-Anderson to inform you that we are coming tomorrow to remove your telephone."

"You're what?"

"We are notifying you about your phone removal, sir. Will your wife be home to give our repair man access to the home?"

"Will my wife . . . Why are you removing my phone?"

"Wey-ell, sir, it seems you have neglected to pay your phone bill."

"That's wrong! I am sure I paid it!"

"Wey-ell, sir, Roane-Anderson does not have a record of any payments for the past three months."

"I remember paying those bills! This is just some crazy mistake at your office."

"Sir, I should not have to inform you that Roane-Anderson does not make mistakes."

"I can bring in my checkbook—my bank statements."

"You certainly can do that, Dr. Thompson, but our service technician will be at your home bright and early tomorrow morning to retrieve our phone."

"Can't you wait a day so I can get you the proof that I paid?"

"I'm afraid not, Dr. Thompson. The service call is already on our schedule."

"But—"

"Of course, if you can verify your payments, sir, we can put you back on the waiting list for another telephone. I believe the wait is approximately . . . seven months at the current time."

They could all hear Arthur's heavy breathing and increasing panic. "Ma'am, I need a phone. I am an essential scientist at Clinton Labs."

"I'm sorry, sir. In that case, you should have paid your phone bill."

"But I did pay my phone bill!" Arthur was roaring now.

"This situation is certainly unfortunate, Dr. Thompson. But please tell your wife to expect our technician tomorrow morning." Doris clicked the receiver down gently and they all burst into laughter.

"I think Susan is going to disappear from the neighborhood tomorrow morning," Joel said.

"She won't dare!" Rochelle disagreed. "She'll be afraid the technician will bust the door down to get the phone."

"Well, she'll be waiting in vain," Doris reminded them.

"You were fantastic, Doris," Rob told her. "I almost forgot you weren't really a Roane-Anderson secretary."

The next morning Arthur was late to work since he had stopped at the telephone office to try to halt the phone removal. When nobody in the office had a record of calling his home, and they verified that his account was paid in full, a light bulb went off. By the time he got to the lab, Sol and Rob had told everyone the whole story and Arthur was greeted with catcalls.

"Hey, Arthur, hoisted by your own petard!"

"That'll teach you to make prank calls!"

Rob told Doris that Harrison had scolded Arthur in front of several people.

"I love jokes as much as the next person, but not when they involve our files at the lab. We won't say any more about it, but I don't expect any repetitions either. If security got wind of this, you might find yourself somewhere other than Oak Ridge, and we need your skills here."

30: February 1945

Betty called Doris and asked if she was free in two days.

"I suppose, except for Barbara. I don't have any piano students scheduled then."

"Could you get a babysitter? Will said I could have the car if I drop him off at the office. I thought we could have a ladies' trip to Knoxville. Will's birthday is coming up and I want to buy him a present. We could go to the department store there. They have a better selection than the shops at Jackson Square."

"You know how to drive?"

"Honey chile, of course I can drive. Can't you?"

"Papa has a Ford, but he wasn't keen on teaching me. I hope after the war Rob and I can afford a car of our own."

"Well, what do you say?"

"Rochelle owes me a babysitting day. Let me check with her."

"Road to Knoxville, Doris!"

"Yes! Just like Bob Hope and Bing Crosby."

"Except we're much better looking!"

The day arrived with cold weather but no rain or snow. Doris bundled up in her Chicago coat and winter gloves. Betty gave a toot of the horn to announce her arrival in her baby-blue Buick sedan. Doris was glad to see her friend in such good spirits. It was contagious. The farther they drove from Oak Ridge, the freer she felt from the gloom of the last several months.

"What kind of present are you going to get for Will?"

"I'm not sure. Let's see what they have."

The two women wandered around downtown, window-shopping and debating a birthday gift.

"Sweaters are always nice," suggested Doris. "I still have my cashmere twin set that I wore in college."

"Mm, that is an idea. Nothing like cuddlin' with a man in a soft sweater . . ." Betty paused to examine a midnight-blue draped cocktail number. "Pretty, but I don't need another party dress."

"I'm too dumpy to wear something like that."

"Oh, Doris—you seriously underestimate yourself! With the right undergarments, it would be stunning on you."

Doris shrugged, and they walked on.

"Is everything back to normal for you guys?" she asked Betty.

"Oh yes. The doctor said we could start trying again."

"But besides the conception part, are you back to having fun?"

"Oh, definitely."

They entered the lingerie section of a department store. Betty pointed to a black lace shortie nightgown. "I think I'm going to try on a couple of these. Do you think black or that nude shade would be more . . . becoming?"

"Nothing says wicked like black, Betty, especially on a blonde. Do you want me to come with you to the dressing room and give you my opinion?"

"Doris! Where is your modesty, girl? You just browse around while I check these out."

Betty headed off to try on her options and Doris idly sorted through a rack of peignoirs on sale. She held up a satiny peach number with ecru lace trim.

"You would look lovely in that, dear. It's your color," said a saleslady, bustling over. "Do you want me to put it in a fitting room?"

Doris looked at the price tag. Even on sale, she shouldn't waste money on something so frivolous. But she had built up quite a savings account between teaching piano and getting a small stipend for helping with the symphonette. She should be able to treat herself once in a while. Maybe if she wore that robe to bed, Rob would put down the engineering articles he pored over nightly before they went to sleep.

"Yes, I'd like to try it."

It fit her perfectly. She loved how the smooth fabric caressed her skin. Doris examined herself in the mirror. With all the walking and housework in Oak Ridge, she was the thinnest she had been since high school. She decided she would splurge. When Betty came out, she showed her the purchase.

"Ooh, Doris, that is definitely you." She turned to the saleslady. "I'm going to take both of these nightgowns."

"The black and the nude, Betty?"

"Why not? It's not easy to find pretty things with the war going on."

"You're so right, ma'am. Your hubbies are going to thank you girls." The saleslady blushed. "I'm sorry, maybe your men are off fighting."

"They're doing important war work right here in Tennessee," Betty assured her.

"Oh, are you Oak Ridgers?"

Doris reflected that the woman didn't seem as hostile as many in Knoxville—just curious.

"What in the heck are people doing over there? Every day, trains full of supplies go in, but we never see anything come out."

"We don't know either," Doris put in quickly. "We're just wives."

"But you wait," said Betty. "When this war gets won, we'll all find out."

"I pray the Lord that happens soon, ladies."

"We all do. Have a blessed day," said Betty.

"Thanks for your help," Doris added.

"And now, to the menswear section."

Betty found a forest-green cashmere sweater for Will. Doris

privately thought it would also look great on Rob, but she gulped at the price. Someday she wanted to be able to just blithely buy things for herself and her family.

Looking for a place to have lunch, the women passed an art supply store. Doris purchased a couple of pads of cheap paper and a set of children's watercolor paints for Barbara. They stopped to lock their parcels in the trunk of Betty's parked car. Then Doris noticed a familiar restaurant. It was the one where Colonel Barton had picked up his liquor supply, but today it was open. "Should we catch a bite there?"

"Looks good to me."

As they waited by the hostess stand for a table, Doris felt a hand tap on her shoulder. She turned abruptly.

"Hi, Doris! This is unexpected." It was Dave Sokol, looking spiffy in his SED uniform. He had apparently just come in the door with a buddy. "Aren't you going to introduce me to your friend?"

"Yes, sorry. I was just startled. This is Mrs. Betty Hunt. Betty, meet Dave Sokol. He works in the same building as Rob."

Dave gave Betty an appreciative smile. "Always nice to meet a friend of Doris. And this is my fellow SED man, Hubert Johnson. Of course, we call him Hubie. Our commanding officer sent us to Knoxville to pick up some equipment, so we decided we were entitled to stop for lunch. Would you lovely ladies mind sharing a table with a couple of homesick engineers?"

Doris raised her eyebrows at Betty, who smiled and exaggerated her Southern accent. "If you don't mind lunch with two very married ladies."

"Married ladies are the best kind." Dave winked at her. "Especially ones with tired husbands."

"Oh, my husband is never all *that* tired, if you know what I mean. He's an engineer, too, with DuPont."

"No wonder," said Hubie. "The DuPont guys have it easy compared to us."

"Speak for yourself," Dave declared.

The hostess led them to a table for four and he sat next to Doris. "I hear that Rob nods off most evenings on the bus ride home. I hope he's not neglecting you."

"That's certainly not your worry."

"I just like to see my friends happy and . . . satisfied."

Doris gave him a quelling look, which he ignored.

"So what have you two been up to today?"

"Why, shopping, of course," Betty replied. "My husband's birthday is next week, so I bought him a present."

"Very nice. But are you telling me that was your only purchase? No party dresses or . . . unmentionables for yourselves?"

"Since you bring it up, we definitely did acquire some unmentionables." Betty fluttered her mascaraed lashes.

"Then where are your packages?"

"Locked safely in the trunk of my car. So don't even think of asking to see what we bought."

Doris tried to suppress a smile at their exchange. So this was what you learned at Sweet Briar.

They all turned their attention to the menu. Once they had ordered and established that Hubie had a son and daughter in New Jersey, Dave asked Betty if she had ever heard Doris play the piano.

"I have not had that pleasure."

Betty and Will did not attend the same parties as the Friedmans' other friends. Doris thought they would be uncomfortable with the X-10 crowd. Although Betty often visited Doris at home, playing piano for her had never come up.

"Do you like music?" Dave asked Betty.

"Of course. I love Sinatra and the big bands."

"No, I mean classical music."

"I went to an opera once in Richmond. *Carmen* I think it was. I liked the story of the gypsy girl. Pretty costumes."

Dave eyed her over his fried chicken. "You don't seem like Doris's type. How did you two get to be friends, anyway?"

"Betty started a bridge club. The only problem is that none of the other women can beat us. It gets a little monotonous."

"I bet I could give you a run for your money if I had the right partner. Maybe I could steal you, Doris."

"The bridge club is ladies only," Betty informed him. "And anyway, why shouldn't Doris and I be friends? You mean because I'm not one of the Jewish people?"

Dave looked taken aback. "No, of course not. I have lots of friends who aren't Jewish."

"Like me," Hubie chimed in. "I'm Lutheran."

"Well, are you implying that I'm not cultured or maybe intellectual"—Betty drew out the word into its component syllables—"enough to be friends with Doris?"

Dave shrugged and squirmed in his seat, and Doris started to laugh. "Honestly, Dave, Betty's the society debutante. I'm just a girl from the South Side of Chicago. But we've become good pals." The women smiled at each other.

"Well, you certainly make a pretty pair."

"Give up, Dave. It will take more than a feeble compliment to dig you out of the ditch you just excavated," Doris told him.

When the waitress brought their check, Dave insisted on paying. The women protested, but Hubie gave a thumbs-up.

When the waitress left, Doris leaned forward and said softly to the others, "You know, this restaurant sells bootleg liquor."

"How do you know?" Hubie asked.

"When Colonel Barton brought me to Knoxville to pick out a piano for the officers, he had his driver go to the side door. He came back with a carton full of bottles. I heard them clink and slosh when he put them in the trunk. I wouldn't mind buying a bottle of whiskey or bourbon to take home."

"How would we get it past the guards at the gate?" asked Betty.

Dave raised his eyebrows. "What kind of a car do you have?"

"A Buick sedan."

"You can hide a bottle under the back-seat cushions. The guards only bother to search there if they get a tip-off. They have a deal with the liquor stores just outside of the dry counties. When people who look like Oak Ridgers buy something, the store owners call the nearest gatehouse and give the guards the car's license plate number. Then the guards search every nook and cranny. When they confiscate the bottles, they give a kickback to the store."

"And probably drink the contents," Doris speculated. "But do you think the restaurant owner would sell me something?"

"He must be the man sitting at that little table in the front. He's been giving us the eye. Leave it to me." Betty draped her coat over her arm and sashayed over to the owner. They followed her. "Are you the proprietor of this fine establishment?" she inquired, bending down so that her bosom was at his eye level.

"Yes, ma'am."

"I thought so. What a delicious lunch we had. As fine as any restaurant in Richmond."

"Are you from Richmond, missus?"

"I am. And I am also a friend of Colonel Barton, who recommended that I stop here for a meal."

"Oh yes. Colonel Barton is a frequent customer. Please give him my regards."

"I certainly shall." She lowered her voice. "The colonel also mentioned that you occasionally have an extra bottle or two in the kitchen for those who like to take a taste of Knoxville home with them."

"Uh . . ." The owner wrenched his gaze from Betty's breasts to her wide gray eyes. "Just what kind of taste do you mean?"

"Something that's been a little aged, say for about four years?" Two dollar bills appeared in Betty's gloved fingers.

"For you, missus, I think we could find something aged eight years, at least." He took the bills and put them in his pocket. "Send one of your soldier friends to the door in the alleyway on the side and we'll see to it."

"Thank you kindly, sir." Betty straightened up.

They waited next to Betty's car until Dave sauntered back to them, carrying a paper sack. "Here you go, ladies. A nice, mellow Canadian whiskey. I expect a shot, Doris, next time I have dinner at your house." He pulled up one of the back-seat cushions and deposited the bottle underneath it.

"Thank you, Dave. And thanks again for lunch," said Doris.

"I don't suppose that earns me a kiss?"

"No, you don't suppose."

"Betty, you are a piece of work!" Doris said when they were back in the car.

"I am, am-n't I?" Betty touched up her hair and lipstick in the rearview mirror.

"Here. I insist on paying you back for the whiskey."

"If it makes you feel better." Betty took the money Doris was holding out.

"It does. And we saved the cost of a nice lunch."

"Watch out for that Dave. He seems to be pursuing you."

"I think he just fancies himself a ladies' man. He never seems to go out with the same date twice."

"If you say so."

"Betty, would you mind one more stop before we go home? I'd like to talk to Mr. Clark at the piano store. I was hoping he might have some office work I could do from home."

"No trouble at all."

"Okay, turn left at the next corner."

When Doris walked in with Betty, Mr. Clark came to greet her.

"Mrs. Friedman! Are you in the market for your very own Steinway? We just got in a baby grand."

"Oh, I wish! Maybe someday. Mr. Clark, this is my friend and neighbor, Mrs. Hunt."

"Pleased to meet you. Are you also a pianist?"

"I'm afraid not. Doris is the one with the musical talent."

"She certainly is. A fine musician."

"Mr. Clark, I've been studying bookkeeping. I set up a filing system and ledgers for the Oak Ridge Symphonette. I was wondering if you needed any extra help like that for your business?"

He rubbed his chin. "Actually, I might have some work for you, at least temporarily. My bookkeeper has been out with pneumonia."

"Oh! I'm sorry to hear that. Would it be work that I could take to Oak Ridge and bring back, maybe every couple of weeks? You know I have a young daughter at home."

"That's not ideal, but we could try it out. Could you come back early next week so I could show you what I need?"

"That would be perfect! I can just take the bus."

Betty was running her hands over the sleek pianos. "Doris, could you play something, since Dave pointed out that I've never heard you?"

Another potential customer had just walked in with a young girl. Doris gave Mr. Clark an inquiring look.

He nodded. "Sure, try out that brand-new baby grand. Show us how it's supposed to sound."

She sat down and played Debussy's *La fille aux cheveux de lin.*

"That was for you, Betty. It's called 'The Girl with the Flaxen Hair.'"

"That's so pretty. Maybe I should broaden my musical tastes! You play beautifully, Doris. Even I can tell that."

"Thanks, Betty, but my piano teacher told me I'd always be second-rate, no matter how hard I tried."

"Well, it sounded first-rate to me."

Doris waved goodbye to Mr. Clark and they went back to the car.

That evening, after Doris got Barbara to sleep, she saw that Rob was already lying in their bed, propped up on pillows doing calculations with his slide rule and recording them in a spiral-bound notebook. She went into the pantry and measured out two small glasses of whiskey. Then she got her new peignoir out of the closet and took it into the bathroom. She put on the filmy robe, picked up the glasses, and returned to the bedroom.

Rob glanced up but simply said, "Hi, honey," continuing with his work.

"I got you a little treat in Knoxville today."

"That's nice." Rob finished making his notation.

"Surprise! I bought a bottle of whiskey at the place Colonel Barton took me. I poured us each a shot."

"Great! Put it on the bedside table. I have to finish this design for the lab. In fact, I should probably wait to drink it until I'm done."

Doris frowned and put Rob's glass next to him.

"Mm, you're wearing that nice perfume."

"Is that all you notice?"

He peered up at her. "Is that a new robe?"

"Do you like it?"

"Pretty colors."

"Rob! Can't you work on your design in the morning?"

He sighed. "I guess so."

"You're hurting my feelings!"

"Aw, I'm sorry, Doris." He gathered up his work and put the items on the other bedside table. She sat on the edge of the bed and handed him his glass. The whiskey was quickly gone and Rob drew Doris down next to him. He started to kiss her. "Here, let's take this off before it gets all wrinkled."

A few minutes later, the sex was over and they were lying side by side.

Doris sat up and drank the rest of her whiskey. She hadn't even had an orgasm. "You know, Rob, you spend more time touching your slide rule than me."

"Geez, Doris, give me a break! You know the kind of pressure we're under at the lab. We have the rest of our lives to have sex."

"Maybe."

"What maybe? What's gotten into you?"

"Never mind. I know you're tired. I'm not sleepy. I'm going to go have a smoke." She hung up the peignoir in the closet, replacing it with the old housecoat she usually wore. She imagined that Betty was having a steamy night with Will in her black lace shortie. Maybe Doris should ask her for seduction lessons. She lay down on the couch in the unlit living room where Rob could not see her. Stealthily, she caressed a breast with one hand and used the other to draw lazy circles around her most sensitive spot. She called up the old excitement of Lenny Stein's kisses. Then she imagined meeting Dave Sokol at a motel somewhere. She was sure he would spend more than two or three minutes getting her hot and bothered. She would guide his hand and show him exactly where to stroke. Then he would take the initiative and push one and then two fingers inside her . . . *Doris—you're so tight and wet* . . . She held her breath so Rob would not hear her come.

31: February 1945

In mid-February, newspaper headlines trumpeted the destruction of the German city of Dresden in a firestorm triggered by Allied bombs. Doris listened to reports on the radio while she dusted and mopped.

"So much of this war is about killing civilians," she told Rob when he got home. "I don't have any pity for the Nazi soldiers, but destroying a city slaughters women and children. After all, a lot of the men are away fighting. Do you think an atomic bomb would be even worse than what we just did?"

"I don't know, honey. All we can do is try to win the war, because if the Germans get the bomb, they could end up ruling the world, even now when they seem to be on the run."

"How would they get it here? Even the V-2 rockets or their new jet planes can't fly all the way across the Atlantic."

"I don't know. Maybe they could sneak a bomb in on a U-boat. But it's not just us, Doris. What about England and Europe? If Germany took them over, they could take their time attacking the United States. They have a lot of engineering know-how, and Hitler pushes for new weapons."

"But we're winning, aren't we?"

"Yes, but if the Nazis are building a bomb, now is when Hitler would try to use it, when he's cornered."

"How is our project going?"

"A lot depends on Los Alamos now. We don't get much news. We did hear that some joker at Los Alamos asked the operator to page

Dr. Werner Heisenberg. Everyone laughed when the announcement came over the loudspeaker."

"I don't understand."

"Heisenberg is the physicist who may be working on a German atomic bomb."

"Oh. Ha ha, very funny."

"We're still making all the stuff we can to send to New Mexico. Joel's friends don't discuss their work in letters or calls, but he says their moods seem to be on a roller coaster."

Perhaps in response to the tension, their weekend parties got wilder. By now they had the punch recipes perfected and there was no shortage of weak beer. It could give you a buzz if you drank enough. One night they had gathered at Arthur's house. The women were exhausted and wanted to call it a night.

"Have you noticed that Neil and Barney never make a move to go home, even when we hint that the party's over?" Susan complained. "You have to practically shove them out the door."

Neil and Barney were two of the bachelors who worked in X-10. Both were awkward types who never had a date.

"Let's shame them into leaving," Susan continued. "What if we danced topless? It will probably be the first time they saw a bare tit since they drank their mother's milk. I bet they hightail it. Let's go into the bedroom and plan." Three of the wives volunteered to join her. All of them had been drinking for several hours. Doris was only slightly tipsy but followed them into the other room.

"I don't want to see their faces," one of the women said. "And hopefully they won't know exactly which woman is which."

"We could wear masks!" another suggested.

"I don't have any masks in the house," Susan told them.

"You could tie scarves over your mouth and nose, like women in a harem," Doris said.

"But then our eyes would be uncovered."

"I know! We can put lampshades on our heads, like the drunk life-of-the-party men!"

"Great idea!" Susan said. "We can use the three lampshades in here. They're even identical." The women pulled off their tops and bras, throwing them on the bed, and donned the lampshades. "I'll introduce you as the Oak Ridge Odalisques!"

Doris was not brave enough to join the dancers but said she would play something appropriate on the piano. "How about Ravel's *Boléro*? I can just keep going until those little weasels slink away!"

Doris slipped back into the living room and arranged herself on the piano bench. Dave Sokol walked over and asked if she needed a page-turner. "No, but I could use a rhythm section," she told him, gesturing to a bongo drum on a nearby shelf. "Do you know Ravel's *Boléro*?"

"Do I know it?" Dave hummed the first bars, tapping an invisible drum with his palms.

"Okay, you're in!"

Susan came out of the bedroom and turned off all the lights except one floor lamp. "And now, for our *final* act of the evening"—she gave her most meaningful stare to the immovable bachelors—"introducing . . . the Oak Ridge Odalisques!"

Doris began to play, and after the first few bars, Dave joined, keeping a steady rhythm on the bongos. The three dancers, each with arms crossed and hands linked to the next woman, only partially hiding their bouncing breasts, edged out of the bedroom door. They step-touch-stepped to the right several times and then reversed course. Between their limited field of vision and state of inebriation, stumbles almost brought the trio to their knees several times. Some of the men gave wolf whistles or cried "Bravo" and "Encore," but Neil and Barney simply watched in silence, smiling with mild approbation.

Susan leaned over to Doris. "Damn! It isn't working."

Doris kept playing but inquired, “Full striptease?”

“No. Those nebbishes are definitely not worth it. Let’s end this.”

Doris drew the music to a close and the dancers retreated into the bedroom to get dressed.

“How come you didn’t dance, Doris?” asked Dave, bending over so he did not have to raise his voice.

“I’m the accompanist.”

“Too bad. I know you dance very well.”

“I’m always happy to foxtrot with you at the tennis courts,” she said, referring to the site of many Jackson Square dance nights.

“I prefer a setting with a little more privacy.”

Doris caught Rob eyeing them and stood so that Dave had to straighten up.

“Susan is dying for us all to go home now. The chorus line didn’t work, so I’m going to help her shoo everyone out.”

“Okay, I get the message. But think about it.”

On their walk home, Rob and Doris laughed about the dance. “I noticed Dave Sokol hanging around you again.”

“Just because he was the percussion section.”

“I don’t like the way he looks at you.”

“Oh, Rob!” Doris hugged him. “Are you still jealous after three years of marriage?”

“Hey, you’re my girl.” He stopped and kissed her.

“Well, if a duet with Dave gets me some attention, I may try it again.”

“Come on, Doris. You know I’m a walking zombie half the time. Maybe we can go to Gatlinburg again soon.”

“I’d love that. But for now, I’ll just be happy to be in our own bed. I’m glad tomorrow is Sunday so we can sleep in a little—if Barbara lets us.”

32: March 1945

One Saturday, Rob was at the lab as usual. Spring flowers dotted their neighborhood, softening the drab construction. Doris had planted a line of daffodil bulbs next to the house. The construction workers had left occasional trees standing, including a dogwood on their lot. That morning, Doris had taken Barbara to the park. Doris chatted with two other mothers, sitting on the benches while the children played. Barbara would be three in several more months. She never had accidents now and wanted to wear her pink ruffled panties daily. Soon she would outgrow them, so Doris wrote Naomi and asked her to send a couple of larger pairs. Doris noticed that Barbara was developing a Tennessee accent and calling people *y'all*.

Doris got lunch ready when they returned home. Barbara ate half a peanut butter and jelly sandwich and drank a small glass of milk. She was still quite thin, but at least her height was average for her age. Doris put some daffodils in a green glass vase on the kitchen table and gave Barbara crayons and paper so she could draw them.

"You can give your picture to Daddy when he gets home."

"Yes! He can take it to work to make his office pretty!"

Doris knew that it would take more than a child's drawing to brighten up Rob's Spartan corner, but she agreed that was a good idea. "Or maybe you would like to send this one to Grandpa? He likes to draw too."

Barbara frowned. "I only remember him a little."

"Well, he sure remembers you! He misses us a lot."

Samuel was a good correspondent, which was lucky since Sophie and Naomi rarely wrote letters. Doris called the family about once a month, but long-distance phone bills were expensive. They had even less contact with Rob's family. Oak Ridge was Doris's world now. It was hard to recall her hopes for her future. She felt relatively content to be in limbo. At the same time, she was ashamed of herself for accepting the limitations of her life.

"When can we go to Chicago on the choo-choo train?"

"I'm not sure, honey. Soon, I hope. But it costs a lot of money, and Daddy is also very busy. It would be more fun if we all go together." Even though she missed Chicago, Doris was not eager to travel by train again in wartime without Rob. "Is your picture all done?"

"Yes."

"You look kind of sleepy. How about if you get in bed for a nap and I'll read you a story."

Soon after Barbara fell asleep, the phone rang. Doris ran to answer it before it woke her daughter. She was surprised to hear Dave Sokol's voice on the line.

"Hi, Doris. I just saw Rob in the lab. I'm getting off early this afternoon and wondered if you wanted to join me and a couple of my chums for bridge. It's such a nice day, we thought we'd play at one of the tables by the pool."

Oak Ridge had built a huge, spring-fed swimming pool the year before. March was still too cool for swimming, but people gathered around it on nice days.

"That sounds tempting, but Barbara is napping. Even when she wakes up, I couldn't watch her around the pool and concentrate on playing bridge."

"I thought about that. Harrison's secretary, Myra, told me she thinks Barbara is adorable. Harrison just left for a meeting and gave her the afternoon off. She said she's available to babysit. I could bring her over when I pick you up."

Doris pondered for a minute. Myra had indeed babysat for Barbara before, so that was fine. A good bridge game sounded appealing. She worried Rob would be annoyed if she joined Dave and his friends. But it was a very public place, so what harm could it do? She deserved a couple of carefree hours. So what if she found Dave attractive? Dancing together occasionally at parties was their only contact outside of the piano lessons. A tingle of anticipation told Doris that she was making excuses, but she heard herself say, "Sure, I'd love to play bridge."

By the time Dave drove up, Barbara was dressed. She ran to greet Myra and proudly showed off her drawing.

"We'll be back before dinnertime," Dave told them.

As Dave had boasted, he was a sharp bridge partner. The men did not talk much during the game, unlike her friends in the bridge club. After Dave and Doris won three games in succession, the other two said they gave up and were returning to the barracks.

"Come on, Doris. I'll take you home." Dave handed her into his jeep and turned the radio to a local station. Instead of turning onto her street, Dave drove higher along the ridge at the end of the houses.

"Where are you going?" Doris asked.

He pulled off the road near a patch of forest and turned off the engine. "I just wanted to talk for a few minutes. I never get you all to myself. Even at our piano lessons, Barbara is there."

"I need to get home. It's almost five o'clock and we promised Myra."

"I told her it might be as late as seven before we got back."

"But Rob will be home for dinner and I haven't even started cooking."

"From what I saw at the lab, I wouldn't expect Rob before seven or eight, if then. They're getting another batch of isotope ready to send to New Mexico. Anyway, Doris, I've been wanting to tell you—you're wasted on Rob. Your looks, your brains, all your talents . . . You're a class act."

Doris looked away. "Thank you, but you're wrong. Rob is modest, but he's super smart. And he's kind and loving."

"Is he a good lover?"

"That's an awfully personal question! What business is it of yours?"

"If he isn't, I could show you a few things. Listen! It's so quiet here you can hear the birds chirp. Do you know this line? *A few light kisses, a few embraces, a reaching around of arms, / The play of shine and shade on the trees as the supple boughs wag . . .*"

"Walt Whitman from *Leaves of Grass.*"

"See? I thought you would recognize it. Whitman is my favorite poet."

He leaned closer and Doris let him kiss her. He certainly knew what he was doing. Her heart pounded and she was not sure if she was glad or relieved when the gear shaft got in the way of their embrace. Even though she craved the old feeling that the world contained endless possibilities, Dave's unfamiliar taste and body shape triggered a wave of guilt.

"Come on, let's get out and walk a little. I promise I'll get you home in plenty of time." He came around to the passenger door and opened it for Doris. "Look, there's a tree trunk over there that would make a good place to sit."

Doris wondered if he often took women to this convenient spot. He walked next to her without touching. "I want to know more about you, Doris. You intrigue me."

She made a face. "I'm hardly very intriguing."

"How did you get to be such a fine pianist?"

"The same way anyone does—practice, practice, and practice. I was lucky to have a great teacher, though. She's well-known in the Chicago music scene. She also happens to be my cousin. But I have a problem with my hands. You see my thumbs? How short they are?"

He took her hand and examined it but didn't let it go. "I do see."

"I'll never be a concert pianist. It's a physical limitation."

"I bet that disappointed you."

"You bet right."

"Such a perfectionist." He started kissing her again. She was wearing a loose shirt. He unbuttoned it and pulled her breast out of her bra. He bent down and teased her nipple with his tongue as he slipped his hand into the elastic waist of her trousers. "Just relax and let me make you feel good." He lightly stroked her with his thumb, pushing a finger inside her. "See? You're all wet for me."

Her fantasy was coming true.

"Wait a sec. I have a blanket in the trunk." He strode over to the jeep and returned with a blanket.

Doris knew she should have followed him to the car and demanded that he take her home, but the warmth between her legs seemed to spread through her bloodstream, urging her to just take this moment for herself.

Dave spread the blanket on a grassy patch and drew her down beside him. As they continued kissing, he pulled off one leg of her pants and gently pushed her legs apart. He slid so that his head was between her splayed thighs.

"Pink and pretty," he murmured.

Doris blushed. Rob rarely said anything during sex. She gasped as Dave put his mouth right on her clitoris and teased her with small licks and then a stronger suck that had her on the edge. Rob had never . . . She always suspected that Rob did not think nice Jewish boys put their mouths on women's private parts. She gave herself over to pure sensation, until she had an intense climax. She put a hand over her own mouth to stifle her moans just in case anyone might be in earshot.

"Nice." Dave put her hand on his erection over his pants. "How are you at blow jobs?"

Despite Rob's never offering oral sex, Doris did routinely provide it. Now, with her desire quenched, the thought of giving Dave a blow job made Doris want to run down the road, back to the safety of her house. Nevertheless, she unzipped his fly. She didn't like the musky tang of his pubic hair. His erection was thicker but shorter than Rob's. *Stop thinking about Rob*, she admonished herself. She tried her best to seem eager, starting with tentative swipes of her tongue and then drawing the whole head of Dave's penis into her mouth. She bobbed her head up and down, but she felt like a two-bit whore. As she sensed Dave getting close to his climax, she tried to switch to more hand-pumping and take her mouth away, but he pressed down on the top of her head. She felt his semen spurt out and tasted the salty, sour fluid. She choked and he let go. She swallowed, needing to get rid of it, but fearing that spitting it out would be an insult.

"Rob doesn't usually come in your mouth, does he?" Dave asked with a patronizing smile. "I could give you quite an education, Doris."

"No thanks. I need to get home. I don't know why I even got out of the car." She buttoned her shirt and tucked it back in.

"Maybe because you're curious—and bored. And your husband is sweet but not very savvy."

"Stop insulting Rob. I don't like how you pretend to be his friend." Doris started to rise, but Dave pulled her down by the wrist, not hard but insistently.

"Like you pretend to be his faithful little wife?"

"That's enough, Dave. I don't know what came over me today. We didn't even have anything to drink. I feel awful."

He shrugged but wadded up the blanket and followed her back to the jeep. "That didn't even count as real sex. But I think you'd enjoy a good fuck. Consider it, Doris. If you change your mind, I'm available."

She glared at him in silence and he started the ignition.

"You talk a good game. I'm surprised you're such a Goody Two-shoes."

"Do you have a sensitive bone in your body? I bet you just read Walt Whitman to have good seduction quotes."

"You don't know the first thing about me, Doris."

"How could I? You hide behind jokes and flirting."

He kept his eyes on the road, but she saw his hands clench the steering wheel. "Some of us don't have the luxury of feeling at home."

"You think I feel at home in Oak Ridge?"

"You have a family, friends, a house . . . All that in the middle of this war. What do you really have to complain about?"

Doris was silent. He had a point. Underneath the bravado, she sensed that Dave was a lonely man. She wondered what had happened to his family. She hopped out of the jeep as soon as they got to her house. She paid Myra, thanking her for helping out. Dave was waiting in the car to take Myra back downtown. The next thing Doris did was to thoroughly brush her teeth and wash her face. She'd acted like a selfish teenager—not a mother and a wife. She felt like bashing her forehead into the wall. Maybe it would knock some sense into her. She'd take a shower before bedtime.

As Dave had predicted, Rob did not get home until eight thirty. He was so tired that he just wolfed down a sandwich and went to bed. She was relieved that he didn't ask about her day. She lay awake, curled around his familiar shape and inhaling his scent. He would be so hurt if he found out what she had done. Now Dave had her in his power. She could only hope that he kept his mouth shut.

33: April 1945

After a meeting of the bridge club, Betty told Doris that she was pregnant again. Her mother-in-law had suggested that Betty come home to Richmond until the baby was born.

"Are you going to do it?" asked Doris.

"Not unless they force me at gunpoint! I have everything I need here—the new hospital and Will. But I am nervous. I'm being really careful about what I eat and drink. The OB told me to take a gentle walk every day. I'm having some morning sickness this time, though, so I don't feel much like walking."

"I'm glad you're sticking around. I'd miss you if you went home. You can walk up to the park with Barbara and me when we have a nice afternoon. We could bring a picnic blanket and a pillow for you because those wood benches aren't the most comfortable."

"It sounds nice. Maybe once I'm feeling better."

At that moment, the front door opened and Will walked in. Doris had met him in passing a couple of times but had never really had a conversation with him.

"Hello, darlin'." Betty waved from where she reclined on the couch. "You're home early. Do you remember my friend Doris?"

"I sure do. Nice to see you again." Will sat in an armchair. "They let us go early today because the big boss is having dinner with some visitors. How are you feeling, Betty?"

"Just peachy. Doris and I won the bridge game today, as usual."

Will smiled at his wife. "I stick to poker."

"He's a gamblin' ramblin' wreck from Georgia Tech," Betty quoted fondly from the Georgia Fight Song.

"And a hell of an engineer," sang Doris.

Will gave her a surprised smile. "How do you know the lyrics?"

"Engineers sing it, even in Chicago."

"Her husband is an electrical engineer."

"Well, he doesn't have his degree yet, but he does that kind of work."

"Is he at X-10?"

"Yes. DuPont works a lot with his group."

"Oh, is he one of Hartnell's bunch?"

"Yes."

"That Hartnell, he's an arrogant SOB."

"He's been very kind to Rob and me. And his men love him," Doris protested.

"He doesn't like having DuPont run things." Will frowned. "We need one of his chemists at another big production plant. We made the fellow a fine offer but he said he'd rather die than work for DuPont. Hartnell didn't even scold him."

Doris had heard this story. Their friend Arthur had been offered a job at the Hanford plant that was making large quantities of plutonium. Although Arthur was Episcopalian, he refused to work for DuPont in solidarity because everyone knew they didn't hire Jews. However, she stayed silent.

"Betty's told me quite a bit about you. Thank you for being a good friend to her these past months."

"It's been my pleasure."

He paused. "Betty told me that you're Jewish."

"Yes, we've had fun comparing notes on our families."

"I hope you know that the DuPont Company is not anti-Semitic. That's just a false rumor."

"Really? I don't hear much about all that. But then, until I met

Betty, I didn't even know there was an organization called the Daughters of the Confederacy." She gave Will her sweetest smile.

"Oh yes. That's just my mother's generation."

"Plenty of women my age in Richmond belong too," Betty contradicted him. "But I only joined to please your mama."

"I know, sweetheart. But, Doris, I'm glad Betty has a friend like you."

"And my husband is delighted that Betty has improved my cooking skills."

"Well, it didn't take much, given where you started!" Betty retorted. "And Doris tells me stories from the Old Testament. Sometimes it's just like Bible study around here, though there's a lot of steamy stuff they didn't mention in Richmond—extra wives and concubines and adultery and all."

Doris thought about their trip to Knoxville, not to mention her slip with Dave. She could feel her cheeks starting to turn red. "I should be getting home so the two of you can enjoy your extra time together!" She went to the bedroom door and the babysitter helped her put on Barbara's coat.

Doris heard the news of FDR's sudden death on the radio. The announcer said that Truman would be sworn in as the new president that same day. She called Rob at the lab to let him know. Radios were not allowed in X-10 because security worried that they could be used to conceal listening devices. However, Doris had not been the first wife in the group to notify the men.

"People are worried about whether Truman will stay committed to the project," Rob said in a low voice. "He's kind of an unknown. Everyone feels so sad about Roosevelt. It's hard to focus on work."

"I know. I think he'll go down in history as one of our greatest presidents—up there with Washington and Lincoln."

"Well, the Republicans would disagree with you! You know there was a rumor that FDR was coming to visit Oak Ridge. They've been building ramps. We thought they might be for his wheelchair."

"Too late now. But after we've come so far, I can't imagine Truman would slack off on the project."

"I guess we'll just keep working. Fingers crossed. I'd better go. See you tonight."

The next day at bridge club, the mood was somber. Betty did not mention her pregnancy but Doris noticed she had hired an extra young woman, Jody, to do all the chores—serving snacks and drinks, clearing dishes—while Clementine kept an eye on the children. After the other women left, Doris carried some plates into the kitchen where Jody was washing up. Betty followed her with some dirty glasses.

"I thought you were taking it easy," Doris said.

"I'm fine. I can't lie on the couch for seven more months. If I do, I'll be the size of an elephant! To think that in college I was known for my tiny waist."

"Don't talk to me about waistlines," Doris moaned. "Especially not after that chocolate cake. But the important thing is having a healthy baby. Anyway, it feels obscene for us to be worrying about weight. At the movies we saw a newsreel called *Nazi Murder Mills* that showed the liberation of concentration camps. I can't stop picturing it. Piles and piles of decaying bodies, so thin you could see they'd starved to death. And those were the ones they didn't incinerate in the ovens. Our soldiers forced the people who lived nearby to come and see the carnage, but they were just standing there, scowling and covering their noses. Though they made some of the local men put the bodies in mass graves."

Betty put her hand over her mouth. "I'm so sorry, Doris. I don't know if I could watch a film like that."

"Me either," Jody chimed in.

"I think every American should watch it. The Nazis rounded up the Jews into ghettos. Then they packed them into trains like sardines. When they got to the camps, the Nazis set up two lines, using whips and vicious police dogs. One was for people healthy enough to be slave labor. The others—children and older people—were told they were going to shower rooms. They filed in, naked, and were gassed to death. Most of the people who didn't die on the first day were starved or beaten to death or just executed. And our government knew for a couple of years and did nothing."

"That's terrible. I will pray for the Jewish people, Doris."

"Not just that we'll all convert, I hope."

"Of course not." Betty hugged her. "What a tragedy."

"We had cousins who wrote us, begging for help. I'm sure they're all dead now. When I think that if my family had stayed in Europe, it could have been me and Rob on those trains . . . and Barbara. Imagine all those mothers, Betty, helplessly watching their children die."

"No, stop, Doris! I just can't think about that right now."

"I know you're worried about your baby. But still, I can't stop thinking about what it would be like. I'm sorry."

The women said goodbye and Doris took Barbara home.

34: April–May 1945

Instead of looking forward to Dave's piano lessons, Doris now dreaded them. They were stiff and awkward with each other. She retreated into a formal mode, focusing on musical technique and avoiding conversation. During the second lesson after their encounter, Dave stopped mid-piece, pressing both hands on the keys to create a discordant crash.

Barbara looked up with wide eyes from the corner where she was playing. "That was a bad boo-boo, Mr. Soldier."

"You're right, kiddo. Doris, I think this should be our last lesson."

"I agree. I think I've taught you all I can." *He's not the only one who made a bad boo-boo*, she reflected.

"And I guess *I've* taught *you* all I can."

"I'm sorry, Dave. It was a mistake. I hope I didn't hurt your feelings."

"Nah. Maybe dinged my pride a little, that's all. It's your loss, in the end."

Doris took a breath. *Keep it civil and get him out of the house.* "I won't charge you for the lesson today."

"If that makes you feel better. I'll see you around. I'm going to New York next week for a little R and R anyway."

"I hope you have a great trip."

Doris did not mention to Rob that Dave's piano lessons had ended. True to his word, Dave was not around often at social events. She began to think that she had dodged a bullet but still had periods of dread that Rob would find out. The thought of Dave's caresses no longer played any role in her sexual fantasies.

By May, Oak Ridge was buzzing about the news of Hitler's suicide and Germany's surrender. The pressures on the project did not ease, however. The administration was pushing everyone to work harder to finish the job—whatever the job was. New billboards had gone up: WHOSE SON WILL DIE IN THE LAST MINUTES OF THE WAR? one asked above a picture of a wounded soldier and his deceased comrades. Another showed maps with a white flag over Berlin and the Rising Sun flag over Tokyo with the message: ONE TO GO NOW—GIVE IT ALL WE'VE GOT! STAY ON THE JOB. FINISH THE JOB. A third showed a helmeted GI peeking out of jungle foliage with a sign: WILL SWAP FOXHOLE HOME WITH OUTSIDE EXPOSURE. NEIGHBORS SOMETIMES NOISY. Even shirts from the Oak Ridge laundry were handed back with a paper band that said, BEAT THE JAPS! Everyone joked that the navy had better be more efficient than the laundry, which often sent back the wrong shirts or familiar ones with new stains and missing buttons.

"The senior guys at the lab are starting to talk about how the bomb should be used," Rob told Doris. "Everyone thinks it will be finished soon. People at X-10 and some leaders from the other plants are proposing a new organization called the Association of Oak Ridge Scientists. I was there for the first meeting."

"What if General Groves or Colonel Nichols gets wind of that?"

"What can they do to us? They can't draft all the scientists on the project and send us to Alaska!"

"It could be a black mark on your record."

"I'm just a small fry, Doris. Nobody notices what I do."

"Security notices everything. Think about it, Rob. For our future. We don't even know yet if an atomic bomb would be that different than what we already did to Dresden and Tokyo."

"Doris, believe me, one atomic bomb is probably going to equal hundreds of the bombs we already have. It's not only bigger. It will release radiation to kill people."

"If it ends the war, it would be worth it. That's why the project exists."

"I felt the same way when it meant defeating the Nazis, but now we have to think. Harrison predicts the Russians will have their own bomb in four or five years. That really worries me. Stalin would be happy to take over the world. A lot of the guys think atomic weapons and energy should belong to a world government, like the United Nations. Maybe that would stop the Russians from trying to make their own bombs."

"That sounds awfully optimistic. Look at the League of Nations. It didn't prevent this war. When the Nazis wanted to break its rules, they just withdrew."

"I don't know yet what's right, but if I think the government is making a mistake, I'm going to speak up."

Doris sighed as she finished washing up the dinner dishes. "It does sound like the right thing to do. I'm just scared you could get blackballed, somehow."

Although there were no crowds in the Oak Ridge streets to celebrate German surrender, a festive dance was held on the tennis courts that weekend. Doris and Rob met Joel and Annette there. The friends guzzled near-beer, Cokes, or lemonade to quench their thirst after dancing in the humid evening air. After a couple of jitterbugs, the disc jockey put on the slower Russian tune "Dark Eyes." Dave Sokol came up and asked if Doris would dance with him. She would rather have declined, but she did not want to annoy him and maybe draw attention to their interactions. She looked over at Rob. He frowned a little, but when she pointed at Dave and raised her eyebrows in inquiry, he waved his assent.

"Eyes that haunt me so, eyes that taunt me so, while they smiled

at me life was ecstasy. Was our whirling dance just a gay romance? Or for me perchance, just a broken dream," a tenor crooned, varying the tempo between languid and gypsy fast. Dave hummed along as he guided Doris in a waltz step, holding her a little closer than was comfortable.

"It's called 'Ochi Chyornye' in Russian," he said, "and that's a terrible translation. It's really more like 'Black and burning eyes, full of passion. I love you and I fear you . . .'" He softly sang along for a few bars in what sounded like fluent Russian.

"You speak Russian?" asked Doris.

He started, as if he had been carried away by the song. "Oh, just a little. I told you—my parents were from Russia."

"I thought you grew up in Kansas."

"I did."

"My grandparents came over from the shtetls, too, but they spoke Yiddish. My mother's father actually knew seven languages . . . but he refused to speak Russian because he hated the tsar."

She felt him shrug. "All Jews hated the tsar. Anyway, I wanted to let you know I'm being transferred in a couple of weeks."

Doris felt a wave of relief. "Oh, really?"

"Yup." The song ended. "Can I have a cigarette?"

"Sure."

"Let's get a little further from the dance floor where it's cooler."

She looked back at Rob, who was watching. She mimed having a smoke. Dave walked her to a bench in a dimly lit corner.

"Have you thought much about our little interlude after the bridge game?"

"Not really," Doris lied. She thought about it daily, imagining how Rob would feel if he found out. "As I said, it was a mistake."

"Your hubby keeps a pretty close watch on you."

"He trusts me. He knows I love him."

Dave raised a skeptical eyebrow and snorted.

"I do! I think maybe he doesn't trust you."

"With good reason. I'd still like to be alone with you."

"Keep your voice down, Dave. Someone might hear you."

"Indeed. Isn't that your friend Annette just over there?" He indicated with his chin, and she saw Annette staring at them. Doris puffed on her cigarette defiantly and gave Annette a jaunty wave.

"So it is. Annette is a nosy parker."

"I bet she'd love to tell Rob she caught us necking."

"Well, there's nothing to see."

"I could give her something to see."

Doris moved farther away. "You wouldn't dare."

"Not if you do me a little favor."

Doris glanced over and saw that Annette was still watching them. Her heart sank.

"What kind of favor?"

"Do you know where Rob keeps the keys to his file cabinet when he's home at night?"

"Why are you asking?"

"How about borrowing them for me? We both know he's exhausted by bedtime. You could just sneak the keys to me once he's asleep. I'd park my jeep on the next street over and meet you behind your house. I'll copy what I need at the lab and return the keys in a couple of hours. He'll never know."

"Why would you want Rob's files?"

"I told you, I love instruments. It would be very helpful to bring those diagrams with me to the new project site."

"Then ask Rob and Harrison for the designs."

"I don't think they'd let me have them. Professional competition between project sites."

"That doesn't make sense. All the sites share the same goal."

"You're being naive, Doris. Even in a war, men want some glory for themselves."

"I wish Rob wanted a little glory. He just wants knowledge and to be a team player. But now I think I understand why you kept flirting with me . . . You're right. I was naive. No, Dave. I will not give you Rob's keys."

"Hmm. I wonder what Rob would do if he knew about us. I think we're going to give Annette a show." He reached for Doris, but she stood up too quickly.

"If you come any closer, I'll stub out my cigarette on your wrist," she murmured with a fake smile.

"I could just go over there and tell him."

"Go ahead. I'll deal with it."

Dave put up his hands in mock surrender. "You're a nasty little cocktease."

"And you are one sick son of a bitch. Excuse me, I'm starting to feel nauseated, especially when I think of what we did." She stalked away, trying to keep her face bland.

Annette joined her. "What did Sokol want?"

"We were just smoking, away from all the noise. He says he's leaving Oak Ridge soon."

"That will make Rob happy. You hang around with him too much. People are noticing."

"Annette, you're a dear friend, but sometimes I wish you'd mind your own business. I'm a grown woman. I don't need a chaperone."

After they got home, Doris kept replaying the conversation with Dave in her mind. Should she tell Rob that Dave wanted his keys? Could Dave be spying for the Soviets? Even though he spoke Russian, it seemed far-fetched. After all, he had a security clearance. Who was Doris to report an SED man? And if she did, Dave was clearly ready to tell Rob about the sex. It seemed they were at a stalemate. Was there a danger that Dave could get into Rob's files even without her help? She knew Rob was scrupulous about keeping his file cabinet locked. Unless Dave was a safecracker like Dick Feynman, it was unlikely he'd get access. And if he had those skills, he wouldn't be bothering with Doris. She decided to keep quiet but didn't sleep much that night. She hoped his transfer happened soon.

35: June 1945

At the next bridge club meeting, Betty's pregnancy was starting to show. The other women knew about her previous miscarriage and tried to be especially supportive, pitching in to set up the card tables and refreshments, as well as cleaning up after the games. Rochelle mentioned that she, too, was pregnant again.

"My kids will be almost four years apart—close enough to play together but not so close that they'll be fighting all the time."

"I hope someday I'm in your shoes," Betty said. "Right now, I'm just happy when I feel queasy, because I know the baby is still there."

"Well, you have that pregnancy bloom," one of the women told her.

"At least the weather will be cooler for both of you by your due dates," said Doris. "Barbara was born right in the middle of July and our apartment was stifling!" She went over and gave Rochelle a hug. "Mazel tov!"

"What did you just say?" asked Betty.

"I said 'mazel tov.' It means 'good luck' in Hebrew, and we kind of use it like *congratulations*."

"What else can you say in Hebrew?"

"Not much. *Shalom?* It means 'hello' or 'peace.' Do you know more Hebrew, Rochelle?"

"Mostly just prayers that we sing in the synagogue."

"That's like church Latin for me," a neighbor said. "I can mumble some words, but I only have a vague idea of what they mean."

“Well, I’m crossing my fingers for healthy babies!” Betty crossed both forefingers and her eyes for good measure.

“Betty, you say you’re a good Christian woman but I think you’re a heathen at heart!” Doris said, and everyone laughed.

After the other women said their goodbyes, taking their children and leftover cake back to their homes, Doris asked, “How are you really feeling, Betty?”

“I’m nervous, of course, but I try to keep my mind off it. I listen to the radio and I’m knitting a baby blanket.” She showed Doris a mint-green-and-white afghan, about eight inches long so far, made of fine wool.

“That’s lovely! I’ve never learned to knit.”

“I could teach you some time if you like.”

“By the end of this war, you’re going to turn me into a balabosta!”

“A what?”

“Balabosta is a Yiddish word that means a superb housewife. Something I’m obviously not!”

“I thought you said you didn’t know any Hebrew.”

“Hebrew is the ancient language of the Jews in Israel. The Jews in Palestine are trying to revive it. Yiddish is mostly German, with Polish and Hebrew words mixed in. My parents grew up speaking Yiddish, and my grandmother still hardly speaks any English. She wanted to talk with her grandchildren, so when she would see my father coming down the street she’d tell us, ‘Is caming der Pa!’”

“Mine usually says things like, ‘Stand up straight, girl’ or ‘Where are your white gloves?’ I try to keep out of her way.”

Even though Betty seemed so confident, Doris sensed that she struggled to meet everyone’s expectations. Maybe it was that insecurity that drew them to each other, even though their backgrounds were so different on the surface.

“Betty, is being a wife and mother the thing you always wanted the most?”

Betty leaned back on the couch and thought. “Well, basically. But in college I did have a dream of becoming an interior decorator.”

“I bet you’d be great at that. You’ve got very good taste.”

“Well, thank you, Doris! But I don’t think my parents or in-laws would like it if I went out and worked to earn money. They all think the man should wear the pants in the family.”

“But what do you think?”

“I think it would be fun to design beautiful rooms. But first I’ll get my own house all furnished—I mean the real one in Richmond. Later on I should have plenty of time to branch out a little.”

“It’s nice to hear you have your own interests. You say I underestimate myself, but I think you also should aim a little higher, Betty.”

“Ooh, I should watch out, Doris, or you’ll turn me into a Yankee gal.”

“Is Will taking good care of you?”

“When he’s home. Things are busy lately.”

“I know. I’d better take Barbara home and give you a rest.”

When Doris brought her daughter out of the bedroom, Barbara asked, “Mrs. Hunt, can I touch your tummy?”

Betty laughed. “Sure, go ahead, sugar.”

Barbara patted Betty’s stomach. “I don’t feel a baby. Benjamin said he’s going to have a baby brother or sister. He said they kick sometimes, while they’re growing. What about us, Mommy? Are we going to have a baby?”

“Would you like that?” Betty asked.

“Um, I don’t think so. Babies cry and have stinky diapers.”

“That’s good, Barbara, because for now, you’re the only kid I need,” Doris told her.

36: June 1945

Rochelle and Sol invited the Friedmans to dinner on a Sunday night. Annette and Joel were there too. Doris started when Dave Sokol walked in. She hoped this would be the last time she would have to tolerate his company. He had brought a date, a bubbly nurse who worked on the hospital's maternity ward.

"Are there lots of babies being born?" Doris asked her. "It seems like I know a lot of pregnant women right now."

"The numbers are certainly going up. We think we'll see a big jump nine months after VE Day."

"I've heard that General Groves is unhappy with the high birth rate at Los Alamos," Joel told them. "Someone wrote a really bad limerick about it: *The General's in a stew / He trusted you and you / He thought you'd be scientific / Instead, you're just prolific / And what is he to do?*"

"Well, there's not much to do in Los Alamos, besides making babies," Dave commented.

"Is that where you're going?" asked Sol. "Or do you prefer not to say?"

"No, the army is sending me to Dayton, Ohio. I leave next week."

Sol nodded knowingly, but Doris had no idea why Dave would be stationed in Ohio. She was just relieved to hear that he would soon be gone. She sat close to Rob during dinner.

After dessert, Rochelle put on some dance music. They pushed the living room furniture against the edges of the room and the couples took turns partnering each other. They kept to slower songs since there wasn't room for more vigorous steps.

When it was Doris's turn to dance with Dave, he asked her quietly under the cover of the music if she had said anything to Rob about his attempt to borrow the keys.

"No, I haven't. Against my better judgment."

"Well, let's make a deal. You keep quiet and I'll keep quiet."

Doris shrugged. "I just want to forget the whole thing."

"I know you think I was just using you."

"Weren't you?"

"That's not all it was. I do think you're special. We had fun, didn't we? A guy has needs, after all."

"You seem to have a steady supply of women to meet your needs."

"But not like you, Doris."

She sighed, and he smiled, steering them into a turn. Being in his arms still made her pulse race, in spite of everything. "Have you ever been serious about a girl?" she asked.

He looked away and just missed stepping on her toe. "Yeah, but I don't want to talk about it."

"Did she leave you for someone else?"

"No. But we can't be together right now."

"Because of the war?"

"Because of things you couldn't begin to imagine."

Doris could feel the tension in Dave's body. "Well, maybe you'll be happier in Ohio. I hope so."

The song ended and she went back to join Rob in the kitchen.

Later that night, she snuggled up to Rob in bed and reached around to stroke him. She felt him start to get an erection.

"Hey, someone's frisky tonight."

"Why not? Aren't you in the mood?"

"Sure I am." He turned and eyed her suspiciously. "You're not trying to get pregnant again, are you?"

"No! I think we should wait until the war is over. Even better, I hope we can wait until we can afford to buy a house. We have plenty of time to have another baby. In fact, I'd like to finish college first."

"That again?"

"Rob! When you asked me to marry you, we agreed I would get my degree."

"That was before we had Barbara."

"I have every intention of taking good care of Barbara. Just like I already do. And what about the promise you made when I agreed to move down here?"

"Of course I'll try to help you finish. But why is it so important? Neither of our mothers worked, although mine helps out in the store sometimes. I should be able to make a decent living and take care of things once we get home."

"I want a better life than either of us had growing up. And how often have I told you that I want to work outside of our home?"

"I know. But let's not make a ten-year plan tonight, okay? I thought you were hot to trot."

"I am! I have to take advantage of every night that you're not buried in an engineering journal or snoring like Rip Van Winkle."

"I'm sorry. I know I'm not much fun lately."

"I love you anyway, Rob."

"Love you, too, of course."

Sex was more enjoyable for Doris than it had been for a while. While Rob was touching her, she remembered how sweetly he had introduced her to lovemaking, just four years ago. Rob also surprised her by kissing his way down from her breasts to between her legs and actually giving a few tentative licks where it counted. She moaned her appreciation to encourage him and reciprocated.

Her pleasure was tainted, however, by the worry that Rob would find out about her episode with Dave. After they finished and Rob was indeed snoring lightly beside her, Doris debated again what to do. If she kept quiet, her marriage would have a chance to recover.

But she doubted she would ever be able to forgive herself. And one of the things she valued most with Rob was their trust in each other. She could feel the guilt distancing her from him. But if she came clean about what happened, she wasn't sure Rob would still love her. Maybe that was what she deserved. She imagined going back to Chicago with Barbara and getting a divorce. Rob would have no trouble finding someone new, but Doris couldn't see herself remarrying. She knew she could manage on her own, but it would be grim and lonely.

Beyond her own concerns, there was the threat to the project. Dave's willingness to drop his effort at blackmail just added to Doris's suspicions. She knew him well enough to sense that he was on edge. All the little hints pointed to his spying for the Russians. She didn't think some utopian world government would ever convince Stalin and his crew to give up their ambitions for a communist empire. What if they used their own atomic bomb to force the world to go along? Even if it felt ridiculous that she, Doris Friedman, could influence the war, she knew it was her patriotic duty to inform someone. She just couldn't bear to tell Rob. She wasn't even sure what he would do with the knowledge. Who would really listen to her and give her wise advice? Harrison was the obvious choice. She decided to talk privately with him as soon as possible, before Dave left town.

37: June 1945

The next morning was one of the play group days. Before dropping Barbara off, Doris called Myra and requested to see Harrison.

"I can't explain on the phone," she said, "but I really need to talk to him as discreetly as possible. It's about security at the lab."

Luckily, Harrison was in town and agreed to see her at eleven in his office. Myra said she would meet Doris at the building entrance and take her to Harrison by the most private route to avoid being seen by people at work.

When they arrived at Harrison's office, he stood up to shake Doris's hand. "Myra said your call sounded serious. You're worried about security?"

"Yes. I've made a horrible mistake. But I'm ready to take the consequences if you think it's best. It's about Dave Sokol. I think he may be a Soviet spy."

Harrison frowned. "He has been fascinated by our instruments and what we're producing in the lab, but I figured he's an engineer—and of course he has a top-secret clearance."

"He asked me to let him secretly borrow the keys to Rob's filing cabinet so he could copy things."

"That does sound suspicious. I think you'd better tell me the whole story."

Doris told him about Dave's flattery, the piano lessons, and his probing questions about Rob's work, including overhearing him asking Rob to view his circuit diagrams. She mentioned his unconvincing declarations that he was a Republican, and his slip in revealing that he spoke Russian.

"Rob and I have been bickering lately," she confessed, "and Dave invited me to play bridge by the pool. It seemed innocent, but on the way home he stopped in a wooded area." She looked down at her lap. "I'm afraid we had quite a make-out session. I'm so ashamed." She looked back up at Harrison, but he just shook his head with a rueful smile.

"These things happen, Doris. My first wife . . . well, let's not talk about that."

"I intend this to be my first and last . . . betrayal. And I think Dave lured me into a compromising situation mainly to blackmail me into giving him the keys."

"But you didn't."

"No, I refused. Then he offered to keep quiet if I also said nothing. It was tempting, especially since he's leaving next week for another project site. But I thought—maybe he could learn more secrets there."

"Where's he going—do you know?"

"He said Dayton, Ohio."

Harrison recoiled. "I can't tell you anything more, Doris, but you made the right call. I'm going to have security detain him."

"Will they want to talk to me?"

"Definitely."

"Then I have to tell Rob, before he hears it from them."

"I'm afraid you do, Doris. Rob's a fine young man."

"He is, but he's also insecure. He was already a little jealous of Dave. Now he's going to be so hurt. It's my fault."

"I hope he gives you the benefit of the doubt, Doris. After all, you could have just kept your mouth shut."

In more ways than one, she mused. "Rob said you believe in the United Nations. Do you think it would be so bad if Russia got a bomb too?"

"Stalin is greedy for power. He's more dictator than socialist. And I work for our government. I have to protect the project, whatever my personal beliefs. I saw Dave in the reactor building a few minutes ago. I need to call the guards and have him picked up. I'll have Myra find a private place for you to talk to Rob. I really need your husband to focus on work right now, but I suppose it can't be helped."

A few minutes later, Doris found herself alone with Rob in a small, windowless office furnished only with a metal desk and swivel chair. She shut the door after he entered.

"Doris, what's wrong? Is someone in the family sick?"

"No, but I have something awful to tell you. I just told Harrison that I think Dave Sokol is a Soviet spy."

Rob sank heavily onto the desk chair. "I can't say I'm totally surprised."

"But there's more. He's been flirting with me for months . . ."

"That's no surprise either."

"And a couple of months ago I ended up alone with him. That day I played bridge by the pool last spring? And we—"

"You had sex with him."

"Not actual intercourse, but . . . pretty bad."

"Annette said you were having an affair, but I didn't believe her. Not my Doris." He wheeled the chair around so she could see only his back.

"Rob, I swear, it was the only time. I felt so awful afterwards. And then he asked me to steal your file cabinet keys and hand them over so he could copy your work at night and return them before you realized."

Rob swiveled back. His eyes were as dull and dark as the coals in their furnace bin. "And did you?"

"No! I told him no. I was hoping the whole thing would go away, but I realized the project was too important, so I told Harrison today."

"Where's Barbara?"

"She's at the play group this morning."

"Go home, Doris. I have work to do. I'll deal with you later."

She took a few steps toward the door and looked back at Rob. "I can take Barbara to Chicago if you want me to leave."

"That's probably what you wanted all along." His tone was even, but Doris could hear that he was suppressing tears.

"No. There's no excuse for what I did. I'm so sorry, Rob. I do love you. Whether you believe me or not."

He glared at her. "Go home. We'll talk later."

Doris walked out of the office, trying to look nonchalant. She was happy that none of their friends had spotted her. She heard a scuffle at the end of the corridor and realized that it was Dave, being dragged toward her between two MPs who held his upper arms.

"You!" he gasped as they approached. His hands were cuffed behind his back.

"Out of the way, ma'am," said one of the guards. "This doesn't concern you."

"Oh, yes, it does," Dave snarled. "She's the bitch who turned me in. What do you think will happen to my family now, Doris?"

Doris shrank back. "You said they were all dead."

"I said a lot of things. Don't you know what's at stake?"

She looked him in the eye. "I do. That's why I told Harrison."

"Well, have a happy little life, Doris. Think of me when you play Tchaikovsky."

The MPs pulled him farther down the hall.

Doris turned and walked blindly the other way. She ducked into a ladies' room that luckily was empty. She washed her face, swiped some powder on her nose, and took a deep breath. Then she marched herself out of the lobby, past the guard at the door.

38: June 1945

Rob did not come home that night until nine. Barbara was asleep in her room and Doris was slumped on the sofa. Rob threw his sweater on a dining room chair and faced her.

"Well?" He stared down at her and she did not look away. "Aren't you going to apologize?"

"I thought I already had. I'm very, very sorry. For what I did and for hurting you." She could feel the tears starting.

"You really gutted me. After being the runt of the litter all my life, I thought finally somebody really wanted me."

"I do want you."

"Me? Or the Doris-Cain-Good-Housekeeping-Seal-of-Approval version?"

"You. As you are. The you I loved from the start . . . We just married so young. And the war and Barbara always came first. I haven't exactly felt wanted, either, you know. I don't even recognize myself anymore."

"Is that your excuse for acting like a slut?" He took several steps toward her, hands fisted.

She sat up. "Rob, if you raise a hand to me, I swear I'll take Barbara and leave and never look back."

At that moment, Barbara stumbled into the living room, rubbing her eyes. "I had a bad dream. Daddy!" She ran to Rob and grabbed him around the knees.

"Not now, Barbara," he growled, and pushed her away.

She lost her balance and fell, hitting her head against the coffee table with a thunk. She began to wail.

Doris snatched her up. "Get out, you bastard! I don't care where you go. Just take your damn slide rule and get out of this house."

"Oh my God! I'm sorry—is she okay?"

"What do you care." Doris took Barbara into the kitchen and put ice cubes in a dish towel, applying it to the bruise on her daughter's head. By the time she'd calmed Barbara down, Rob was gone. She tucked Barbara into bed and sang a lullaby until she fell asleep. Then she sat in the dark living room. She could feel the house shaking. She saw cracks running across the ceiling and Cemesto walls crumbling to join the dust and gravel of Oak Ridge, the Clinch River running backward, fissures opening in the earth. She had an urge to grab Barbara, but in the end went out to the porch alone, checking for copperheads before she sat on the top step and had a smoke.

In the morning, as she was making pancakes for Barbara, Rob knocked on the door. Joel was with him. She was relieved to see that at least Annette had not accompanied them.

"Can I come in?" Rob asked. His eyes were red.

"Do as you please. It's your house."

Joel and Rob came inside.

Joel took a deep breath. "Rob told me what happened."

"Are you here to call me a slut, too, or to lord it over me like your busybody wife?"

"No, Doris. Annette thinks you and Rob quarreled because she told him about you and Dave. She doesn't know you reported Sokol or that he's a spy. I promised Rob I'd keep that secret. Annette is miserable. She couldn't bring herself to face you and apologize."

"Really, Joel? Do you actually believe that?"

He gave her a helpless look.

"Well, don't worry. Annette didn't need to tattle. I told on myself. And Barbara and I are out of here as soon as I can get a train ticket."

"You can't leave, Doris," said Rob. "Security is going to want to interview you. Harrison asked to meet here with both of us in a few days. And . . . I'm begging you to stay." His voice broke. "I didn't mean what I said and I never meant to hurt Barbara."

"Don't go, Doris," Joel added. "You let that son of a bitch get to you, but you did the right thing. You could have kept it all a secret and nobody would have known."

"And a lot of it was my fault," Rob added. "If I had taken better care of you . . . listened to you . . . paid attention . . ." His voice was shaking.

"I'll stay until the Sokol mess is cleaned up, but I'm not making any more promises than that."

Rob picked Barbara up and kissed her forehead. "I'm so sorry, Barbara. I didn't mean to push you. At least that black-and-blue mark doesn't look too bad."

She turned her face away. "You made me hurt my head. And you called Mommy a bad word."

"He did," Doris affirmed, "but I did something wrong that made Daddy very mad. It's over now. The grown-ups will deal with it. Daddy and I both love you very much."

Rob and Joel left for the lab. Doris got through the next few days somehow, filling the time with chores and cooking. Each piano lesson was a welcome distraction. She caught up on the investment advice columns and added a few shares to the ones she had already purchased. She might need that money to live on if she and Rob broke up.

On the night of their meeting with Harrison, she had fed Barbara and sung her to sleep by the time the men arrived. Doris offered them something to drink. Harrison and Rob each took a glass of near-beer and they sat down.

"I wanted to give the two of you a private update," Harrison said. "Doris, you were right. When the FBI checked on Sokol's history, they discovered with very little effort that he'd had communist sympathies since he was a teenager. He was even arrested once at a labor protest. I don't know how in hell they missed all that when he got his clearance."

"Did he really grow up in Kansas?" asked Doris.

"He did, but his whole family got disillusioned by discrimination there against Jews. After Dave finished college, he moved all the way back to Russia with his parents and brother. He lied on his forms about those years. He told the FBI agent that they lived in miserable conditions. His father had fallen for Russian propaganda about a province set aside to be a new home for the Jews. But it was really a freezing wasteland near Mongolia. His family is still stuck there, but Dave used his education to try to escape. Just before America entered the war, he was smuggled into the States."

"Wouldn't his passport have been a tip-off?" Rob wondered.

"He and the Russians managed it so there were no obvious records of his leaving or his return. He had just the right training for the SED too. But the FBI thinks the assignment to Oak Ridge was a lucky break. As a radiation safety officer, he had access to every building. We think he gave information to his handlers when he took a trip to New York recently. If you hadn't reported him, he would have undoubtedly done even more damage at his next posting. Oh—and by the way—he's married. His wife is in Russia too."

"Do you think he did it for money?" asked Rob.

"I doubt it," Harrison answered. "He strikes me more as a true believer."

Doris remembered Dave spouting Marx. He hadn't been joking. And now his comments about his family and the woman he loved made sense.

"I wonder if the authorities were threatening to harm his family if he didn't become a spy. Is he in jail?" Doris asked.

"To protect the project, the army has been sending suspected spies to remote military bases where they can be isolated—so he's probably traveling to a barracks in Alaska as we speak. Since everyone around here knew he was leaving for another assignment, his absence won't even be remarked. So please keep this to yourselves."

"Will security come after me or Rob?"

"Don't worry, Doris. You're a hero in this story, not a villain. But I imagine you'd rather remain an unsung hero."

"Definitely."

"And nobody is sending your husband to Alaska."

Doris realized that Harrison also knew about Rob's attempted enlistment.

"Rob, I need you more than ever until this project gets finished. And I hope the two of you can patch things up. I've always thought you made a great couple."

39: July 1945

Doris gave up the idea of leaving Oak Ridge, but she and Rob were still walking on eggshells with each other. They only talked about day-to-day issues and slept on opposite sides of their bed. On a Monday night in July, he came home from the lab with a bounce in his step for the first time in a while.

"I heard some news today, but as usual, you can't tell anyone. You swear?"

"Don't I always? What is it?"

"Last week they tested the bomb near Los Alamos, and it was a big success. Most people in Oak Ridge don't know. At X-10, guys are just muttering in corners, but one of the SED men told me that their group has a betting pool on when they drop it on Japan."

"Let's listen to the war news at ten o'clock."

They sat on the couch and turned on the radio. A reporter was interviewing a naval spokesman.

"The United States Navy is blockading all Japanese harbors. Most of their cities are in ruins from our bombing. They're rationing food and it's rumored that people are starving to death all over the nation," the spokesman summarized.

"Do you think surrender is imminent?" asked the reporter.

"You would think so, but their generals are fanatics. They've been training civilians to fight to the death with hand grenades and even bamboo spears. Kamikaze pilots are sinking our ships. And you know what happens when the Japs lose battles. Most of the soldiers commit suicide rather than get taken prisoner. If we have to invade, who knows how many will die on both sides. Some estimates are as high as a million."

"That doesn't sound promising," replied the reporter. "And let me remind our listeners that, at the moment, President Truman is attending the Potsdam Conference, along with Stalin and Churchill. The world is awaiting their decisions."

Doris shivered and clicked the radio off. "How bad do you think one bomb would be?"

"The word is that the explosion was equal to twenty thousand tons of TNT. All the bombs put together that caused the Tokyo firestorm were less than two thousand tons."

"So one atomic bomb might be ten times worse than that?"

"Yup. And nobody knows how much radiation will be released or how long it will linger. Sol said he feels sick imagining it."

"It is horrifying."

"A bunch of people from Chicago Met Lab have signed a petition to Truman. It says that America has a moral responsibility in introducing such a dangerous weapon. It asks the government to demonstrate the bomb to the world to preserve peace in the future. No bomb should be dropped on Japan before showing them exactly what will happen and giving them a chance to surrender. We discussed it and passed our own version around our group today."

"But look how cruel the Japanese have been. Maybe using the atomic bomb on a military base or something could save our soldiers."

"Most Japanese military bases and factories are in the middle of cities. Groves will probably pick a big target to show off the bomb."

"Are you going to sign the petition?"

Rob sighed. "I know you're worried about it, but I already signed, along with most of the guys in the lab—but only those of us who are civilians. Harrison wouldn't let any of the army men sign because they could be court-martialed. He signed first. It has sixty-seven Oak Ridge signatures now."

"I think it's the right thing to do. I just hope it doesn't come back to haunt you."

"If I didn't sign, it would haunt me. Like I said before, what can they do to us? They need us to finish the bomb."

"But it's already finished, isn't it?"

"They only have a couple of them. They may need more if the Japanese stay so stubborn."

"Do you think Truman will listen?"

"I don't know, Doris, but I'm glad we're trying to have a say. There wouldn't be a bomb without all the physicists, chemists, and engineers."

"All the people and all the money! Won't the army be bound and determined to use the bomb to justify what they've spent?

"You're probably right, honey." Rob gave Doris a quick kiss on the cheek. "I'm beat. Let's have dinner and go to bed early."

That weekend they went to see *Anchors Aweigh* with Annette and Joel. Afterward the two couples went back to the Friedmans' house to relieve the babysitter. Barbara was asleep, so they sat in the living room and talked, sipping beers.

"Who did you like better, Doris, Gene Kelly or Frank Sinatra?" asked Annette.

"Oh, Gene Kelly. I love to watch him dance." Doris had been giving her old friend the silent treatment as much as she could. Annette was being sweet as sugar—without her usual digs. Neither woman brought up Annette's accusations about Dave.

"Hey, Joel, did you sign the petition too?" Doris asked. When it was just the four of them, the old friends had become more open about discussing the bomb.

"I did. Though frankly I don't expect it to have much influence."

"Do you think the government will try to blackball the signers?"

"I doubt it. It's more likely that Truman will never see it. I heard Groves had a fit and made sure it was stamped *top secret*. He said the information in it could tip off the enemy that the bomb is ready. He doesn't want anything to stop the bomb from being used."

"I'm proud of Joel for signing," Annette declared.

"I'm proud of Rob too. I'm just worried for the future."

"For a few days I couldn't talk with my friends at Los Alamos," Joel went on. "That was a tip-off that the test was about to happen. Now the phone lines are open again. I heard on the grapevine that Oppie wouldn't let the petition circulate there. He's too cozy with Groves."

"Do you think Oppenheimer wants to drop a bomb on Japan?" asked Rob.

"Before the war, I would have pegged him as more of a pacifist type. He's a strange bird, all into left-wing politics and Sanskrit poetry. I wouldn't begin to guess what he wants now, but he must be incredibly relieved that the test worked."

"Rob says one bomb could destroy a whole city," Doris said.

"Not quite. Maybe a few square miles." Joel got up and threw his empty beer can in the trash.

"Would you like another?" Doris asked.

"No, thanks." Joel sat back down and put his arm around Annette. "The thing is, these first bombs are just the start. Now that we know we can make them, the army is going to want bigger and better ones. Pretty soon, one bomb will be able to take out a city."

"What an awful thought."

"And now you need a huge bomber to deliver one, but look at the progress the Germans have made with rockets. Imagine an atomic bomb on a rocket. How could we defend ourselves from that? I want to study theoretical physics when the war is over. No more weapons development for me. How about you, Rob?"

"I haven't thought that far. I'd like to work for a company that designs new kinds of electronics."

"I want Rob to go to college," Doris said. "I'm willing to get a job to help put him through school. He says he knows more already than most guys with an engineering degree, but if he doesn't have one, he'll always be a second-class citizen."

"Doris—stop nagging me."

"Who would take care of Barbara if you work, Doris?" asked Annette.

It annoyed Doris how Annette was always so eager to ally with Rob.

"The two of you really got yourselves into a fix by starting your family so young." So the gloves were back off.

"You're always such a voice of cheer, Annette."

"We'll all cross these bridges when we come to them," said Joel. "The next couple of weeks should be interesting though."

40: August 1945

The morning of August 7 was clear but muggy in Oak Ridge. Rob left for the lab while Doris and Barbara were still having breakfast. After clearing up the dishes, Doris got out a pad of paper and some crayons for her daughter.

"What do you want to draw today?" she asked.

"My birthday cake. Now I'm three!"

Doris did not know who was prouder: Barbara, for having had a small party and blowing out four candles—one for each year and one for good luck—or Doris, for having baked the cake and frosted it with flowers and a legible HAPPY BIRTHDAY written in icing. Barbara's presents included a baby doll that cried if you turned it on its back and an illustrated book of fairy tales. Doris and Rob had also taken her to see *Snow White*, her first movie.

"Would it be okay if I put on the radio while you draw?"

"Okay."

Given Rob's expertise with radios, the Friedmans had two. The larger one was broken. Rob had taken it with him to the lab that morning where he had tools to fix it. Rob had built their second radio from a crystal kit, so the sound quality was poor, but it could pick up the AM station in Knoxville. At nine thirty a country music broadcast was interrupted by an announcement that the president had a special message for the nation. His gravelly voice came on the air:

"Sixteen hours ago an American airplane dropped one bomb on Hiroshima and destroyed its usefulness to the enemy. That bomb had more power than twenty thousand tons of TNT." Truman said the bomb was atomic, harnessing the basic power of the universe. He noted that the Japanese had rejected the ultimatum from the Potsdam Conference and could now expect total destruction if they did not surrender. "We have spent two billion dollars on the greatest scientific gamble in history, and won."

"They did it," Doris whispered. She felt several warring emotions—pride that Rob had been part of such an important project, hope that the Japanese would now surrender, and sadness for the people in Hiroshima.

"Did what, Mommy?"

"I think the big war is going to be over soon, Barbara."

"Yippee! We can go see Grandma and Grandpa and Bubbe. And Aunt Naomi."

"I hope so. Soon. Let me just listen a little bit more."

The president's short statement ended, but the press had clearly been briefed on the Manhattan Project ahead of the planned announcement. The crew of the *Enola Gay* bomber gave eyewitness accounts of a mushroom-shaped cloud that rose seven miles into the sky. They said that Hiroshima, a city the size of Seattle or Memphis, had been all but vaporized. Other reporters revealed that the bomb had been developed in the secret cities of Oak Ridge, Los Alamos, and Hanford. Doris wondered if Rob and the others at the lab had heard the news.

A few minutes later, the phone rang. It was Annette.

"Doris! Did you hear? They bombed Hiroshima."

"Yes, I had the radio on."

"Oh, you have one at home? I thought Rob brought it to the lab today."

"You know Rob and radios. We have another small one here."

"Rob is the hero of the hour! One of the wives was calling Myra every few minutes with news updates, but meanwhile Rob fixed your radio. Now everyone is gathered around, listening to the broadcast.

Nobody cares today if we have a verboten radio in the lab. My mother even called from Chicago. Of course, she didn't know what we were doing here until now. According to her, you'd think Joel won the war single-handed! She was going to call your parents as soon as she hung up."

"Uh-oh. I'll brace myself. I'm sure my mother will think we're all about to die of radiation poisoning. She'll probably mail me a lead apron."

"You're assuming she'll understand what an atomic bomb is."

"That's true. Here's to blessed ignorance!"

"Let's hope the Japanese surrender quickly now."

That night the younger men in Harrison's lab gathered at his house to celebrate. He and Nora Joy went to a party for the bosses, leaving Myra in charge of their baby. She also had instructions to let the men enjoy the Hartnell liquor supply. Wives were not invited, but Doris didn't mind, since she suspected she wouldn't enjoy the rowdy gathering. She and Annette and Rochelle met at her house, putting Barbara and Benjamin to sleep in the bedroom. They talked about life after Oak Ridge. Annette was starting to think more about having a baby, but she knew she would need to work to help Joel while he got his physics PhD. Rochelle hoped Sol would get a new faculty job in California, with its warm, sunny beaches.

"Did you know about the bomb, Rochelle?" asked Doris.

"I figured the project was some type of weapon, but no, I didn't have any of the details."

"Harrison told Rob and Doris the whole story when he first met with them in Chicago," said Annette.

"Really? You've known all this time?"

"Yes, I think Harrison was worried that Rob wouldn't leave his job making battleship speakers. You know Rob. He's always loyal to his group. But when we heard about the project, we knew it was more important."

"Doris and Joel wouldn't fill me in. I had to wait until I came to work in the lab and got a security clearance." Annette's nose was obviously still out of joint.

"We were just being patriotic, Annette. After all, you could be a secret Soviet agent!"

"Right. From my mouth to Uncle Joe's ears."

They all chuckled.

"You do love telling secrets, Annette." Doris could not resist the dig.

Annette shrugged and looked away.

"One of the commentators said we dropped the bomb mainly to intimidate the Russians and keep them out of Asia," Rochelle said. "He said the Japanese would have had to surrender anyway, with our navy blockading all their ports."

"Rob said that General Groves wanted to see how the bomb performed in action. I pity the people of Hiroshima. Did Sol sign the petition?" asked Doris.

"No. He said it was futile and Truman would just do whatever he wanted. Sol is a realist."

"Looks like he was right. I just wish we'd had the bomb in time to save some of the people in the camps," Doris said.

Rochelle shrugged. "Some people think we should have bombed the railway lines and interrupted the transports, but it's all wishful thinking now."

"I don't think the Germans will be fighting another war any time soon," Annette put in. "So, Doris, what will you and Rob do now?"

"He'll look for a job in Chicago. I could help support us too. I've even started trying my hand in the stock market."

"Really, Doris? After living through the Depression? Both our families lost a lot of money."

"That's because they bought stocks on margin. They only paid for ten percent of the stock shares up front. It's like taking out a loan.

When the market crashed, they couldn't pay what they owed and lost everything. I just want to invest in the safest stuff, like blue chip stocks, or maybe even some real estate."

Rochelle smiled at her. "I think in ten years we'll be visiting Doris and Rob in their mansion by Lake Michigan."

"I'll believe that when I see it," Annette scoffed.

"I'm sure you'll be watching. Watching for flaws and tearing me down to Rob like you always do."

"Girls! We're about to win World War II. Let's not start a battle at home."

"You're right, Rochelle. Would either of you like another Coke?"

41: August 1945

Doris walked over to Betty's house. In her seventh month of pregnancy, Betty was doing well, but the heat was miserable.

"If we had a car, we could go to the pool," Doris told her. "It's too far for you to walk in this humidity though. Could Will come home at lunch and drop us off? Then we could take a taxi home."

"I hate to bother him. Also, I feel like a whale. My ankles are swollen. I don't want to be seen in public in my hideous maternity bathing suit. I haven't even had my hair done in a couple of weeks. And my mascara would run." Betty indeed had a scarf wrapped around her hair. Her eyebrows, normally meticulously drawn arches, were barely visible without her usual makeup.

"Oh, Betty. Relaxing in the cool water could be good for your health, or at least your mood. Who cares how you look? You could keep a robe on until you were ready to get in the pool."

"I'll think about it, Doris." Betty put an ice pack on her forehead.

"So what do you make of the bomb?"

"I suppose you already knew all about it, Chicago girl."

"It's true. I heard about it before we even came here."

"See? I knew it."

"But that doesn't mean I really understand it."

"The whole thing gives me the heebie-jeebies. I'm trying not to dwell on it. I want to keep calm for the baby."

"Are you still planning to give birth at the Oak Ridge hospital?"

"Yes. I told them to just put me out for the duration."

"Really? You don't want to be awake?"

"I do not like pain. How bad was it when you had Barbara?"

"I won't lie. It hurt a lot, but the fear that she could die from being born so early was worse than the pain. They kept her in an incubator for the first several days. I could only hold her for a few minutes at a time. It felt so strange being a mother, like it wasn't real."

"I bet you were relieved to get her home."

"Half relieved and half panicked. I was afraid I wouldn't be able to keep her alive. I used to wake up and check her in the bassinet every couple of hours during the night to make sure she was breathing . . . You know, Betty, some nights I was so blue I actually wondered if I'd be better off if she died." Doris fumbled in her purse for a cigarette. "I still feel guilty for even thinking like that."

"But, Doris, look at Barbara now. You managed to get her, and yourself, through all the tough times. She's a little skinny, but so pretty and bright."

"And stubborn."

"Like her mama! Let's talk about something more cheerful. Did you go to a lot of dances in college?"

"Some, but I was living at home, so I couldn't stay out very late. When I started college, I had never even gone out with a boy."

"Really?"

"Yes. And a lot of my social life in college was playing cards with friends and going to concerts. I bet there were a lot of dances at Sweet Briar."

"Well, of course it was all girls, but we had formals with the boys at Washington and Lee, or we went to dances at the University of Virginia. I had such pretty gowns. My favorite was a white chiffon with a ballerina skirt and silver trim. It showed off my figure. Now look at me."

"Betty, you're going to have a plump, healthy baby. Ever since I've met you, this was your dearest wish."

"You're right, Doris. I'm going to stop this wallowing. I'm going to be a strong, independent woman like you."

"I'm no paragon. In fact, Betty . . . can I tell you something? Would you promise not to think too badly of me? I can't tell my other friends, but maybe you would understand."

"Cross my heart. I will keep your secret and try not to judge."

"Remember Dave Sokol from that lunch in Knoxville?"

"Mm."

"I kissed him a couple of months ago."

"I warned you about him. Just kissed?"

"Basically. And some touching."

"Above or below the waist?"

"Never mind."

"That was naughty. I am surprised at you, Doris. Was it fun at least?"

"For a few minutes. Then I started to feel awful . . . But we didn't have, you know, real sex."

"Why did you do anything with him?"

"He'd been flirting with me for months. Rob's been so tired and distracted. I felt like I missed out on life by getting married so young. Here was this good-looking, sophisticated man, interested in me."

"Did Rob find out?"

"In the end, I had to tell him. Dave tried to blackmail me into giving him the keys to Rob's file cabinet at the lab. And he let on that he speaks Russian. I reported him to security and they arrested him. Then the whole thing came out."

Betty was quiet for a moment.

"Please don't say anything to Will."

"I won't. This is just between us girls. Was Rob very mad?"

"He was terribly hurt. And he called me a slut. I almost left for Chicago, but we're trying to work things out . . . Betty—I feel like a slut."

"Doris, you just gave some very good reasons that you slipped."

"Ugh. You wanted a nice, light conversation and I told you I wished my baby was dead and I cheated on my husband."

"You told me you felt desperate as a very young mother with a sick baby. And that you were gullible when an attractive man tried to seduce you."

"That's a nice Southern way of cleaning up my story!"

"We all make mistakes. Do you still love Rob?"

"I do. He makes me mad as hell sometimes, but I love his big heart, and his sense of humor, and even his insecurity—and I still think he's very handsome, in his skinny way."

"The love is what's important. Give him some time. I think he'll forgive you. Come here and give me a hug, Doris—that is if you can reach around my middle!"

The two women sat for a moment, comforting each other in a sweaty embrace.

42: August 1945

The next day, the bombing of Nagasaki was announced. At dinner, Doris asked Rob what he thought.

"Truman jumped the gun. He could have waited a few more days for a surrender. I bet he never even saw the petition. At the lab they're saying Groves pushed for this. He was in a rush to find out what a plutonium bomb could do."

"Wasn't Hiroshima a plutonium bomb?"

"No. Hiroshima was a uranium bomb. The test bomb at Los Alamos and the one we just used on Nagasaki were plutonium. But that's not been announced in the news so far."

"If they already tested a plutonium bomb, why did they need to see how it performed?"

"Because the test site at Los Alamos was empty desert. Nagasaki is a city with a port and factories, and of course lots of houses and civilians."

"That's appalling!"

"They're claiming they did it to show Japan what will happen if they don't surrender. They're threatening to use more bombs."

"Do we have more?"

"Who knows? Only people like Oppie or Groves have that kind of information."

"The *Oak Ridge Journal* had an article about Nagasaki today. Colonel Nichols told the reporter that none of us should mention anything that's not already in the official news."

"Exactly. That's why we shouldn't talk to anyone about the two different kinds of bombs. Now the big question is whether we keep atomic secrets for the US alone or create some kind of international body for world peace."

"Maybe atomic power will make people's lives better, like with cheap electricity."

"Or maybe the Soviets will get the bomb and we'll have Hiroshima and Nagasaki in New York and Washington, DC. This war may be ending, but life just got a lot scarier."

Barbara looked from one parent to the other. "What's a bomb, Daddy?"

"It's something that goes bang and stops bad people from hurting our family."

"Oh!" She smiled. "Can we go see Grandpa and Bubbe now?"

"Sometime soon, Barbara, but we don't know exactly when."

Doris, along with the rest of Oak Ridge, was elated when Truman announced the surrender of Japan on the evening of August 14. She and Rob took Barbara to Jackson Square to join the crowds. Doris was worried that the press of people would be too much for a small child, but Rob perched his daughter on his shoulders. They ran into Joel and Annette.

"They're selling copies of the *Knoxville Journal* for a dollar!" Annette told them. "I bought one, even though the price is ridiculous. I want to show it to my children someday."

"I don't know if Barbara will remember this when she's older, but I wanted her to see it," Rob told them. "Sometimes I felt chickenhearted for not being in the service, but today I'm proud."

Doris sighed. She had come to understand the insecurity that prompted Rob's desire to fight on the front lines, but she still resented his attempt to enlist behind her back.

"It is pretty incredible that we built the bomb in three years," Joel agreed.

“Those bombs saved a million of our boys’ lives!” shouted a man standing next to them.

“And we kept it all a secret too,” added Annette.

“At least as far as we know,” Doris said.

“I wouldn’t be surprised if they find some spies after the war,” Joel agreed, “but it doesn’t matter so much now that we beat the Nazis and the Japs.”

“What about the Russians though?”

“Doris, the Russians will get a bomb eventually,” Joel replied. “So will other countries. But hopefully they’ll think two or three times before starting a war. Especially with the kind of bombs that are coming next!”

“Boom!” shrieked Barbara. “Bombs got the bad people!”

Several women standing next to them laughed. “What a darling child,” one of them cooed to Rob. “I hope I find a handsome hubby like you when I get home,” said her friend, saluting Rob with her open beer can. He blushed.

Annette nudged Doris. “We are pretty lucky.”

“Yes, I hope you’re counting your blessings, wifeys,” said Joel, striking a pose. “But if you other young ladies want to pat someone’s butt, try mine. I’m afraid Rob might drop Barbara if you startle him.” More giggling ensued.

Someone had hung a crude effigy of the Japanese prime minister from a lamp pole with the label TOJO. A group of boys stood under it, whooping and banging on garbage can lids. High school kids piled out of an old jalopy with ATOM SMASHER painted on the door. Not only beers but also jugs of moonshine were being handed around.

“I think we should take Barbara home,” Doris told Rob. “It’s getting wilder. Or if you want to stay, I can walk her back.”

“No, I’ll go with you.”

They trudged back up the hill.

"Do you still feel proud of the project?" asked Doris after they had put Barbara to bed.

"Of course! Don't you?"

"I think the science part is amazing, but I just keep thinking of all the people who died in this war . . . and I wonder if the atomic bomb was really needed in the end."

"I don't think we'll know for a long time. But I agree with Joel—this is the start of a new threat in the world. When weapons are invented, they get used."

"I think you're right. They banned chemical weapons after World War I . . . But the Nazis gassed the Jews in the camps."

"And the Japanese used poison gas and anthrax. I don't doubt for a minute that the Japs or the Nazis would have used the bomb if they got it first."

"I just want to be happy today that the war is over and the right side won. My parents called yesterday. They said your brother is back home."

"Yes, I know. My father is proud of him, but he still talks like I'm a draft dodger."

Doris snuggled closer to Rob on the couch and rested her head on his shoulder. "Don't let him hurt your feelings. I don't think he even understands what you've been doing. My mother is fretting that I might bring radiation back to Chicago! I've never told them about the dose you got."

"Does she think being in Oak Ridge might have hurt Barbara?"

"You know, she didn't even mention that. Honestly, I think she's mainly worried about herself. If it weren't for Papa and Naomi and Bubbe, I'd claim to be radioactive so she would stay away."

"Doris, you should cut the family a little more slack."

"I suppose. How about you and I have a little celebration of our own tonight? You kept saying that our time would come after the war!"

"Uh-oh, I need a new excuse now."

"Then never mind." She started to get up but Rob pulled her back to him.

"Doris! I was just kidding. Let's make a new start. I just hope Sokol is freezing his balls off in an igloo somewhere."

"Forget about him." She turned and gave him a lingering kiss. "You're worth a hundred Dave Sokols."

"Hey, how about putting on that fancy robe you bought in Knoxville?"

"You got it, sweetie."

43: September 1945

Everyone was talking about what they would do now that the war was over.

"I sent applications for a few jobs in Chicago," Rob told Doris. "Joel is going to work on his physics PhD. Argonne National Labs is going to be a center for physics, but I don't think it's the place for me."

"Where could you get an engineering degree?"

"I'd probably have to go to the University of Illinois or DePaul. I don't know how we'd afford the tuition without the GI Bill. I'm more interested in a research job."

"Would you at least take some night courses?"

"Maybe."

"Rob, I think you have an inferiority complex. You're afraid you wouldn't do well in college. Hasn't working here shown you that you're just as smart as these guys with fancy diplomas?"

"Don't try your psychology on me." Rob ruffled her hair.

"Oh! You're so frustrating! I'm sure you could get some kind of scholarship. Have you talked to Harrison about it?"

"No. He's a chemist and I'm an engineer."

"He's someone who values you and cares about you. I bet he'd have some good advice."

"I don't want to bother him. And he already knows too much about our personal lives."

"You know I can work part-time to help with money."

"Taking care of the family is my job as a man, Doris."

"I thought we were a team."

"We are. But I'm the quarterback."

She wanted to argue with him, but newspapers and women's magazines were full of articles pushing wives to be homemakers. Women should retreat so the men coming home from war could take back their rightful jobs. Doris didn't buy it. She tried to back off and let Rob choose his own path, but his head was in the clouds sometimes. She also knew that her affair with Dave had diminished her influence with Rob. Maybe she should just be glad that he had taken her back. Still, a small voice whispered that she should have a say in their family's future.

Will phoned to tell Doris that Betty had her baby, a healthy, seven-pound boy they named William the Third. They would call him Bill to distinguish him from his father. The next day, Doris visited the hospital. Betty was wearing a frilly aqua bed jacket and had put on makeup, although she had a turban over her hair. Baby Bill was sleeping in a bassinet next to the hospital bed.

"Don't hug me!" Betty whispered, putting her hand up. "I'm sure I smell awful."

Doris sat in the chair next to the bed. She kept her voice low, too, to avoid waking the baby. "You look amazingly well put together. And Bill is beautiful. He looks like a Kewpie doll. I love his blond curl. You should have seen Barbara when she was a newborn. Scrawny and covered with fuzz, with purple medicine on her face. Are you happy?"

"So happy, Doris. And relieved. My mother-in-law decided not to come see the baby since we're leaving for Richmond next month. Back to our own house and all my friends. And now I'm a mother, too, like I always wanted."

"Is Will proud?"

"He is pleased as punch! He thinks Bill looks like his side of the family."

"How was your labor?"

"It hurt some at the start. My waters broke, so Will came home and took me to the hospital. But when it got worse, the nice doctor put me to sleep, just like I planned."

"You weren't worried about the baby?"

"I trust the doctors here. They gave me laughing gas and something else. I don't recollect a thing except waking up. The baby was right there, all clean and wrapped in a blanket. Wasn't it like that for you?"

"No, I was awake. I saw her all crusted with white and red stuff, and I heard her cry. I was relieved she made it because she came so early. Are you going to try to breastfeed?"

Betty made a face. "Bottles for me. They say breastfeeding makes you saggy. And we're hiring a baby nurse to help with night feedings."

"I bet you wish your mother could be here."

"Now you're going to make me boo-hoo." Betty carefully wiped a tear from her cheek. "I've just got to believe she's looking down on us. I swear I smelled her perfume when they gave me the gas to put me to sleep."

The baby moved his legs. Betty leaned over to check on him, but he quieted.

"Was your mother a big help when Barbara was born?"

"My mother felt ashamed. Her mahjong friends gossiped about my getting married so suddenly and counted the months from wedding to birth. When I took Barbara home from the hospital, Mama sent my Bubbe to help, but she's full of old-country superstitions. I couldn't trust her with a sick newborn. Rob's mother was working in their family store, so I was pretty much on my own. A visiting nurse came a couple of times those first weeks. I was worried that the health department would take Barbara away because she wasn't putting on enough weight."

"Look how well everything turned out though. Is something wrong, Doris? You look upset."

"You don't need to be bothered with my problems today."

"Hey, Chicago girl, spit it out!"

"It's just that I'm concerned about Rob. He's been offered a job in an engineering company."

"Well, that's good, isn't it?"

"Yes, but it's a junior position. I've been trying to convince him to get his college degree. Otherwise I'm afraid he'll never have the kind of career he deserves."

"Do you want me to ask Will to talk with him?"

"Thanks, but Rob's already annoyed with me. I think advice from Will would just make him madder. Rob's a sweetheart, but he has a temper. When he throws things around or sulks, it drives me crazy."

"What's his job title going to be?"

"Engineer."

"Well, that sounds good."

"That's what Rob says. He got a certificate of appreciation from the War Department for his contribution to producing the atomic bomb. They gave them to all the X-10 lab people. He thinks it's as good as a college diploma, but it's just a piece of paper! I look at the other couples—like you and Will, Sol and Rochelle, or Joel and Annette. You're all going to get ahead and give your children the best chances. I want that too."

"Well, you know what a good wife does . . ."

"Stays quiet and stands by her man?"

"No! That's what she appears to be doing. She says, 'Yes, dear,' and then does what's needed."

"You mean she's the power behind the throne?"

"You could put it that way. Not that I think men are kings—they're just boys who need to feel like kings. I'll give you an example. When we were looking for a house in Richmond, one came up for sale on the same street as my in-laws. You can imagine the pressure Will's mother put on us to buy that property."

"From what you've told me about her, that sounds like a nightmare!"

"I knew I had to do something fast. I wondered why the house was underpriced, so I went to the newspaper archives and looked up the address. Lucky for me, I hit pay dirt. It turned out that a man committed suicide in that house in 1930. He'd lost a lot of money in the stock crash, but the newspaper also hinted he had a suspiciously close friendship with another man—a lawyer in town. His own wife had filed for divorce. At the next family dinner, I told them the story. I ended with a tearful declaration that I could never ever sleep soundly in such a house of horror and shame."

Doris started to laugh and Betty shushed her. "Don't wake Bill."

"Sorry," she whispered.

"So you just go back to Chicago and let Rob start his new job. Give him some time, Doris, and let him have his pride. Men need that. I don't think you learn that up North, like we Southern girls do. If they don't treat him right at work, he may get a lot more eager to go to school. Meanwhile, keep on learning how to make money. In another couple of years, Barbara will be in kindergarten, and you'll be free to finish your own degree if you want."

"I could do that. I just have to find the patience."

"You and Rob are still so young. Start by making a home for your family in Chicago and see what happens."

Baby Bill let out a thin cry.

"Oh my stars," exclaimed Betty. "It's time for his bottle." She rang for the nurse.

"You must be exhausted, Betty. Thanks for listening to me when you're lying in a hospital bed!"

"Lucky you—I was a captive audience!"

"I'm really going to miss you."

"Don't borrow trouble. We still have a month left until we leave."

44: October 1945

Doris stood in the living room of the house on West Malta. She was surrounded by moving crates. Rob had taken Barbara for a last trip to the playground. Doris had already said teary goodbyes to Rochelle and Betty. The movers were about to arrive. The Friedmans would be on a train to Chicago that evening. It seemed like yesterday that they had been moving into their new home—but she also felt like she'd aged thirty years rather than three. She had run into Colonel Barton the week before at Jackson Square. He was with a downtrodden-looking woman in a frumpy dress who must have been his wife.

"Headed back to Chicago, Mrs. Friedman?" he'd inquired.

"Yes, sir. I'll miss that Steinway, though."

"I'm sure you'll soon have a passel of babies to keep you too busy to play piano."

Doris smiled, though anyone that knew her would notice it did not reach her eyes. "My daughter already does a good job of that. Good luck to you and Mrs. Barton."

She saw Alice coming down the boardwalk, her two boys trotting next to her. "Alice! I'm glad I ran into you! Just look at the size of the twins," she marveled. "We're going back to Chicago. No more farm-fresh chickens."

"Too bad," Alice replied. "You were one of the good ones, Doris. But this place will keep growing. I'm glad of the new schools for the boys. They'll learn a lot more than I ever did. If you come back to visit, look us up."

Doris wondered what kind of family would move into their house. She'd left the rooms as clean as she could. She gazed at their piano, wrapped in padding for the move, and could hear Dave Sokol's deadpan rendition of "The Dance of the Sugar Plum Fairy." Where was he now? Shivering in the Aleutian Islands and cursing her? It was her fault—no, she told herself—it was mostly his fault for involving her in his schemes. She could not help feeling sad for him though. What a waste of all his drive and intelligence. She heard Rob and Barbara's steps on the porch and mentally finished her goodbyes.

Soon after they arrived in Chicago, Doris's twenty-one-year-old sister, Naomi, married her boyfriend, who had just returned from the Pacific. The reception at the synagogue was far fancier than the one her parents had hurriedly put together after Doris's wedding at city hall. Naomi looked joyful in a beige silk suit and hat with a short veil. Sophie was wearing a blue and silver brocade sheath. Doris privately thought it emphasized her thick middle. Doris's own moss-green wool suit dated from before her pregnancy. She was proud that it fit again.

"You could have worn something more formal," Sophie commented in a sour tone.

"Mama, I don't have any cocktail dresses, and right now I can't afford to buy one."

"Are those real pearls?" Sophie asked.

"I'm afraid not, Mama."

"I didn't think so."

"Leave Doris alone," scolded Naomi. "That shade of green brings out your eyes, Sis."

Doris and Rob circulated among the guests, sipping on their glasses of wine. Doris's youngest aunt, Mamie, greeted them.

"You look nice, Doris," she commented. "You've lost some weight, I see."

Doris was grateful that Rob put his arm around her waist and said, "Yes, doesn't she look beautiful? You know our daughter turned three in July."

"Uh-oh, time for the next one. Watch out for that baby weight though."

"We're going to wait to have another child until our lives are settled and we can afford to buy a house," Doris told her.

"Well, don't wait too long!"

"She has plenty of time," Rob interjected. "She's only twenty-three."

"Really? I lose track of time. You look older, Doris. You were in the South, weren't you? Too much sun ages your skin."

"Excuse us, Aunt Mamie. I see my father's brothers over in the corner and I haven't said hello yet." As they walked away, Doris said, "She's such a *klafte*. I'm not sure it was the best idea coming back to Chicago."

"Come on, honey. Every family has an Aunt Mamie."

"Mamie and my mother at the same party is my idea of hell."

"I see some good-looking lox at the buffet. Do you want some?"

"No, but go ahead before it's all gone!"

Doris spied Harry momentarily by himself, looking at some antique Torah crowns in a glass case.

"Uncle Harry!" She gave him a quick hug.

"My favorite niece!"

"Ssh, don't say that where someone can hear at Naomi's wedding."

"Well, you were the first grandchild on your side of the family, so that's always made you special. That and your brainy *yiddishe kop*! I understand your husband helped invent the A-bomb."

"That's quite an exaggeration. But he was in a group that did important work on it."

"And now you're back home. Will the university let you register for your final year?"

"I haven't looked into it yet. But I wanted to ask you something."

"Oh?"

"When we were at Oak Ridge, I went through the accounting course you sent. I helped organize the business side of their amateur orchestra. Now I'm keeping the books for a couple of music businesses here in Chicago, but I wonder if you could give me a part-time job in your office. I'd like to make some more money so Rob could get his engineering degree."

Harry wrinkled his brow. "We had this discussion before. You're a mother now. Any jobs that need doing should go to the boys coming home from the war. Finish your college."

"What about giving me some stock tips?"

"Stock tips? What, you want me to commit insider trading now?"

"No, Uncle Harry. Just a little advice on good stocks for investing."

"I don't know, Doris. You shouldn't take risks with the little you're saving."

"Harry!" The rabbi approached them. "Come and meet one of our newest members of the temple. He loves staying at your hotels."

Doris stood there for a moment after the rabbi hustled Harry away. Well, at least she had tried. She wondered how Harry expected her to get through a rigorous year at the university without being able to afford a babysitter. She supposed that he had his family and staff to take care of such mundane concerns. It was clear she was on her own.

45: January 1946

Dear Betty,

Now it is three months since we came home. I hope you, Will, and Bill had a wonderful Christmas season in Richmond. We are living in a small apartment again. I actually miss our house in Oak Ridge. Barbara has started preschool three mornings a week. I use that time to give piano lessons or do bookkeeping work. I also have continued buying stocks, being very careful and conservative. It is paying off. I often think about our conversation about letting Rob be king of our castle. I have not told him about my investments, though normally I avoid keeping secrets.

He is happy so far at his new job, though I still think they are underpaying him. His top-secret clearance came through. I was relieved because he signed a petition in Oak Ridge asking Truman to give Japan a chance to surrender before using the bombs. I thought the government might hold that against him.

Barbara is still underweight, but otherwise is doing well. I think she will learn to read soon, but I won't let her skip any grades. Better to be a little bored in school than to always be younger than everyone else. She has made some friends in her class but still misses Rochelle's son, Benjamin. Sol and Rochelle are living in California again. He got back his job teaching at Caltech. Rochelle just gave birth to a little girl, named Aliza. It sounds like they are very content with life. Barbara still says "y'all" sometimes. She is taking kiddie lessons at the Art Institute. In a couple of years, I plan to start her on the piano.

I think Rob has forgiven me for what happened in Oak Ridge. He is not one to talk openly about problems, except in a crisis. I do notice he has gotten a little more inventive in our private life, which is a welcome change. I miss you, Betty! I don't have any friends here who understand me so well. I wish we could go on a road trip to downtown Chicago. I think you would love all the stores, like Marshall Field's. Is your mother-in-law driving you nuts? How is little Bill?

Love, Doris

Dear Doris,

I loved hearing all your news. Please keep writing. Of course, Will's mother is still the same interfering battle-ax. Will can do no wrong in her eyes, but I am always falling short. She wants us to go to her church every Sunday. Now that Bill is getting heavy and wiggly, sitting through the service is becoming quite a trial. He always wants me to hold him, so Will gets to have a baby-free lap. I remember you asking about preachers who give sermons about hellfire. Well, the pastor at Mama-in-law's church is definitely one of them. I had to take Bill out of the service when he started to cry, and I could feel that man's eyes boring into my back. I was just waiting for lightning to strike me down.

I am enjoying our lovely house. We belong to a country club with a pool and tennis courts. I play bridge with some of the other women my age. After Oak Ridge, I must confess that I find most of them boring. Also, none of my bridge partners are anywhere near as smart as you, Doris!

Will got a promotion at DuPont when we came home. I suspect he'll make vice president eventually. For New Year's we had a party at home for his group. I was glad we had a caterer and some help to serve the food and liquor. A far cry from having to smuggle bootleg bottles into the Edgemoor gate! One of my friends from Sweet Briar has started a decorating business in town and I am helping her out. It is a bright spot in my life. Will teases me that you were a bad influence. Maybe one of these days a business trip will take Will to Chicago. Then I could travel with him and see you again.

Love, Betty

46: May 1946

With settling in Chicago, caring for Barbara, and working to improve the family finances, the months passed quickly. On a rainy day in May, Doris was surprised when Joel drove Rob home from work. Both men looked somber and Rob asked Doris to get out their precious bottle of scotch.

"Remember Louis Slotin?" Rob asked her.

"Of course! Who could forget Louis?" Doris had always enjoyed his tales about fighting in the Spanish civil war and being an aircraft gunner. It was never clear how much was real and how much he made up, but it didn't really matter. She had also never understood why he risked diving into the reactor's shielding tank. "I was sad when he left Oak Ridge to work at Los Alamos. Isn't he getting married soon? You said he was tired of working on bombs and wanted to come back here."

"He died today," said Joel.

"Oh no! What happened?"

"Remember the guy who was killed in a radiation accident at Los Alamos a few months ago?"

"Vaguely. We didn't know him. Did you, Joel?"

"No, I never met him either. He was testing a plutonium bomb core and dropped a shielding brick on it. The thing went critical and let off a huge dose of radiation, but he was alone in the room, so nobody else got hurt. Louis was working with the same core. It's a small ball of plutonium. He was doing an experiment Feynman called tickling the dragon's tail. The goal was to use two half spheres made of beryllium to surround the core and to see how close together you could get them, without the half spheres touching. If they touch, neutrons can't escape and the core goes critical. Louis was holding the top half with one hand and just using a screwdriver to allow it to get closer to the bottom half. The screwdriver slipped and the top of the sphere dropped onto the bottom. Louis threw the top aside, but it was too late. He knew right away he'd probably gotten a fatal dose. It's taken him nine days to die miserably."

"And this time six other people were in the room and got exposed too," added Rob. "A couple of them are still in the hospital."

"What was he thinking?" Joel drank his scotch in one swallow and thumped the glass down on the coffee table. "The army says he's a hero for saving everyone else, but after the first accident, safety measures were supposed to be in place. They all ignored them. Nobody was even wearing their radiation badge. A test like that should only be done with a remote control system—not by hand."

"He always was a daredevil." Rob drained his glass too.

"Yeah, but he was a sweet guy. Great sense of humor," Joel added. "You know he assembled the core for the Trinity Test."

"His poor fiancée. His poor parents." Doris poured herself a small glass of scotch. She wiped a tear away.

"Groves sent a plane to get his parents in Montreal. They got to be with him, before he got delirious," Joel told them.

"I'll miss him," said Rob. "I was really looking forward to his moving back here."

After Joel left, Doris asked Rob to cuddle with her on the couch. "I'm so glad you're healthy," she told him.

"Yup. You'll probably be stuck with me for a long time."

"I hope so. We're stuck with each other. I want to do a better job of enjoying every day."

"I agree, Doris. You spend too much time worrying and trying to control everything."

"I think I'm getting better, though."

Doris's self-confidence was slowly increasing, along with her secret bank account. Rob also had regained his interest in sex, now that his work schedule was less hectic. Doris tried not to judge her attractiveness by his attentions but still found them reassuring.

"I notice you haven't asked me to get a college degree for at least two or three months."

"Don't remind me!"

They laughed, but neither could forget the tragedy of Louis's passing.

47: July 1946

That summer, Doris read in the paper that the army had tested a plutonium bomb under the ocean near the Marshall Islands. They even gave the device a name—Helen of Bikini. The explosion caused an unanticipated tsunami that contaminated a wide area with radiation. The islanders might never be able to return to their homes. That same week Doris threw a small fourth birthday party for Barbara at a picnic table in Lincoln Park. It would have been miserable to have everyone in their small apartment on a hot summer's day.

Sophie relayed the latest gossip about Harry's oldest daughter who had joined a modern dance troupe in West Berlin.

"It's shameful for a Jewish girl to live in that Nazi city! And who knows if she's shacking up with boys, like an alley cat. I don't understand how Harry can let her be so wild."

"Well, she's twenty-one," Doris said. "How would he stop her?"

"You know how. Cut off the cash." Doris's mother rubbed her fingers together. "At least my daughters are married to good men."

"You weren't so happy when I married Rob. And when I had Barbara."

"Not happy? What nonsense are you talking, Doris?"

Doris let it go. She would never get a satisfactory response from her mother anyway. She started to cut herself another wedge of cake.

"Ah-ah! One piece is enough for you." Her mother took the spatula out of Doris's hand. "Are you even wearing a girdle? That skirt looks tight."

"It's time for us all to walk over to the zoo," Doris announced.

She hoped her mother would refrain from comparing Doris's figure to the elephants. Yet Sophie's barbs no longer bothered her nearly as much as they once had. Sometimes she even felt sorry for her mother. Sophie spent so much energy putting on a good show.

"Who wants to see Bushman the gorilla?" Doris asked. "He's Barbara's favorite animal."

The enthusiasm was unanimous. They watched, fascinated, as the huge gorilla ate individual grapes from a bunch on the floor of his pen. Posted on his cage was an award from the United Service Organizations for Bushman's helping the morale of Chicago servicemen during the war. The party group also visited the giraffes and the big cats.

Doris was watching the spider monkeys swing on branches in their enclosure when she heard a commotion. She turned around. Barbara had squeezed between the bars of a cage holding some small deer. She was petting one while onlookers laughed and pointed.

A zookeeper came in and angrily picked her up, yelling, "Where are this child's parents?" He took Barbara out of the deer pen, carefully locking the gate behind them.

Doris rushed over and took Barbara from his arms. "I'm her mother. I only took my eyes off her for a moment." She was frustrated that nobody else in the family had been watching out for Barbara, though she knew it was her own fault for expecting anything else.

Rob was not far behind. "Sorry, sir. But you should have a better barrier. It's not safe if a four-year-old can get into the cage!"

"We expect parents to watch their children. You are a skinny little girl." He wagged a finger at Barbara. "Don't you try getting into the lion's cage, now!"

"I'd like to pet a lion!" Barbara told him.

The zookeeper glared and she stuck out her tongue.

"Barbara! Apologize!" Doris said. "It may be your birthday, but all those presents could be left at Grandpa's house if you don't behave."

Barbara told the zookeeper she was sorry. For the rest of the zoo visit, Doris kept Barbara continually in her line of vision.

"I will say she's fearless," Rob remarked to Doris when nobody else could hear.

"I'm glad she's not an anxious child, but a little fear is a good thing."

After the party, Samuel brought them back to their apartment. Barbara had fallen asleep en route, so Rob carried her inside. Samuel left Sophie in the car while he helped Doris bring the birthday presents upstairs.

"It was a nice day," he said. "It's good to see you happy, Doris. When you got back from Oak Ridge, I was worried about you. I felt like something had come between you and Rob."

"I don't want to talk about it, but you're right. It was my fault, but it's better now."

"Don't sell yourself short. Rob is lucky to have you. You're lovely, smart, and talented."

"I wish I could see myself that way. I'm a plump college dropout who teaches piano. And I'm a lousy mother."

Samuel sighed. "You've never really appreciated your own strengths. I know your mother's nagging doesn't help. I probably should have been firmer with her."

Doris put a stack of presents on the dining table and turned to hug her father. "You've always done your best, Papa, to make me feel loved. Probably I'm my own worst enemy."

48: August 1946

When Doris heard a radio report about a new edition of the *New Yorker* devoted to Hiroshima, she ran to the store to buy a copy before it sold out. Barbara was at preschool, so Doris was free to devour the magazine from cover to cover. A year after the war, the author, John Hersey, was portraying the Japanese as ordinary human beings, no different than Americans would be if an atomic bomb fell on their homes. His stories of six survivors vividly revealed their suffering, showing the real and ongoing extent of the tragedy. Doris realized that other articles had glossed over the city's devastation and minimized the lingering horrors of radiation. And these were just the consequences this first year. What would happen to these people in the years to come? And what about the children they would have? Doris thought about Louis Slotin and started worrying again about Rob's health. Should they even consider having a second baby?

When Rob came home that night, she handed him the magazine, with its innocuous cover illustration of New Yorkers enjoying Central Park in the summer. He was in the middle of reading the article when she finished putting Barbara to bed.

"Are you surprised?" she asked, sitting next to him on the couch.

"No, I'm not. The government doesn't want people thinking about radiation from the bombs. Did you know that one of the chemists in the Y-12 plant gave an interview to the local Tennessee press last year saying that Hiroshima would be contaminated with radiation for fifty years?"

"No, I didn't hear about that."

"Security came and took him away. The scuttlebutt was that he had a heart attack after they gave him the third degree. Anyway, he was fired."

"Was he right?"

"Apparently not. The project sent a team to Hiroshima and Nagasaki six or eight weeks after the bombings, and even by then, levels were pretty low outside of the area near ground zero. They exploded the bombs about a third of a mile in the air, so a lot of radiation didn't reach the cities."

"Do you still think the bomb was worthwhile?"

Rob looked thoughtful. "I do. Remember that first night when Harrison warned us the Nazis could get it first? We had to go for it. And in the end, the bomb helped us defeat the Japanese and end the war."

"But most of the victims ended up being women and children—doctors, teachers. Imagine if an atomic bomb fell on Chicago."

"War doesn't just kill soldiers. Even wars in ancient times had rapes and famines."

"But now we bomb cities instead of besieging them."

"We just have to hope that fear of the bomb brings peace in the world."

"Right, like peace came after the First World War. I feel so helpless. I just hope you don't get sick from the radiation at Oak Ridge."

Rob gave her a comforting hug. "Doris, the dose I got was miniscule compared to what those people experienced. I'm fine, and I'll continue to be fine."

"Do you think it would still be okay for me to get pregnant?"

"Because of the radiation I got?"

She nodded.

"The only thing that worries me is whether I can get you pregnant. The doctor said I might be shooting blanks for a while."

"I'm not ready to try anyway."

"You just tell me when you are, and we'll throw away the rubbers. It would probably be good for Barbara to have a brother or sister. Sometimes I think we spoil her."

That night Doris had a nightmare. She was in the middle of a smoldering, gray wasteland of ruined houses. She was scooping aside ashes and pulling boards off a pile, knowing that Barbara and her father, Samuel, were underneath. She heard air-raid sirens and could see multiple mushroom clouds in the distance, but she kept digging until she saw her daughter's face, covered with dirt and blood. "No! Barbara! Get up! Papa!" She woke, choking off a scream. Rob stirred but remained asleep.

She sat up and took a deep breath. She was afraid to go back to sleep and perhaps fall into the nightmare again, so she slid out of bed as silently as she could and went to the living room. She spent the rest of the night on the couch, trying to distract herself by reading *The Chrysanthemum and the Sword*, a book about Japan recently published by an American anthropologist, but she could not concentrate. The code of Bushido and the cult of the emperor seemed quaintly antique, even though she supposed that both had contributed to the Japanese determination to rule the Far East.

Her own concerns about buying a house or having a second child seemed petty. She supposed she had been closer to the center of events than most people, especially if Dave's espionage could have hastened a Russian bomb. But she had no delusions that one housewife could influence the course of history. She still thought about Dave now and then, wondering where he was and whether he still hated her. She bit her lip. Maybe Harrison knew something, but he had taken a job at MIT and the Friedmans had no contact with him.

49 September 1949

Rob continued to work for the same engineering company, getting small raises but no major promotions. Although Barbara was starting second grade now, it never seemed like the right time for Doris to finish her degree. Her days were filled with teaching piano, bookkeeping, and investing. She couldn't quite get motivated to return to the world of studying and exams. With careful budgeting, she had saved enough from Rob's salary and her own earnings for a down payment on a modest house on the Near North Side of the city. Her investment fund remained an untouched, secret reserve. When Betty's letters described her increasingly luxurious life, it was hard not to be a little envious. However, Doris replied with cheerful missives, padded with minor details about her daily routines.

Doris was hanging pictures in their new home when the radio announced a special message from President Truman. The Soviets had detonated an atomic bomb. The president claimed he always expected other nations would develop their own bombs. Doris thought less often these days about Dave Sokol, but she spent the rest of the afternoon recalling their times together and speculating about what might have happened to him after the war. Maybe he was part of the Russian atomic program now—or maybe he was still stuck in some military prison. She remained angry that he had tried to manipulate her. She wondered if he had really believed in communism or if he had been pressured into his role. It seemed as if his family had not felt welcome in the United States or Russia. If she could talk to him, she would apologize for upending his life. She doubted that his arrest had made any difference in the outcome. As Joel had predicted, the Soviets had their own bomb now, regardless.

When Rob got home, he looked grim. "I think we're in for an arms buildup. Remember what Joel said in Oak Ridge? Hydrogen bombs will be next. Edward Teller is obsessed with them. If they can get the design right, hydrogen bombs will be cheaper to build than atomic ones. They'll make Hiroshima and Nagasaki look puny."

"Let's hope the cold war stays that way."

The centerpiece of the new living room was a black-and-white television in a heavy, oak cabinet. Although Doris had protested at the expense, Rob persuaded her that television was going to replace radio as the next big thing. That evening, Doris was glad to be able to watch the late-night news. The commentator reminded the nation that General Groves had predicted it would take the Soviets at least forty years to develop an atomic bomb.

"He was dead wrong on that one," said Doris.

"Most people thought it might be five to ten years, so this test is just a couple of years early. You did your best to stop Sokol, but I doubt he was the only spy the Soviets had in the project." Rob looked around the room. "You did a great job with the decorating, honey. I don't tell you enough how much I appreciate you. Now we have our own house, and Barbara will be in a good school district."

He kissed Doris and turned off the television. They went upstairs and had sex for the first time in their new bed. Doris tried to lose herself in the sensations.

"I just want to forget about nuclear war," she told Rob afterward, lying with her head on his shoulder and his arm around her.

"Think about this instead: transistors! In a few years they'll replace vacuum tubes. Everything—radios, TVs, computers, rocket guidance systems—will be much smaller and more advanced."

"Only an engineer can have sex and then get passionate about transistors! Who makes them anyway?"

"Bell Labs in New Jersey developed them, but it may be several more years before they get used commercially."

Doris resolved to keep an eye on the transistor market and, if possible, to buy stock in Bell Labs. Her growing knowledge about finance was a bright spot, but she wished she could find a more challenging job. Betty was now a partner in her Richmond decorating business, although she would be the first to admit that she had the advantage of her family's social connections. Rob continued to insist that he was satisfied with his work and was too tired to take college classes. Oak Ridge felt like a thousand years ago but also like just yesterday.

50: February 1950

Doris and Rob attended a cocktail reception at the company where he was working. Rob spent most of the evening talking shop with the other engineers. Doris chitchatted with the wives, but the talk of fashion, childbirth, and Dr. Spock did not engage her. Not one of the women seemed to care about literature or music or even politics. Doris imagined that she would disagree with most of them anyway. She had not realized how much she would miss Oak Ridge with its shared mission and interesting people.

Now that the Friedmans had been in their new house for over a year, she was also disgruntled with their neighbors. Last week two women had rung her doorbell. They asked Doris to put up awnings over the front windows and to repaint the house trim from green to brown to match a color scheme for their block. Doris politely declined. Not only did she think it was a waste of money, but she liked their house the way it was.

Just yesterday, Barbara had come home from school in tears. Two girls in her class who had been friendly told her that her dad was a commie and she was no longer invited over to play. That evening, Doris called one of the mothers, although they were only slightly acquainted.

"Diane, could you please explain why your daughter told Barbara we were communists and that she is no longer allowed in your home?"

There was a short silence. "Well!" Diane huffed. "I told her not to say anything."

"She obviously ignored you." Doris's tone was glacial. "But more importantly, where did you come up with this information?"

"An FBI agent came to several of our houses. He wanted to know all about your family, Doris. Not just your politics, but what kind of car you drive and whether you seem to spend a lot of money. He even asked if Rob told dirty jokes! It's obvious you're on some kind of list. And I've heard you say you'd like to see Adlai Stevenson run for president."

"Do you think Stevenson is a commie?"

"No . . . but he wouldn't be my choice."

"That doesn't surprise me. Diane, are you aware that my husband, Rob, worked on the atomic bomb?"

"Well . . . no."

"Yes, we were at Oak Ridge, Tennessee, during the war. And Rob continues to work on government projects, so he needs a security clearance. That's why those agents were asking questions."

"Well, how was I to know that?"

"Look, I don't care what you think of me or Rob. Frankly, I don't value your opinion. But you leave my daughter out of it. You should be ashamed of yourself, spreading rumors and making an innocent child cry."

"I'm sorry. I—I'll invite Barbara to come over after school."

Doris left it at that, but she was so angry that she was shaking. She wanted to yell, "Don't bother. Barbara is no longer allowed to play with your little brat," but she just said a grim thank-you. She even restrained herself from slamming down the receiver. Rob still thought she had overreacted, but Doris vowed to find a way to move their family to a nicer neighborhood in the suburbs. She would have to do some research, because she heard that Lake County was a bastion of the Republican Party. Meanwhile, she just hoped the fuss would blow over at Barbara's school. She would go in and talk to the teacher.

The cocktail party was winding down and Doris reminded Rob

that they needed to get home. When they arrived, the babysitter, a teenager from down the block, met them at the door.

"Barbara says she swallowed a bobby pin."

"Would you repeat that?" asked Doris.

"I put her to bed, and I guess she was lying on her back and for some reason she was playing with a bobby pin. She says she swallowed it."

"Did you see a bobby pin in her bedroom?"

"No, but I wasn't looking for one."

"Was she choking?"

"No, she was very calm. She just told me she swallowed it."

After hastily paying the girl, Barbara and Rob ran upstairs to Barbara's room. She was sleeping peacefully. Doris gently shook her awake.

"Barbara, is it true that you swallowed a bobby pin?"

"Yes. I'm sorry, Mommy. I was just playing with it and it dropped right into my mouth."

"Is anything hurting you, Barbara? Your tummy or your throat?" asked Rob.

"No, but it tasted bad, like metal."

"I'm going to call her pediatrician's emergency number," said Doris.

"It can probably wait until morning."

"Let's let them decide."

"Is the doctor going to have to cut me open?" asked Barbara, starting to cry.

"I don't think so, Barbara, but we need to know what to do."

Doris talked to the doctor on call, who told her that a bobby pin could perforate Barbara's intestine, which would be serious. "Bring her to the emergency room and we'll see if we can spot it on an X-ray."

They bundled Barbara into the car and took her to the hospital. After waiting an hour, they were taken into the room.

"That machine looks scary. I don't want to lie on the table."

"Don't worry, Barbara," Rob reassured her. "The doctor is just going to take your picture with a special kind of camera. It uses a little bit of radiation like Daddy got in Oak Ridge. You won't feel a thing."

The radiologist looked askance at Rob.

"My daddy helped build the atomic bomb," Barbara informed him.

"Well, your daddy is right. You won't feel anything when the X-ray machine goes on. But your parents will wait outside so they don't get x-rayed too."

"Be brave, honey." Rob lifted her up to sit on the table.

"It will be over before you know it," Doris added.

"I can't believe she swallowed a bobby pin! It almost seemed like she did it on purpose," Doris said as they waited in the consultation room. "She does a lot of things to get attention, even though I try so hard to give her what she needs. Sometimes I think we just got off to an awful start with each other."

"I bet she imagined the whole thing."

After a few minutes the nurse brought a subdued Barbara in to join them. She looked younger than her seven years, wrapped in a flannel blanket. "They're developing the X-ray now and the doctor will come in to talk with you in a few minutes."

The doctor entered and clipped the X-ray film to a light box on the wall. "Well, young lady, you did quite a job." He pointed to a dark shape inside of a shadowy structure. "This is your small intestine where you start to digest your food. And here's your bobby pin. We can't just leave it there or wait to see if you poop it out."

"Ugh!" Barbara exclaimed.

"If it moves wrong, it could poke a hole and cause an infection."

"Does she need surgery?" asked Doris.

"Well, we hate to operate on a young child if we can avoid it.

There's a new kind of X-ray called a fluoroscope. Only a few hospitals have them. The nearest is the children's hospital in Cincinnati. They can use it to picture the bobby pin. They'll put Barbara to sleep and thread a rubber tube down her throat with a magnet at the end. Hopefully it can grab the bobby pin and lift it gently out of her body. I'm going to call a doctor I know there. I think you should fly out tomorrow."

"Damn it, Barbara! Now look what you've done!"

Doris knew Rob yelled when he was frightened, but she saw Barbara's face crumple.

"Accidents happen, Rob. Calm down. We need to get home and make plane reservations." She turned to her daughter. "Our first plane ride, Barbara! Maybe the stewardess will give you one of those pins with wings."

"Just don't put it anywhere near your mouth," said the doctor.

Doris took Barbara on a propeller plane to Cincinnati. As they sat on the plane, she recalled their wartime train trip with the drunken soldiers. This was certainly more civilized. She kept an eye on Barbara for any symptoms, but her daughter just cuddled her favorite stuffed tiger and stared out the window.

"Mommy, look at the toy cars and houses down there."

Luckily the weather was good. Still, Doris clutched the armrest whenever there was a bump.

Barbara noticed and laughed. "Daddy and I like roller coasters, but you're a scaredy-cat."

"Then you'll just have to be brave for both of us."

After they retrieved their suitcase at the airport, they took a cab directly to the hospital. Barbara was admitted to a private room with a large recliner where Doris would be able to sleep. She held Barbara's hand, walking next to the gurney as they wheeled her daughter to the operating room.

"Here's where we say goodbye," she told Barbara at the door. "I'll be in the waiting room. They'll give you some medicine to put you to sleep and the next thing you know, you'll be back in your bed minus one nasty bobby pin."

Doris tried to read a dog-eared magazine but had a hard time sitting still. She was worried about Barbara but also realized how much more competent she felt as a mother than she had in Oak Ridge. She patted herself on the back for handling the emergency efficiently. When the radiologist came out and said all had gone smoothly, she heaved a sigh of relief.

"Thank you so much, Doctor."

"She'll be in the recovery room for several hours, so if you want to go down to the cafeteria or call your husband, feel free."

"I can't see her now?"

"She's still unconscious. And she'll be groggy and maybe nauseated when she wakes up. We don't let parents come into the recovery area."

"Tell me, Doctor, what company makes those fluoroscopes?"

He gave her a puzzled look.

"I'm asking because I invest a little in the stock market. These machines seem like an important invention."

"Smart idea, Mrs. Friedman. They're made by a division of DuPont."

"Oh! I already own some DuPont shares. We got familiar with them when we were at Oak Ridge."

"You worked there?"

"My husband did. It was an amazing place. Thanks for the information."

Doris called Rob to tell him that the procedure was a success. He gave an audible sigh of relief.

"We can take the train home to Chicago now that it's not an emergency," she said. "It will be a lot less expensive."

"Okay. Your father said he'd pick you up if you get home while I'm at work. By the way, did you see that Scotland Yard arrested a physicist, Klaus Fuchs, who was at Los Alamos? He's been working in England. They say he gave atomic secrets to the Russians."

"You're kidding!"

"He was a major player in designing the bomb. That's probably how the Soviets got theirs so fast."

"I wonder why he did it!"

"He's a refugee from Germany and, obviously, a communist. Even though he's not Jewish, he hated the Nazis. He said that atomic energy should belong to the whole world, not just America."

"Sounds familiar, doesn't it? Even Harrison felt that way. I wonder what happened to Dave Sokol after the war."

"Maybe they let him go back to Russia, since he couldn't do any more damage."

"Russia is pretty grim these days. Not much better than Alaska. And I don't imagine their spy agency would be happy with him for getting caught." Doris hoped Dave's fate was not as dark as she imagined. She felt sorry for his wife. Did she know how Dave had behaved at Oak Ridge? Maybe it had been an act to cover up his spying, but Doris thought a lot of the flirting was real. Even though Rob continued to be absent-minded and absorbed in his work, she preferred his loyalty to Dave's flattery. "Well, I'll let you know when they say Barbara can go home. I think they'll keep us here for a day or two."

"We're just lucky they had the fluoroscope and that our doctors knew about it. You were so right to call when we found out. Poor baby. I hope she doesn't feel too sick when she wakes up."

51: April 1951

After over a year of trying, Doris was finally pregnant. She was only three months along, still feeling queasy. They were driving in their rattletrap of a car to visit Joel and Annette. Joel had finished his PhD and they had moved to the suburbs with their two-year-old daughter. Doris and Rob only got together with the Levitts every few months. Doris actually found herself missing Annette. Their long history together outweighed her occasional barbs.

Doris struggled to avoid being carsick. They still had almost an hour of driving to go. She tried to distract herself by thinking of the stock shares she had bought last week. She continued to multiply the money she earned by investing it but did not tell Rob. He said he was happy about having a second child but was rarely home. Not only did his job involve long hours and frequent trips to New Mexico to test rocket components, but he was designing radios for a friend, Mort, who had started a company. Doris was upset about the second job, especially since Mort was not paying Rob as promised.

"I thought you were supposed to get a check last month," she reminded her husband.

"When the company takes off, I'll get part ownership," Rob said, his reply muffled by the engine of a delivery truck in the next lane.

Doris raised her voice. "If the company takes off. It has a lot of competition from much bigger firms. And do you have a written contract about the share you'll get?"

"We don't need a contract. Gentleman's agreement."

"Rob! I'm worried that you're being a patsy!"

"You don't understand. This is a great opportunity. And the work is fun for me."

"It may be fun, but what about your family? You're gone most evenings and weekends. How will I manage after the baby comes? If you're going to work a second job, at least get one that pays! Or better yet, you could be taking courses to get your degree. Then you'd make more money at your regular job."

"You're harping on college again? You're never satisfied. First, we had to buy a house. Now you want to move to a bigger house in the suburbs."

"I'm disappointed with Barbara's school. And I'm sick of our gossiping neighbors. You don't have to deal with them every day."

"I like my school," Barbara piped up from the back seat. "I don't want to move. And I'll help you with the baby, Mom."

"See?" Rob took his eyes off the road to give Doris a hostile look.

"And stop fighting all the time!"

"I'm sorry, Barbara. You're right. Mom and Dad should not fight in front of you. Rob, could you find a gas station? I'm not feeling well."

Rob jerked the car into the next lane, turned into a service station, and braked sharply.

"Dad! Don't drive like that!"

Doris lunged out of the car door and ran for the bathroom, where she heaved up her breakfast. When she felt like her digestion had calmed down, she rinsed out her mouth and trudged back.

Rob had the radio on. He and Barbara were singing along to "The Tennessee Waltz."

"I hate that song," Doris said, slamming her door shut.

"Really? Reminds me of Oak Ridge," said Rob.

"Why? Nobody stole your sweetheart."

"You have a short memory."

"You're never going to let that go, are you?"

"You said you would stop fighting," Barbara reminded them.

They spent the rest of the ride in silence, with the radio playing in the background. When they got to the Levitts' home, Annette showed off her spotless housekeeping. Joel took Rob into his den while Doris and Barbara played with Annette's daughter.

"I think I'm going to like being a big sister," Barbara said, helping the toddler with a wooden jigsaw. "Just don't ask me to change diapers."

"Do you want a brother or a sister, Barbara?" Annette asked.

"Oh, I don't know. Maybe a girl. My friends' little brothers can be awfully annoying."

"Well, babies are fun," Annette told her.

Doris grimaced. "They're fun to visit."

"You look exhausted, Doris."

"I'm just having some morning sickness."

"And she and Dad are always yelling at each other," Barbara said.

"I'm surprised, Doris. Rob works so hard. He never has a bad word to say about you."

"I would be more grateful if he worked for people who paid him. Never mind, Annette. Let's just enjoy our visit. Do you miss being at the lab or are you happy staying home?"

As Annette enumerated the joys of her new vacuum cleaner, Italian cooking classes, and her daughter's successful toilet training, Doris remembered why she had limited tolerance for spending time with her old friend.

At dinner, the conversation turned to the conviction and sentencing of Ethel and Julius Rosenberg for providing secret information about the atomic bomb to the Soviets.

"They clearly gave away valuable secrets," Rob said.

"Julius did, but I think the evidence against Ethel is weak. So maybe she typed up their notes. Does that mean she deserves to die?" Doris asked. She had a vision of Dave Sokol, being led to his execution in some godforsaken prison. She was horrified to think that she could have doomed him to that. “What will happen to their children?”

“They should have thought of that before they betrayed their country,” countered Rob.

“Their sentence is much too extreme,” said Joel. “Fuchs only got fourteen years in prison.”

“But that’s England,” Doris pointed out. “They don’t have McCarthy and the House Un-American Activities Committee.”

“Yeah, and Fuchs isn’t a Jew,” Joel added.

“What’s the electric chair?” asked Barbara.

“Well, it’s a special chair that gives a big jolt of current through electrodes—”

“Rob! She doesn’t need a technical explanation. Barbara, where did you hear about the electric chair?” asked Doris.

“Kids at school said they’re gonna use it to fry the Rosenbergs.”

“I’m sorry you had to hear something so ugly. The electric chair is supposed to be a painless way of executing someone who did a terrible crime.”

“But is it? Painless? Being fried sounds like it would hurt a lot.”

“It’s probably not painless,” Doris admitted.

“Did the Rosenbergs do something terrible?”

“They helped the Russians get an atomic bomb,” Rob explained. “And that means the Soviets could strike our cities.”

“Will they bomb Chicago?”

“No, because then we would bomb Moscow.”

“And then bombs would fall on New York, and then St. Petersburg, and then Washington, and then Sverdlovsk . . . and then the end of civilization as we know it,” Joel put in.

Barbara looked around at the adults. “Okay, fry them.”

“But it’s not that simple,” Doris said. “The Russians would have built their own bomb without any help from spies. It just would have taken them a few years longer.”

"And executing the Rosenbergs won't change anything now, Barbara," Joel said. "They would never have a chance to be spies again. They didn't kill anyone. It's just politics. Our government could punish them by putting them in jail for a while."

"In school they showed us a new movie, *Duck and Cover*, with Bert the Turtle. They said if an atomic bomb explodes, we should get under our desks and cover our heads like a turtle going into its shell. That warning siren sound is scary!"

"What a bunch of hooey," Rob muttered.

"Dad! It's important to know what to do if the enemy attacks."

"Nothing can protect people from an atomic bomb."

Doris looked at her husband and mouthed *stop*. "Hopefully we'll never have to worry about that, but I'm glad you watched the movie carefully."

Rob gave her a disgruntled look but did not say anything more.

Their drive home was uneventful. After Barbara went to bed, Doris and Rob sat on the living room couch.

"I think we need to talk," Doris said. "We seem to be hurting each other all the time. Maybe our goals are too different."

"Not really. When I saw Joel's house today, I realized why you want to move to some place like that."

She was going to say it out loud—the question that had played in her head so many times over the years. "Would we be better off getting a divorce?"

"No!" Rob grabbed her shoulders and turned her to face him. "How could you think that? Have you forgotten how we fell in love?"

"I haven't forgotten. But your work is the center of your life."

"No, Doris. You and Barbara and this new baby are the center. I'm going to look for a job that pays more. And I'll tell Mort I can't do any more work for his company."

"And then you'll resent me."

"I won't resent you. I promise."

Doris felt tears gathering. She wanted to express herself without getting so emotional. It was probably pregnancy hormones, but she took a deep breath. "I worry that I'm the wrong woman for you. That you'd be happier with a wife who just enjoys staying home and taking care of the kids."

"You do a great job managing our home. I keep telling you."

"But it's not enough for me, Rob. I want to make some kind of dent in the world."

"I'd be bored with a little wifey like the other engineers have. You challenge me, and that's good."

"Is it? We were so young when we met. I thought I could just change the parts of you that didn't fit my vision of the future. But now I see that we can only change so much. I hate being your nagging wife—but I can't seem to stop. Maybe we're too different to be a good team." Her tears started to flow in earnest. She fished a handkerchief out of her pocket and swiped at her eyes.

"I think you're wrong. Look at all we've done together. We helped win the war. You took care of me and Barbara when things were tough. Maybe our families have different values, but frankly, neither side is such a bargain."

"That's certainly true." Doris wiped her eyes.

"You're right, we were just kids when we married. But we've grown up together. If we split, you'd be miserable trying to take care of two children. And I'd be miserable without you. I love you, Doris. I don't say it enough. And you're the only person who's ever loved me as I am . . . if you still do."

"I do still love you, Rob. I'm not sure how much I love myself."

"Oh, honey." Rob kissed Doris on the forehead and she rested her head on his shoulder. They sat in silence for a few minutes.

"Rob?"

"Yes, Doris?"

"I've been keeping something from you."

"Something more about Sokol?"

"No! There was one make-out session. And it was the biggest mistake of my life."

"I don't blame you anymore, Doris. When I give you a hard time, I'm really mad at myself—for neglecting you. For not being good enough to keep you satisfied. At work I usually know what to do, but with you . . ."

"You were overwhelmed at the lab in Oak Ridge. That's no excuse for my trying to get attention from another man."

"And now I'm ignoring you again. I'll do better. I don't want to lose you, Doris."

"You forgive me for Sokol?"

"Absolutely."

"Anyway, my secret has nothing to do with that. I was going to tell you that I've been making quite a bit of money buying stocks. And this house was a good investment, too, even if I'm not happy here. If we sell it along with what's in my portfolio, we can buy a house in a nice suburb by the lake. We can even finally get a dog. Maybe a collie like Tippy."

Rob hugged her close. "That's incredible, Doris. Let's do it."

"I was worried that my success would hurt your pride."

He moved her back so they could look into each other's eyes. "What gave you that idea?"

"Betty and I used to talk about men needing to feel like the kings of the castle."

"Not me. I've been in awe of you ever since we met—your smarts, your drive, and your music. I just felt lucky that you wanted me too."

"But you kept telling me it was your job to support our family. Remember, you said you were the quarterback?"

"I guess I did. But like you said, that was my inferiority complex speaking. I'm always afraid I'll let you down. When I'm nervous, I just pretend I know better than you do."

"What a pair we are. We have to start talking to each other instead of at each other."

"Just let me love you, Doris, until it seeps in. My sweet Doris." He stroked her cheek.

"I don't feel very sweet."

"You are, honey. I know how to design a circuit, but when it comes to dealing with the rest of it . . . I depend on you. You're like a plutonium core, radiating all that hidden power inside its shell, but power for good."

"Oh great—now I'm a deadly bomb." She hiccupped.

"No, that's not what I meant. You're like—a force of nature. You supply the power that runs our family. You know, nuclear reactors are going to be used soon for electricity. And it will be safe. You'll see. We're learning to control fission."

"I don't think I'd want to live next to a reactor."

"Come on, you did in Oak Ridge."

"And I always worried there would be an earthquake or something."

"We waste too much time waiting for a catastrophe. We have to enjoy all the progress since the war. We're living in the atomic age now."

Doris imagined all the neutrons, whizzing around and colliding when she and Rob cracked open each other's hearts. But maybe love was like a reactor's lead shield or its cooling tank of water, taming anger and insecurities into life-sustaining energy. She pictured their new house with a green lawn and a garden, and a baby grand in the living room. She would plant rosebushes and coax them to grow fat pink and yellow blooms. Barbara would chase the puppy while Rob barbecued and the baby laughed in a playpen on the patio. Life was far from perfect, but why not have some ordinary happiness? Sarah, her piano teacher, had been right. A family was a blessing.

Rob and Doris sat in each other's arms for a while longer, contemplating their future in the world they had put at risk but also helped save.

Please consider leaving a review of *Fission: A Novel of Atomic Heartbreak* on your preferred site. New authors, indie authors, and our novels can only thrive with the support of people who take the time and energy to let others know about them. If you enjoyed this book, please spread the word in whatever way feels good to you.

Author's Note

My father, Donald Schover, was a research associate in Dr. Charles D. Coryell's group in the Manhattan Project at the Chicago Met Lab and then the X-10 nuclear reactor and laboratory at Oak Ridge. He was one of the sixty-seven signers of the Oak Ridge version of the Szilárd petition asking that the power of the atomic bomb be demonstrated to the Japanese before targeting civilians. He and my mother, Janet Moss Schover, married at ages twenty-two and nineteen. My older sister, Michal, was born eight months later, in July 1942. I was not born until 1952.

Stories of Oak Ridge were part of our family lore during my childhood. This novel is my attempt to fill in the sketchy outlines of those tales. Therefore, I have used fictional names except for a few people who were well-known historical figures. It is also my effort to understand the origins of my parents' contentious fifty-year marriage, and the difficult relationship between my mother and older sister. In writing *Fission*, I was struck by the loss of my mother's early dreams for herself and the limited horizons for a young woman during that era.

My parents recounted that Dr. Coryell had them over to dinner in early 1943 and told them everything—about the mission to build an atomic bomb before the Nazis, his task to create the first gram of plutonium, and the need for his team to go to a secret base for the project. It surprises me that Dr. Coryell chose to disclose so much to a young couple, especially since my father had only a year of electronics training. However, an extensive series of interviews with Dr. Coryell have been published. He mentions my father briefly several times. He notes that instrumentation was his group's weak point. My father, junior as he was, became their electronics expert in Oak Ridge, so recruiting him may have seemed important. I have no idea how my parents were vetted before being recruited, but Coryell mentions he relied a lot on personal referrals. A good friend of my parents was already working in his group. The detailed conversation in chapter 3 is my fantasy of how the disclosure might have come about, incorporating anecdotes from my parents' real lives. In reading about Oak Ridge, most of the wives did not know as much as my mother. However, the scientists at X-10, like the group at Los Alamos, knew the purpose of the Manhattan Project.

One of the most important contributions of the Coryell group is described in Chapter 26. They produced large quantities of barium-140, a radioactive isotope of the element barium. It decays into lanthanum-140, an even more radioactive substance that was used at Los Alamos to test the implosion trigger design for the plutonium-based bombs used in the Trinity Test and at Nagasaki.

Many events in the book were based on my parents' anecdotes, although relationships with their family are largely fiction. My parents returned to Chicago in 1945 and I know very little about their friends from Oak Ridge, so secondary characters are invented. I do know that my mother made friends with some Southern women and came to admire their toughness and humor. One did indeed ask her about her missing "Jew horns." She also mentioned that one of the other wives in their group had an episode of hysterical blindness, so I wove that into the character of Betty. Many of the homemakers of Oak Ridge had mental health issues. My mother described her own episodes of seeing the house collapsing. They sounded like classic panic attacks. My parents held progressive values and deplored segregation but never talked about the miserable treatment of African

Americans at Oak Ridge. I think they had good intentions but were limited by the blinders of their time. I have used the word *colored* in the novel because it was one of the least racist terms employed in that era.

To my knowledge, my mother never even contemplated having an affair in Oak Ridge. The idea for the spy plot came from recent revelations about Oscar Seborer and George Koval, Soviet atomic spies who spent time in Oak Ridge. Both were just a little older than my father. Like him, both came from Eastern European Jewish families and were experts in electronics engineering. Koval (*Sleeper Agent* by Ann Hagedorn, 2021) worked as a radiation health officer at X-10 during or soon after a time when my father was exposed to a hefty dose of radiation as described in the novel. Thus, my parents may well have known one or both of them. Koval was a (secretly married) womanizer and a bridge player, although I do not think he was a classical music enthusiast. He was a baseball fan in reality. He did provide information to the Soviets on instrumentation and plutonium output at Oak Ridge, but his main espionage accomplishment came after his transfer to Dayton, Ohio, where he had access to the design of the trigger for the plutonium bomb at a top-secret plant that produced polonium, a radioactive substance. The design of the bomb trigger may have been the most important secret of the Manhattan Project. Even when other aspects were revealed to the public, the role of the Dayton site remained classified for decades. In Chapter 37, Harrison cannot tell Doris why Dayton is so crucial, because of this secrecy.

In contrast to the character Dave Sokol in *Fission*, Koval was extremely careful to hide his background and to blend in socially. He was never caught and managed to flee back to the Soviet Union in 1948, just as other Manhattan Project spies were being arrested. In the interests of the story, I have Sokol arrive in Oak Ridge in late 1943, but Koval actually was not assigned there until August 1944. He then proceeded to Dayton, Ohio, in June 1945.

I do not understand why my father never went back to get a college degree after the war. He spent his long career as a successful but self-taught electronics and systems engineer, learning new technologies as they developed, from vacuum tubes to integrated circuits. He directed projects that measured seismic waves of underground atomic weapons tests, tested instruments on rocket sleds, sent unmanned probes to the moon, separated sludge from sewage, and created electronic controls for letter-sorting machines. However, he was always underpaid and somewhat undervalued because of his limited credentials. My mother never finished her degree either. She ended up teaching herself accounting, but much later in life than in the plot of *Fission*. She started off as a bookkeeper for auto agencies and became the first female comptroller of an industrial company in Illinois. Her lack of an accounting degree also ended up limiting her career. Unlike Doris, she shunned the stock market because of her family's experience during the Depression.

Fear of atomic war was a constant when I was growing up in the "duck and cover" era. I recall asking my father why we weren't building a bomb shelter. I was devastated when he told me, "Honey, it wouldn't help." I also have a vivid memory of the family watching TV as the Cuban missile crisis unfolded when I was ten. When I was seventeen, a sixteen-minute Japanese film of the human aftermath of Hiroshima and Nagasaki was declassified and shown on public TV. My father and I sat together and watched. I asked him how he felt about working on the Manhattan Project. He told me his whole motivation, like his peers, was to get the bomb before the Nazis. He was against using the bomb on Hiroshima and believed that Nagasaki was targeted mainly to see how the plutonium bomb (already tested at Trinity) would perform in war. However, we did not discuss the view that the bomb was used more to checkmate Stalin than to force the Japanese to surrender. He did believe the bomb had saved American soldiers. I have his tattered copy of the Smyth Report. I do not recall discussing Oppenheimer or the Rosenbergs with him, but he and my mother thought Edward Teller was diabolical. My father used to make business trips to White Sands, New Mexico. On one occasion he took a guided tour of Los Alamos. He was upset at the lack of a memorial to his friend Louis Slotin, who died in the "tickling the dragon's tail" tragedy.

When I was in high school, my father spent several years working on a project with Toshiba. He made friends with the Japanese engineers and took several extended trips to Japan. He visited Hiroshima and was deeply affected. My mother refused to accompany him to Japan. She focused on the unfairness of gender roles there, but I think she felt anxious and resentful that my father was spending so much time away from home. She died at age sixty-nine. My father lived to be eighty-seven and never had cancer, despite his radiation exposure. In the last years of his life, he spent a lot of time reminiscing about the Manhattan Project. He put together a presentation that he gave to groups of senior citizens. I wanted to videotape him, but he had an unexpected, catastrophic fall before I had a chance. My mother died when I was pregnant with my only child, but my father was in our lives until my son turned fourteen. I am grateful for that time together.

Book Club Discussion Questions

1. How might Doris's choices when she has an unintended pregnancy in 1941 be different from those she would have today in the same situation?

2. Why do you think Doris gives in to her attraction to Dave Sokol?

3. Given what we learn about Dave Sokol's life history, do you think he is a traitor to spy for the Soviets?

4. How does the early Cold War period affect Doris and Rob's marriage?

5. How do Rob and Doris differ in their opinions about using the atomic bomb?

6. What would you predict about the future happiness of Rob and Doris's marriage?

Leslie Schover loves to meet readers and would be happy to talk with book clubs over the internet. Please contact her through her author website: www.leslieschoverauthor.com/contact.

Acknowledgments

I would like to thank my father's colleague, the late Howard Gest, PhD, who kindly contacted me when he saw my father's obituary in 2007. His sons, especially Ted Gest, graciously responded to an email I sent and pointed me to an essay Dr. Gest wrote about the Szilárd petition (https://biology.indiana.edu/documents/historical-materials/gest_pdfs/hgSzilard.pdf).

I have also been grateful to meet online with Charles D. Coryell's remarkable daughter, Julie E. Coryell. I profited greatly from the interviews with her father that she published with Joan Bainbridge, as well as a commemorative lecture she gave in her father's honor. I want to thank Knoxville historian Jack Neely for providing information about piano stores in Knoxville and the availability of Steinways during the war. Oak Ridge historian D. Ray Smith kindly answered a variety of questions and gave me a link to the Clinton Labs phone book that listed the home addresses and work and phone numbers for my parents and several other people I recognized from their stories. He also checked earlier drafts of *Fission* for historical accuracy and caught a couple of errors. I hope to visit Oak Ridge and thank him in person. Ann Hagedorn, author of *Sleeper Agent*, also took the time to have an online meeting to discuss her research on the spy George Koval.

While writing this novel, I also benefited from the wisdom of author Linda Watanabe McFerrin and literary agent (and cousin by marriage) Andy Ross. I attended their writers' workshop in Provence as well as an online course afterward with Linda. Andy edited an earlier draft of *Fission* and helped me transform it from a quasi-memoir to a more dramatic piece of fiction. And finally, I want to thank my fellow writers Michelene Esposito and Janice Prudhomme. We met in Provence and have created our own inspirational writers' group.

Sources

Books

Albright, Joseph, and Marcia Kunstel. *Bombshell: The Secret Story of America's Unknown Atomic Spy Conspiracy.* New York: Times Books, 1997.

Blume, Lesley M. M. *Fallout: The Hiroshima Cover-Up and the Reporter Who Revealed It to the World.* New York: Simon & Schuster, 2020.

Cook, Richard. *Ignored Heroes of World War II: The Manhattan Project Workers of Oak Ridge.* Self-Published ebook, Kindle Direct, 2015.

Hagedorn, Ann. *Sleeper Agent.* New York: Simon & Schuster, 2021.

Hersey, John. *Hiroshima.* New York: Vintage Reprint Edition, 2019.

Johnson, Charles W., and Charles O. Jackson. *City Behind a Fence: Oak Ridge Tennessee 1942–1946.* Knoxville: The University of Tennessee Press, 1981.

Joseph, Timothy. *Historic Photos of the Manhattan Project.* Nashville: Turner Publishing Company, 2009.

Kelley, Cynthia C., ed. *The Manhattan Project: The Birth of the Atomic Bomb in the Words of Its Creators, Eyewitnesses, and Historians.* New York: Black Dog & Leventhal Publishers, 2020.

Kiernan, Denise. *The Girls of Atomic City: The Untold Story of the*

Women Who Helped Win World War II. New York: Atria Books, 2014.

Robinson, George O. *The Oak Ridge Story: The Saga of a People Who Share in History.* Philadelphia: Pantianos Classics, 1950.

Safford, Joan Bainbridge, and Julie E. Coryell, eds. *A Chemist's Role in the Birth of Atomic Energy: Interviews with Charles DuBois Coryell.* Seattle: Promethium Press, 2012. https://juliecoryell.com/2018/10/charles-d-coryell-the-book-and-the-movie/.

Strasser, Emily. *Half-Life of a Secret: Reckoning with a Hidden History.* Lexington: University Press of Kentucky, 2023.

Westcott, Ed. *Oak Ridge (Images of America).* Mount Pleasant, TN: Arcadia Publishing, 2005.

Online and Media Sources

Broad, William J. "Fourth Spy at Los Alamos Knew A-Bomb's Inner Secrets." https://www.nytimes.com/2020/01/27/science/manhattan-project-nuclear-spy.html.

Broad, William J. "Fourth Spy Unearthed in U.S. Atomic Bomb Project." https://www.nytimes.com/2019/11/23/science/manhattan-project-atomic-spy.html.

Campfire Stories: *Astonishing History. "The Radioactive Story of Louis Slotin, Harry Daghlian and the Demon Core of Los Alamos."* https://campfirestoriespodcast.medium.com/the-radioactive-story-of-louis-slotin-harry-daghlian-and-the-demon-core-of-los-alamos-e6f9f38989b7.

A Compassionate Spy: Documentary. Magnolia Pictures, 2023.

Duck and Cover, Bert the Turtle. https://www.youtube.com/watch?v=IKqXu-5jw60. 1951.

Gest, Howard. *The July 1945 Szilard Petition on the Atomic Bomb: Memoir by a Signer in Oak Ridge.* https://biology.indiana.edu/documents/historical-materials/gest_pdfs/hgSzilard.pdf.

Klehr, H., and JE Haynes. "On the Trail of a Fourth Soviet Spy at Los Alamos." *Studies in Intelligence* 63(3), 2019.

Money, Richard. Richard Money's Interview. *Voices of the Manhattan Project.* https://ahf.nuclearmuseum.org/voices/oral-histories/richard-moneys-interview/.

Nazi Murder Mills. Newsreel. https://archive.org/details/1945-04-26_Nazi_Murder_Mills. April 26, 1945.

Secret City: The Oak Ridge Story—The War Years. https://www.pbs.org/video/east-tennessee-public-television-secret-city-oak-ridge-story_war_years/.

Silverman, Mike. "A History of the Oak Ridge Symphony." https://www.orcma.org/history.

Zellig, M. "Dr. Louis Slotin and the 'invisible Killer.'" Canada's History. August/September 1995. https://www.canadashistory.ca/explore/science-technology/dr-louis-slotin-and-the-invisible-killer.

About the Author

photo credit: Pixel Studio Productions

Leslie R. Schover is a clinical psychologist who brings her knowledge of people, relationships, and sexuality to her first novel. *Fission* draws on her parents' stories of Oak Ridge during the Manhattan Project. She was Professor of Behavioral Science at the University of Texas MD Anderson Cancer Center and published three self-help books. Her digital health company, Will2Love.com won an Innovation Prize in the Astellas C3 Changing Cancer Care contest. She lives in Houston, Texas, with her faithful dog, Luc.

Looking for your next great read?

We can help!

Visit www.shewritespress.com/next-read
or scan the QR code below for a list
of our recommended titles.

She Writes Press is an award-winning
independent publishing company founded to
serve women writers everywhere.